"I don't know hov
Jesse's brow furrowed.

"I do." Though Louise hated remembering the reason. "I made several funeral wreaths for the fallen."

Again he stiffened, making her wonder if he'd served in the war. Few soldiers wanted to talk about what they'd seen.

"This will be a festive, cheerful time. People will want to come here, especially if we make it known in Chicago what is happening." Then she made her plea. "Your knowledge of plants will be invaluable."

That brought back the smile. "Are you sure you don't just want me along to carry the boughs?"

"Oh, dear. You deciphered my real purpose." Louise immediately regretted the playful jab. He didn't appear to understand her humor, judging from the look on his face. She braced herself.

Instead of chastising her, he roared with laughter. "Of course I'll help. Anything for a friend who speaks her mind."

A friend. He'd called her a friend. She should be glad. Yet deep down she wanted more.

A small-town girl, **Christine Johnson** has lived in every corner of Michigan's Lower Peninsula. She enjoys creating stories that bring history to life while exploring the characters' spiritual journeys. Though Michigan is still her home base, she and her seafaring husband also spend time exploring the Florida Keys and other fascinating locations. You can contact her through her website at christineelizabethjohnson.com.

Books by Christine Johnson

Love Inspired Historical

Boom Town Brides

Mail Order Mix-Up
Mail Order Mommy
Mail Order Sweetheart
Would-Be Mistletoe Wife

The Dressmaker's Daughters

Groom by Design
Suitor by Design
Love by Design

Visit the Author Profile page at Harlequin.com for more titles.

CHRISTINE JOHNSON

Would-Be Mistletoe Wife

HARLEQUIN® LOVE INSPIRED® HISTORICAL

Recycling programs
for this product may
not exist in your area.

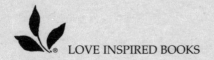 LOVE INSPIRED BOOKS

ISBN-13: 978-0-373-42552-5

Would-Be Mistletoe Wife

Copyright © 2017 by Christine Elizabeth Johnson

www.Harlequin.com

Printed in U.S.A.

Wait on the Lord: be of good courage, and he shall strengthen thine heart. Wait, I say, on the Lord.
—*Psalms* 27:14

For my aunties, whose encouragement
and support carried me through difficult times
and made the good times even better.

Chapter One

❧

September 1871
Singapore, Michigan

Louise Smythe spotted her quarry and motioned her students to follow her across the sand dune. The sun shone hot for so late in the year, and the sand reflected the heat, bringing beads of perspiration to her brow.

As expected, her instructions were met with a chorus of complaints from the handful of young ladies currently enrolled in Mrs. Evans's School for Ladies. Ranging from fifteen to eighteen years of age, the students had come to Singapore, Michigan, to better themselves. Louise taught the intellectual courses, such as literature, writing and mathematics, while Fiona Evans covered the arts. In addition, Louise included an occasional class on the sciences in order to improve the ladies' ability to converse on all topics.

"My feet ache," whined Linore Pace. The eighteen-year-old had landed in Singapore last fall after their ship foundered. She and five other young women were bound for the utopian colony of Harmony on Low Island. After completing the voyage on another ship, Linore had re-

turned to Singapore in August after finding the island—
and the man selected to become her husband—not at all
to her liking.

"Mine too," her cohort, Dinah, seconded. "I can't figure how all this traipsin' around is gonna get me a husband."

"How this will procure a husband," Louise corrected.

"Huh? Cure a husband o' what?"

Louise inwardly groaned. A full summer of demonstrating proper grammar coupled with three weeks of formal instruction had failed to improve Dinah's speech. Her
writing was even worse. Suggesting that a man valued a
woman who could speak properly was useless, since most
of the men in town—including Dinah's former beau—
were lumberjacks and sawyers with even worse grammar.

One of the wealthier girls snorted and whispered to
her pair of friends, doubtless to emphasize Dinah's lowly
estate. The three paying students always managed to separate themselves from the orphans, Dinah and Linore,
whose tuition was paid by scholarship. No matter what
Louise did to pull the ladies together, they always ended
up in two distinct groups.

"Enough chatter!" Louise clapped her hands and
stopped before her quarry, a rather sad example of the
tall wormwood plant. "This is our specimen today."

The whispers turned to giggles.

Louise was about to reprimand them when Priscilla,
her perfectly curled blond hair on full display beneath a
tiny straw hat, pointed past her.

"Now, *that* is a fine specimen." Priscilla Bennington
gave her two friends, Adeline and Esther, a look that cau-
tioned them she had first claim on whatever she'd spotted.

All five girls sighed as one.

Clearly Priscilla was not talking about the wormwood

plant. Like the rest, her attention focused on humans, especially the masculine variety. Louise turned just enough
to spot what had quieted the girls' complaints without
letting them out of her peripheral vision.

Heading her way was a giant of a man, surely the tall-
est man she'd ever seen. Her late husband had been tall
at six foot. This man must be well over six feet, perhaps
even six and a half. The white shirt and navy blue trousers only accentuated his broad shoulders and muscular
limbs. It being an overly warm day, he wore no jacket or
coat. In spite of sleeves rolled to his elbows, he managed
to look proper and formal. Atop his head sat a navy blue
cap, like that worn by Mr. Blackthorn, the lighthouse
keeper. Louise had heard there was a new assistant at
the lighthouse. This must be the man. Neatly trimmed
sandy blond hair peeked from beneath the cap on either
side of his rugged, clean-shaven face.

If she'd been the girls' age, she would have sighed
too. This man was exceedingly handsome. He was also
storming toward them in a most intimidating manner.

"He's positively the most gorgeous man I've ever
seen," Adeline sighed. The sixteen-year-old found every
man she saw more handsome than the last.

Louise turned, finger to her lips, to hush such untoward comments. "A lady conducts herself with dignity at
all times."

"Even when hiking across the wilderness?" Priscilla,
with her matching hats, bags and gowns, managed to irritate Louise on a daily, if not hourly, basis. "There's sand
in my shoes, and my stockings are ruined. That doesn't
even begin to address the damage to my complexion."
She tilted her parasol so it now shaded her face.

The girl came from wealth and no doubt the Evanses
needed the income that such a student brought, but she

was a handful. The new school had been blessed with a benefactress in Fiona Evans's mother-in-law, who had helped to get it started and instituted the scholarships, but she could not support its continuing operation. To survive, the school must turn a profit. That meant accepting and enduring spoiled girls like Priscilla Bennington. In three weeks, the eighteen-year-old had thrown nearly a dozen tantrums and refused to follow direction. Louise suspected Priscilla had been refused by or expelled from every school in Chicago. Here, she headed up the haughty trio.

"This is hardly the wilderness," Louise pointed out for the benefit of the other students, for whom she still had hope. "We are only a short distance from the school."

She might as well have been talking to herself, for all five girls bunched together whispering and giggling. Louise's calm temperament frazzled.

"Then perhaps you should return to that school." The strong bass voice sent a jolt through Louise and brought a sudden halt to the giggling. This man was not pleased. Not at all.

Louise had endured enough opposition for one day. Though he towered over her, she would not let a perfect stranger determine what she would and would not teach her students.

She squared her shoulders. "We will return as soon as we finish examining this example of *artemisia campestris*." She pointed to the tall wormwood. "As you can see, the drought has stunted its growth, making it an ideal subject for study."

The man stared at her as if she'd spoken a foreign language—not an unusual reaction from the men in Singapore. This lumber town didn't boast many educated men or women. Before Mrs. Elder grew gravely ill and left for Chicago with her husband, Louise had kept house for her and the Captain. Both were well-read and their home boasted a large library, but they'd sent for their books this summer, leaving the town woefully deficient in reading material.

"You're standing on federal government property," the man stated. "That's trespassing."

"I am a teacher from Mrs. Evans's School for Ladies. We are conducting the day's study in the field."

His scowl showed no sign of departing. "I don't care if you're Mrs. Evans herself, this is still government property. Regulation states that you must obtain permission to be here. Mr. Blackthorn didn't tell me he'd given anyone permission to walk on lighthouse property."

Louise set her jaw. "He has never objected to my presence in the past."

"He gave you permission then?"

"No one has ever needed permission before. Why, many walk to the lighthouse in order to visit with members of the Blackthorn family."

"That's different," he acknowledged. "The walkways are open to everyone, but you are not on them."

The man was being most impertinent. "According to the late President Lincoln, our nation's government is *of* the people, *by* the people and *for* the people. Thus, government property belongs to the people of this country."

The girls twittered. A most inopportune reaction, for it clearly incensed the man standing before her.

His face darkened. "And the people have elected representatives to put laws in place. Those laws state that the land surrounding a lighthouse is set aside as federal government property. The marking posts and signs are clear." He pointed to a half-buried post. "You are trespassing."

"We are a small group of women. What harm can we do?"

"Don't you know that the previous lighthouse collapsed into the river thanks to erosion?"

Louise did not, but she saw no relevance in this point. "I'm certain a small group of women were not responsible for undermining the structure."

"Footsteps break down the surface of the dune, making it easier for the sand to slide downhill."

The hulking man was grasping at straws, and she had no intention of letting him push her from her purpose. Ordinarily she preferred calm to the storm, but this man was utterly unreasonable.

"Fine. I will speak with Mr. Blackthorn, then." Louise began walking in the direction of the lighthouse, expecting this newcomer, whoever he might be, to stand aside.

He did not. "*I* will speak to Mr. Blackthorn. If he approves your *study*, I will personally deliver that news to the school. Until then you may return to your classroom."

Odious, impossible man! She pointed her magnifying glass at his far-too-broad chest. "There are no plants inside the classroom. That is why we are in the field."

"Then choose another field outside government property."

"This happens to be the sole specimen of *artemisia campestris* within easy walking distance."

He bent to grab the plant, as if to yank it from the sand.

"Stop!" Louise grabbed his hand and was shocked by its warmth and strength. "Don't kill it."

"It's a plant."

She removed her hand and felt the heat flood her cheeks. What had possessed her to touch a man she didn't even know? A handsome man. A man that her students found more than attractive.

The whispering behind her had begun again. She could just imagine what they were saying. Priscilla might consider it a breach of etiquette. The girl could make trouble for her—or for the school.

"Are you all right?" The man peered at her.

She looked at the dune, at the sky, at anything other than the comely visage before her. She pressed a hand to her midsection, though it was her heart that raced.

"Perhaps I did overexert myself."

His lips twitched, as if a smile wanted to break out. "In that case, let me escort you down the dune. Simply point out the building where your school is housed, Miss…?"

He must be terribly new to town if he didn't know that Mrs. Evans's School for Ladies was the closest building to the lighthouse, excepting a lumber warehouse and the second sawmill.

He extended an arm. "Miss?"

She cleared her throat, realizing she hadn't introduced herself. "Mrs., actually. Mrs. Smythe. I'm widowed."

My, that had come out just as flustered as she felt. And her cheeks must be blazing red. What an outstanding mess of things she'd made.

The twittering behind her had stopped, so she hazarded a glance at the man. He was smiling—no, grinning—as if he thought he'd triumphed by making her blush!

Louise squared her shoulders again. She would not let this giant of a man affect her. "I thank you for your offer, but I am greatly recovered. Once we complete our field examination, we will be off your precious dune."

She then held up her magnifying glass and turned to the girls, who were huddled together, many of them slack-jawed and more than one starry-eyed. "Ladies!"

The group shot to attention and pulled out their magnifying glasses.

"We will examine the flowers of the tall wormwood first," Louise instructed. "Use your glasses to determine if it is in bloom or has gone to seed and then draw a likeness in your field notebook." She held up her well-worn notebook that contained sketches and notes on each species she encountered.

Not one girl moved.

"Come now, don't be afraid." Louise motioned in the direction of the plant and then turned toward it only to find herself looking at the buttons of the man's shirt not one foot from her nose. "Oh, you're still here."

"And you're still trespassing."

"As I said, we will be done shortly and then will vacate the property. If you have a problem with that, then I suggest you bring it up with Mr. Blackthorn." She ducked around the man and began demonstrating the use of the magnifying glass.

Priscilla marched past the man, but not without casting a flirtatious look his way. Since she led, the others followed, with Dinah dragging her feet in the rear. Her gaze lingered on the man, as if he was an oddity. Perhaps one could say he was, for Louise had never seen so tall a man, especially one who looked so perturbed.

"Mrs. Smythe."

"Sir?" she answered. "I have introduced myself, but it seems you have neglected to do likewise."

This time his color heightened, bringing giggles from the girls.

"Mr. Hammond. Mr. Jesse Hammond, Assistant Lighthouse Keeper."

Each word came out so stiffly that a laugh bubbled to her lips. "Are you always so formal?"

He looked affronted. "I am precise, Mrs. Smythe, to the letter of the law, which I have sworn to uphold."

"Really, Mr. Hammond, this is getting tedious. As I said, Mr. Blackthorn will have no objection to us hiking upon the dune to further our education. I promise we will not go near any of the buildings. You are quite safe."

His color heightened. "I am not concerned about my safety, madam." He sniffed the air.

Louise sniffed too. Something was burning.

"Fire," Mr. Jesse Hammond said even as he scanned the horizon in all directions.

Louise looked back at her students only to discover a dried leaf aflame at Dinah's feet. "Dinah!"

The girl shrieked and jumped, thankfully in the right direction. The other girls followed suit.

"Put it out, Mr. Hammond," Priscilla pleaded with several well-timed bats of her eyelids.

Before the man could issue yet another reprimand, Louise strode over, lifted her skirts slightly and stomped on the leaf until the flame was extinguished.

"There," she noted, spinning to face Mr. Hammond. "The problem is solved."

"This time, but it demonstrates why you shouldn't be here."

My, that man could aggravate! Louise focused on Dinah. "How did this happen?"

The girl had gone pale as snow. "I—I was just lookin' at things like you told us to do."

"Looking?"

"Aye." Dinah demonstrated holding out her glass.

"Your magnifying glass!" Louise turned so she stood in the same direction Dinah had been standing when the leaf caught fire. She held out her own magnifying glass. Sure enough, the sun's rays reflected and concentrated on the surface in a bright dot. "That's what happened. The sun must have reflected off the glass at just the right angle to set the leaf ablaze."

"Carelessness," Jesse Hammond stated. "Unchecked, it could have damaged one of the outbuildings or even spread toward town."

Louise was about to counter that statement with the obvious truth that a sea of dry sand lay between the burnt leaf and any building, but the girls had begun murmuring amongst themselves again.

Priscilla smiled coyly at Mr. Hammond. "What would we have done without your assistance, Mr. Hammond? We are ever so grateful."

Louise gritted her teeth. Pointing out that she had put out the fire would not endear her to Priscilla or Mr. Hammond. Since the girls' attention was lost, nothing more could be learned today.

"Very well, ladies, we shall shorten our study today."

That drew a grudging nod from the man. "I will hold you to that, Mrs. Smythe."

"And I will speak with Mr. Blackthorn at first opportunity."

He nodded again. "Please excuse me, ma'am. Ladies." He then strode off toward the lighthouse without a single backward glance.

Louise didn't know what she'd expected. The warmth of his hand and moment of compassion had vanished under the weight of his adherence to regulation. Jesse Hammond was a most unreasonable man.

"Isn't he about the most handsome man you ever saw?" Linore sighed.

"Too tall," Priscilla noted, as if she hadn't done her best to attract his attention.

Certainly he had towered over Louise. Now that he

was gone, her limbs set to trembling. The sheer force of the man brought back terrible fear. She closed her eyes and drew in a deep breath, telling herself to forget the past. Jesse Hammond was not her late husband. Other than stature, they likely shared nothing else. Moreover, she had no connection to this man. She need have no dealings with him.

In the future she would avoid any possibility of crossing Jesse Hammond's path.

Jesse had never been so skillfully outmaneuvered, especially by a tiny slip of a woman. He could appreciate that she'd stomped out the burning leaf rather than cry out like the girls, but that sensible act had only reminded him of his failure. He hadn't leapt into action—not six years ago and not now.

Moreover, Louise Smythe had managed to counter every argument he put forth. She was probably right that the keeper wouldn't mind. Blackthorn didn't follow every regulation exactly as written. Sometimes, he didn't follow them at all. That was a problem. A keeper was responsible for lives.

The smallest missed detail could lead to disaster, as Jesse well knew from that horrible night on the *Sultana*. The steamboat had left Vicksburg and then Memphis severely overloaded with soldiers eager to return home. They'd ignored the crowded conditions and sagging decks. After all, they'd endured the horrors of the prisoner of war camps. What was a little temporary discomfort when they soon would be home? Then came the explosion.

The memory still shook him from deep sleep, drenched in perspiration. Why had he survived when so many had died? He, above all, should have perished. Jesse asked

God for an answer, but he'd received none. The best he could do was save others. In the lighthouse service, he could warn ships of danger and rescue people from foundered vessels.

Blackthorn's indifference to regulation rubbed him wrong. Such callous disregard had cost lives six years ago. Jesse would make sure that never happened again. So, even though allowing a few ladies to walk across government property seemed innocuous, that burnt leaf pointed out how something small could lead to disaster.

Jesse located the keeper in the oil shed, drawing oil for the lamps. There wasn't enough room for two small men inside the shed, least of all someone his size, so he waited outside.

Blackthorn capped the brass transfer can he used to transport oil. "What can I do for you, Jesse?" He rose with the exaggerated groans of a timeworn elder. "Bones are getting creaky."

Jesse hoped that meant Blackthorn was considering retirement. It had surely led to the placement of an assistant, though Blackthorn had refused to relinquish many duties thus far.

Jesse returned his attention to the matter at hand. "I found some women walking on the dune just below the lighthouse."

"Any pretty ones?"

Jesse felt the heat rise and coughed to hide his discomfort. "They're young. Students." And thus far too young for him. Mrs. Smythe, on the other hand, was rather attractive, though he could never condone her disregard for rules.

"Must be the girls from the boarding school." Blackthorn exited the oil house and pulled the door shut. He then reached above the door, where he kept the key on a hook, and locked the door before putting the key back on its hook.

Jesse had tried to change this procedure, saying it didn't do much for security to keep the key within reach. By now, the whole town must know it was there. But his pleas had been met with a laugh and an assurance that "we've always done it this way." Blackthorn was too set in his ways. The lighthouse needed fresh eyes willing to see things in safer and more efficient ways.

"Was their teacher with them?" Blackthorn asked.

"Yes."

"Mrs. Smythe." Blackthorn shook his head. "Odd sort, that one. She'll spend hours staring at a clump of dune grass, making notes in some book of hers."

No doubt that was the journal she'd waved at her students. It looked well-used. Louise Smythe was not the type of woman he'd expected to find in a town like Singapore.

"She has an unusual interest in science." That had intrigued Jesse.

Blackthorn squinted at him. "You don't say. The lady hardly says a word."

"That's not my experience. She said plenty to me."

"Maybe she's getting more like the rest of the women she came here with."

"The rest? There's more like her?"

Blackthorn chuckled. "In a manner of speaking. Back, oh, I'd say a year ago, Mrs. Smythe arrived in town with Pearl Lawson, Amanda Porter and Fiona O'Keefe. They were answering an advertisement for a bride." Again he laughed.

"That's humorous?"

"It was at the time. Seems they all thought Roland Decker was the prospective groom when in fact it was his brother Garrett. You should've seen them running from one man to the other. Fact was, neither brother wanted to get married."

"Then why place an advertisement?"

"They didn't." Blackthorn began walking back to the tower. "Turns out Garrett Decker's children did. They wanted a new mama. Got one too. And Roland Decker and Sawyer Evans claimed two of the other three. There's only Mrs. Smythe left. Of course, she's the oldest. Must be around thirty."

Then Jesse hadn't been mistaken about her age. "What else do you know about her?" When Blackthorn gave him a quick look, Jesse regretted his question. "I need to know how to deal with her," he added, feeling the heat again creep up his neck. "She's…difficult."

"Is she? Always seemed quiet as a mouse to me. Would rather poke her nose in a book than speak to anyone. Skips most of the church suppers and the like. Maybe the missus knows more."

They'd reached the lighthouse. Rather than enter the tower, Blackthorn stuck his head into the door to the keeper's quarters.

"Jane!"

Jesse waved his hands, trying to get Blackthorn to stop. He did not want Mrs. Blackthorn involved. She would start matching him to every eligible girl in town.

Blackthorn came out of the open doorway. "Go on in, Jane'll tell you anything you want to know."

"Uh, that's not what I wanted."

"Ambitious young man like you oughta be lookin' for a wife."

Jesse squared his shoulders. "First I need to be able to provide." Unlike his father and mother, whose impetuous decision cost dearly. "Maybe when I'm head keeper I'll be able to consider a wife."

Blackthorn shook his head. "You got a lot ta learn, son. A man's got a leg up on gettin' the head job if he's got a wife and family."

"He does?" That was news to Jesse, troubling news, for he couldn't afford a wife.

"Oh, you won't catch anyone sayin' it right out, but you just look around, especially at them remote lights, and you'll see what I mean. One man can't run this place. Not when the service expects you ta be on duty twenty-four hours a day."

Now Jesse understood. The man was back to his favorite annoyance—Jesse's arrival. "That's why there are assistants."

"Assistants! Bah!" Blackthorn waved off the idea as he headed for the tower.

Jesse followed, his thoughts drifting back to the earlier conflict on the dune. "What I really need to know is if you approve of Mrs. Smythe trespassing on government property."

Blackthorn shook his head. "You gotta get your head out of those books of yours and into real life. Those ladies aren't doing no harm. This here's a small town. Everyone knows everyone else. It pays to be on people's good side."

"But the property—"

"This isn't a fort. It's a lighthouse. People are curious. They stop by all the time. Treat 'em like a neighbor, and they'll do the same for you."

Blackthorn then opened the door to the tower. Each day he poured some of the oil into a smaller filling can and then carried it up the circular iron staircase to begin filling the lamps. The process took several trips up and down the tower staircase. According to Article IV of the manual, the filling of the lamps was supposed to be done as soon as the lamps were cleaned except when cold weather would make the oil too thick to flow. That meant late morning, but Blackthorn didn't keep a regular schedule. Moreover, today's warm temperatures offered no excuse for tardiness. If Jesse was head keeper, he'd follow the manual's instructions to the letter. As assistant, he could only stand by.

"Let me help you." Jesse stooped slightly to get through the door.

"No need."

Jesse swallowed frustration. The keeper hadn't let him touch anything in the lantern. If Jesse was ever going to be head keeper, he had to know more than could be gleaned from the manual. He needed experience. Even without that experience, he'd discovered some inefficiencies that could be rectified. "I could show you a faster way to handle the oil."

Blackthorn practically glared at him. "I've been tending lighthouses for more than twenty years. Don't you think that I know what works best and what doesn't?"

Jesse choked back the retort that clearly Blackthorn didn't. If he would carry the large can up the stairs and transfer the oil to the smaller filling can when he reached the top, he wouldn't have to go up and down the staircase so many times. Since pointing this out had gotten Jesse nowhere, he wouldn't rankle the keeper again.

So Jesse swallowed his pride. "I suppose you do, sir."

"That's right. Jane said she needed something from the store. Find out what it is and go fetch it." The man finished pouring the first batch of oil into the filling can and began the long climb up the circular staircase, the soles of his boots ringing against the iron steps.

Jesse backed out. Though he'd only been here six days,

he was sick of being nothing more than an errand boy. Other than polishing lamps, which the children could do, Blackthorn hadn't let him near any of the equipment. Jesse closed the tower door against the ever-drifting sand.

"What do you want to know about Louise?" Mrs. Blackthorn's voice made him jump. "Didn't mean to startle you. I thought you were expecting me."

"I was?"

"Samuel said it was something about Louise Smythe?"

"Oh. I suppose I did, ma'am." Jesse couldn't recall what he'd intended to ask about Louise. Since Blackthorn approved her climbing all over the dunes, Jesse had lost that argument. He searched for something else. "I, uh, understand she's a teacher." That sounded pretty feeble.

"Down at the boarding school in the west wing of the hotel." Mrs. Blackthorn pointed it out, as if he hadn't noticed the place before.

It hadn't taken long to ascertain that Singapore was tiny. It boasted few businesses beyond the general store, the boardinghouse and the hotel. There were a few saloons, but Jesse didn't frequent those, and the church looked like the rest of the bunkhouses used by the lumberjacks and saw operators when they came to town. Boardwalks stretched between businesses so people didn't have to walk through the sand. The streets served more pedestrians than wheeled transportation. Jesse had yet to see a buggy or horse other than the wagon down at the docks. Then again, the town was only a few blocks long and even fewer deep.

It was a good place to begin remaking his life.

"I hear tell she's a war widow," Mrs. Blackthorn said.

The words shot through Jesse like lead. Not the war. He'd done all he could to escape the harrowing memories. A lighthouse offered a chance to get away from the endless war stories and sorrow. He'd hoped to land at a remote island lighthouse but instead was assigned here.

"You all right, Mr. Hammond?"

Jesse managed a smile. "Just lost in thought."

"Just like her."

"Like who?"

"Like who?" Mrs. Blackthorn shook her head. "Like Louise. That's who we've been talking about, isn't it?"

Jesse had to agree that it was, but Mrs. Blackthorn's description of her didn't match his experience. "She didn't seem very quiet to me."

That made Mrs. Blackthorn smile. "Well now, isn't that interesting. Might be you managed to catch her eye. She is looking to marry, you know."

Jesse grimaced. "That's what your husband said. But I'm not. I need to get established as a keeper first."

"Isn't that just like a man."

Jesse stiffened. "A man needs to be able to provide."

"Love doesn't wait for our schedule. Neither does the lighthouse service."

That was the second Blackthorn who had mentioned marriage in connection with being a keeper. "Why do you say that?"

"Samuel would never have been named keeper if he hadn't had a wife and family."

Jesse was still skeptical. The woman could be using it as an excuse to match make. "Are you certain?"

"As certain as day and night. Why, they came right out and asked him if he was married."

Jesse's heart sank. He wasn't ready for marriage. He hadn't saved nearly enough to support a wife, but if he wanted to get promoted to head keeper, he was going to have to set aside his reservations. This town didn't look big enough to offer much of a choice, not if men were willing to advertise for a wife.

"Louise would make a fine catch. Did you notice the cut of her clothing?"

Jesse couldn't say he had.

"Quality," Mrs. Blackthorn said. "Pure quality. That says something."

So did the fact that she was a war widow. If he must marry, he would look anywhere else for a wife.

Chapter Two

The remainder of the day, Priscilla had remained smugly silent, her gaze boring into Louise with such intensity that she feared the girl was up to no good. To cut off possible problems, Louise went to the headmistress's office once classes had ended and the girls were upstairs freshening up before supper.

Fiona Evans sat at the desk perusing what appeared to be a ledger. Her brow was furrowed, and she rubbed her temple while eliciting a sigh.

Dread settled in the pit of Louise's stomach. She'd heard rumors that Fiona and Sawyer's hotel was not doing well. Since the school was in the same building, her livelihood could be at risk, especially if Priscilla said anything negative to her parents. Though nothing untoward had happened on the dune, Priscilla could twist the truth into something ugly. The Benningtons could do great damage to the school's reputation. Their approval of the new school had led to Adeline and Esther's enrollment. At their word, every paying student could leave. That made this conversation both important and difficult.

Louise rapped on the door frame. "You seem worried."

Fiona looked up and closed the ledger. "More like perplexed. I don't have a mind for figures. Please come in." The beautiful redhead motioned to the chair positioned at the side of her desk. "My apologies for the hot room. I had hoped autumn would bring cooler temperatures. I don't know when I've seen so many hot, dry days this time of year."

"It is unusual." Louise's shoes rapped on the waxed wood floor as she crossed the room.

She then settled on the chair. Though she and Fiona had become friends before the school came into existence, it didn't make this conversation any easier. She searched for a way to begin.

Fiona gave her the opening she needed. "What's bothering you? Trouble with one of the students?"

"I hope not, but I'm afraid something happened today that might give them a reason to complain."

"Oh?" Fiona arched one of her perfect eyebrows.

The former star of the New York stage was the most beautiful woman Louise had ever seen. That she chose to marry a lumber mill sawyer and settle in Singapore was surprising. That she called Louise her friend was just as unlikely, but they'd formed a bond during the hardships of last spring, when a steamship foundered on an offshore sandbar and they joined together to care for the stranded passengers.

Louise began slowly, feeling her way through what had happened. "I brought the girls on the dune to survey a particular plant for our science class, but the assistant lighthouse keeper told us we had to leave the property."

"The assistant keeper joined your class?"

"Unexpectedly." And unwelcome, Louise thought as she recalled his inflexibility. "He objected to our presence."

"Go on."

"I…saw no reason to interrupt our studies. Mr. Blackthorn never objected to my crossing the property in the past, and I told him that."

Mirth sparkled in Fiona's eyes. "I see. Was this man handsome?"

Louise felt her cheeks heat. "That is not the point. I…well, I inadvertently touched the man."

"Touched?"

"Well, more like grabbed onto him. He was going to pull out the plant, and I had to stop him. He was going to kill it."

"Kill it." Fiona's lips twitched. Was she going to laugh?

Louise explained, "I couldn't let him needlessly destroy a living thing, so I stopped him."

"He must have been surprised."

That was not the half of it. "I believe some of the girls found my reaction a bit too forward and not becoming a teacher."

"It was innocent."

"Exactly." Louise was relieved that Fiona saw it that way. "However, I wanted to let you know what happened in case anyone complained."

"I see." Fiona rose. "Is that all?"

It wasn't. "There might be another complaint. From the man."

"Oh?"

Louise could see a spark of excitement light up Fiona's eyes. Now that Fiona and the rest of the women who'd come to Singapore were married, they'd taken it upon themselves to match Louise with every eligible bachelor. Though she had no idea if Mr. Hammond was married or not, he could never be her match.

"He's more than a little rude. He threatened to remove my students and me from the dune."

Fiona's lips twitched. She *was* going to laugh!

"And then there was the fire."

That sobered Fiona. "The fire?"

"Dinah's magnifying glass accidentally caught a leaf on fire, but I stomped it out at once."

"I'm sure that impressed him. What did you say his name was again?"

"Mr. Hammond. Mr. Jesse Hammond."

"Oh! Mr. Hammond." Fiona beamed. "I met him this afternoon at the store. He arrived less than a week ago and is unmarried."

Naturally Fiona would ask about that. Louise pretended indifference. "So are most of the sawyers and lumberjacks."

Fiona laughed. "True, but Mr. Hammond seems unusually intellectual. He talked at great length about the weather."

"The weather."

"Yes. He explained in great detail why it's been so hot and dry this year. I found it fascinating and believe our students will also, so I asked him to give a lecture."

"Here?" The word barely squeaked through Louise's constricted throat.

"Of course it would be here." Fiona peered at her. "Is that a problem?"

Louise couldn't begin to articulate all the reasons why this was a bad idea, starting with the fact that the girls wouldn't hear one word he said. Oh, they'd be quiet as mice. They'd be busy daydreaming over the handsome lighthouse assistant. But that was a petty objection. Young ladies would always sigh over a man before listening to him.

Louise had a more personal reason. "I too know a

great deal about the weather, thanks to Captain Elder's instruction. I can prepare the lecture."

"Splendid! Since it's also an interest of yours, I suggest you collaborate with Mr. Hammond."

The room grew intolerably hot. Louise couldn't draw a breath, could barely think. All that came to mind was the impossibility of Fiona's plan. Jesse Hammond was large and demanding. He would not listen to a word she had to say. He would counter and crush her every suggestion.

"Collaborate?" she managed to gasp.

"It's the perfect solution. He plans to stop by the school tomorrow morning, but I'll be leading music instruction at that time. Since you'll be free, you can discuss the lecture with him."

Louise struggled to draw in a breath. The idea was entirely intolerable. She and Jesse Hammond? Working together to present a lecture? "He agreed to work with me?"

"Don't underestimate your abilities. You have much to offer, and he will be grateful for your guidance."

"What guidance?"

"For one, you can ensure he doesn't speak over the ladies' heads. Help him steer his knowledge into something that will engage the students."

After the way Jesse Hammond treated her earlier today, Louise would have enjoyed seeing him fail in front of her students. Her conscience pricked. That wasn't very kind.

"You will do it?" Fiona prodded.

Louise didn't want to, but this school had given her strength and purpose. Rather than relying on marriage to a man she did not know, she could support herself through teaching. She owed Fiona a great deal.

She nodded her assent. A few minutes with Jesse

Hammond couldn't be that terrible. She would use the time to persuade the man not to give that lecture.

How had Jesse let himself get talked into lecturing in front of a bunch of girls? Mrs. Evans hadn't accepted his polite refusal, and then the woman manning the store counter had chimed in with how much a guest lecturer would enrich the ladies' education. They'd shamed him into it.

Worst of all, he saw no way to avoid Louise Smythe, since she worked at the school. Not that the widow wasn't pretty, but she was a widow—a childless widow. And both Mrs. Evans and the store clerk had been far too eager to corral him into the lecture for him to believe their motives were strictly educational.

Jesse picked at his food, which drew the notice of Mrs. Blackthorn, yet another matchmaker.

"You feeling all right, Mr. Hammond? You've hardly touched a thing on your plate."

"I'm fine." To demonstrate, he shoved a forkful of potatoes into his mouth.

"Good trout," Mr. Blackthorn mumbled between heaping bites of the fried fish and mashed potatoes.

The boys, both adolescents, were too preoccupied with eating as much as possible to pay any attention to the conversation.

Jesse swallowed the potatoes. "Yes, ma'am. It's very good."

Mrs. Blackthorn beamed while her daughter sighed and gave him that dreamy look the girls from the boarding school had given him. Over the years he'd grown accustomed to that reaction. Maybe that was why Louise stuck in his mind. She hadn't fawned and sighed over him. Quite the reverse. Although refreshing, it puzzled him. How does a man respond to a woman who doesn't show the slightest interest in him? It was easy enough to dismiss the hopeful, but the disinterested presented a new challenge.

"You do seem a little out of sorts, Mr. Hammond," Mrs. Blackthorn said as she slathered butter on a dinner roll. "You've hardly said a word."

Jesse didn't usually speak during meals, but there was no use pointing that out. "I'm fine."

Mr. Blackthorn peered at him. "Did you go and get someone else irritated at you?"

"No, sir." He still wasn't accustomed to eating with the family, but board was part of his compensation.

"Good." Blackthorn pointed a fork at him. "It pays to stay on everyone's good side."

Mrs. Blackthorn nodded. "Did you happen to see Louise Smythe when you were at the store?"

"No, ma'am." Jesse clenched his jaw. He'd have to ask Blackthorn for an hour off tomorrow morning. Now was as good a time as any. "I did meet Mrs. Evans, though. She asked me to give a short lecture on weather to the students."

Blackthorn peered at him. "You don't say. Never asked me to do that."

Jesse wasn't about to mention his suspicion that Mrs. Evans, like Mrs. Blackthorn, was trying to match him with Louise Smythe. "It just came up in conversation. If you object, I'll tell her I can't do it." He tried not to sound as hopeful as he felt.

"No, no." Blackthorn waved off the suggestion. "How long can it take? An hour? As long as we don't have a storm brewing, it's fine with me."

Jesse tried not to show his disappointment. "Thank you, sir."

"It'll spread a little goodwill." Blackthorn cocked his head. "Maybe you can have the girls polish some of the brass pitchers."

"Samuel! The girls are supposed to learn, not do your work for you," his wife scolded. She then turned a smile in Jesse's direction. "That means you'll have a chance to see Louise."

Jesse was not about to reveal that he wanted as little contact as possible with Mrs. Smythe.

"You should pay her a call," Mrs. Blackthorn continued, oblivious to his discomfort, "one evening or this weekend."

"I'm not planning to call on any woman just yet."

"Oh?" Mrs. Blackthorn looked to her husband.

"I thought you aimed to be head keeper." Blackthorn's fork jabbed his way again. "You'll need someone to watch the light when you're sleeping, like during a storm."

"And help with all the cleaning," Mrs. Blackthorn added.

"Like I told ya, the service looks kindly on those that're married," Blackthorn added.

Jesse tried his best not to let on that he knew they were conspiring to get him married. "There's still plenty of time."

After all, it had taken over a year for Jesse to wind his way through the political connections needed to get a nomination from the customs collector and then to secure approval from the lighthouse board.

"You're thirty-one," Mrs. Blackthorn stated. "Louise's age. A woman like her won't wait forever."

It took herculean effort not to plead an end to this matchmaking. Instead, he focused on fact. "I only have a small room. That's no place to bring a wife."

"We began that way," Mrs. Blackthorn pointed out.

Clearly Jesse was going to lose the argument unless he could come up with a solid excuse. "It would cost the service more in provisions."

"Not as much as bringing in an assistant," Blackthorn said. "Take my word. If you want to be appointed head keeper somewhere, get married and have children."

Jesse had long dreamed of having a large family with children running everywhere, but he'd first postponed it due to the war and then in favor of getting into the lighthouse service. It'd been years since he'd courted anyone.

"I wouldn't know where to start," he murmured.

"Start with Louise Smythe." Mrs. Blackthorn returned to her favorite topic. "She's looking to marry. You're the same age. Perfect match."

Except she was a war widow. The nightmares already plagued him. Widows often asked how men died in the war. Even the question brought back painful memories.

"There must be other eligible women."

Blackthorn shook his head. "Not in Singapore. You won't find many unmarried women here. Except the girls at the school."

Jesse blanched. "They're far too young. I have in mind someone more…mature."

"Well, if it doesn't work out with Louise," Mrs. Blackthorn said hesitantly, "you could always try advertising for a bride."

Advertising. It sounded perfectly logical and businesslike. No messy emotions involved. And it had apparently worked for three men in town. It would be a simple transaction for the betterment of both parties. The woman could have a family, and he could get a head keeper's position elsewhere in the district.

That evening, instead of napping before his midnight watch, Jesse stared at a piece of paper, trying to come up with the right words. It felt uncomfortable to advertise for a wife, but he told himself that it was the best solution.

"Wife needed," he wrote.

What next? He supposed he should list the qualifications any prospective candidate ought to possess. Hardiness, homemaking abilities, skilled with children. All those came into play.

He jotted a few down and tried to picture the woman who might answer. Why did Louise Smythe come to mind?

Frustrated, he crumpled the paper. Then he recalled he only had a few sheets of paper on hand. He'd better draft the wording on this sheet and save the rest for the clean copies of the advertisement to mail out.

So, he smoothed the crumpled paper and tried again. Maybe he should point out his own assets too. So Jesse rewrote the advertisement.

When satisfied, he copied it three times and put those copies into three envelopes addressed to different Chicago newspapers. In the morning, he would put them into the outgoing mail.

Louise tidied up the classroom late the following morning. If she didn't know such a thing was impossible, she'd think Priscilla had given her headache to her. Louise had ignored the girl's countless pleas to be excused from writing and mathematics, too preoccupied with Jesse Hammond's imminent arrival to deal with anything else. She would let Fiona handle Priscilla.

Louise squared her shoulders. She would not be pushed around. Not by a manipulative girl and not by a demanding man.

She squeezed her eyes shut against the sting of memory. *No tears. Please, no tears.* That's the last thing she needed Jesse Hammond to see. She was strong. She'd endured every blow her late husband, Warren, had thrown at her and survived. She instinctively touched her jaw, which still ached on occasion, particularly when the weather was cool and damp.

Weather! What did Jesse Hammond know about the weather that she didn't? She would demonstrate that knowledge and send Mr. Hammond running back to the lighthouse.

A clearing of the throat indicated the guest lecturer had arrived.

Louise turned and fixed her gaze on him.

My, oh my. The man had seemed large in the open air, but framed by the doorway, he was positively gigantic. He wasn't heavy or overweight, but was so tall that the top of his head grazed the lintel. He leaned on one jamb, his arms crossed and his hat dangling from one hand.

A boyish grin rested on his lips. "You looked so engrossed that I hated to interrupt you."

What could she tell him? Certainly not the truth, that she'd relived a harrowing episode from her past. No, she must be strong and secure. God was her strength and her shield. He would protect her from all harm. Though images of the martyrs flashed through her mind, she pushed those aside. She was in a school after all. Nothing could happen to her here.

"I was merely considering how best to approach the topic so the young ladies understand what you're telling them." She affixed him with a steady gaze, a technique that she had seen Fiona use to maintain control. "That is my role, as I understand it."

Jesse Hammond didn't back down. "Unnecessary. You can continue doing whatever it is you were doing."

"Then you fully understand what a young woman

wants to learn and how best to instruct her. Perhaps you lectured many younger sisters?"

"My sister is older and long married."

"Then you have no idea."

He tugged at the neckline of his shirt, though he hadn't attached a stiff collar or donned a tie. "I will explain cloud formations and how they can tell which ones are likely to bring rain, so they can avoid going out-of-doors. That's all they'll care about."

"Then you think the sole interest of any woman is the condition of her hat and gown. Did it not occur to you that a woman might want to learn? That she is fully capable of any and all intellectual pursuits? Or are you as patronizing as the rest of the men I've encountered?"

His jaw actually dropped. Perhaps she'd gone too far. Then again, such ridiculous beliefs had held back progress far too long.

"Once women join the scientific movement in force," she continued, "advances will come at a rapid pace. Imagine curing disease. Or saving the lives of sailors."

"That's my job, ma'am." He looked like he was struggling not to laugh. Laugh!

"I'll have you know, Mr. Hammond, that I know as much, if not more than you do on the subject of the weather. Captain Elder, the husband of the dear woman I took care of for many months, spoke with me at great length and let me read his volumes on the subject."

"Then explain the different types of clouds and what type of weather each signals."

Though Louise knew this forward and backward, her mind went blank in the face of his challenge.

"Just what I thought," he said after a short pause. "All empty-headed talk."

If Louise was not a proper lady, she would have come

back with a scathing retort or at least stomped her foot at his insolence.

Instead, she stiffened her spine. "Are you saying that Captain Elder did not teach me correctly? I'll have you know that he explained cumulous, stratus, nimbus and cirrus clouds."

His eyebrows lifted and so did the corners of his mouth.

She was not done. "A sea captain must know weather patterns far more intimately than a lighthouse keeper, who is safely ashore. His life and the lives of his crew are at stake."

"Those same lives are at stake if the light is improperly lit or stays dark."

"Yes, of course, but your life is not in danger."

"Except when plunging into the seas to save the lives of others."

She recalled the rescue effort last spring that had brought many passengers to safety—including Linore and Dinah—from a stranded steamboat.

"True," she admitted, "but not on as frequent a basis. Moreover, if what I heard was correct, Mr. Blackthorn advised against attempting the rescue of passengers on a stranded ship last spring."

Judging from his look of distaste, he didn't think much of that decision. "Saving lives is our purpose."

Louise's anger abated. Jesse wasn't as arrogant and uncaring as he'd seemed. He simply followed the dictates of society and consequently rubbed on her nerves. Society insisted women had lesser intellects. It was only natural that Jesse would believe what he'd been taught since birth. She must show him otherwise.

She strode across the room to the bookshelves. Classroom texts and leisure reading filled the lower shelves, but on top were a few precious volumes.

She dragged a step stool in front of the bookcase. "Captain Elder donated a few of his volumes to the school, including one on the climate."

She climbed one step but still could not reach the shelf.

"Allow me." Jesse Hammond crossed the room. "I can easily fetch the volume for you."

She could feel him uncomfortably close. "I can get it." She climbed another step and reached.

She must have set the stool on one of the uneven floor planks, for it tilted beneath her. She cried out as the whole thing gave way. Then, before even one foot touched the ground, strong arms caught her and held her close.

Oh, my!

She could feel his heart beating. His breath tickled her cheek. Every nerve ending inside her came to life.

Oh, my!

If she was the fainting sort, she'd have swooned at once. Instead, an incredible warmth rushed through her, as if she had spent too much time in the summer sun. She had never once felt that way with Warren. What was happening to her?

He set her on the ground but did not release her. She looked up at him. A strange expression was on his face, and she caught her breath. He felt it too! She looked away, her heart racing. This was wrong, terribly wrong. Then why did she feel like a schoolgirl hoping he would continue to hold her close and even kiss her?

She could not breathe, could not speak, could barely think.

"You should be more careful." His voice was rough.

She recognized all too well the signs of attraction. For all his faults, Warren had once been smitten with her. She hesitantly looked up. He looked down at her, his sky-blue eyes darkening as his pupils dilated. His expression softened.

Her pulse raced. Her limbs shook.

He leaned close, lips brushing past her forehead.

"Mrs. Smythe?" The girl's voice pierced through the cloud of emotion.

Priscilla! Louise shot out of Jesse's embrace and smoothed her skirts.

The girl stood in the doorway, smirking and apparently free of the headache she'd claimed all morning.

Louise hurried to control the damage. "Thank you, Mr. Hammond, for saving me from a terrible spill." She picked up the stool. "How careless of me to place it on a wobbly board."

She hoped that would spare her from Priscilla's manipulations.

"You are excused, Miss Bennington."

"Of course, Mrs. Smythe." But that smirk didn't leave her lips as she flounced off toward the dining room.

"I hope I didn't get you into trouble," Jesse said.

Louise closed her eyes and took in a deep breath. Too late. If only he'd risen to Louise's defense, Priscilla might have believed her story. Instead, this little episode could prove costly, if not for her personally then for the school.

Chapter Three

What had he been thinking? That was the trouble. Jesse wasn't thinking. If he had been, he would never have remained so close to Louise Smythe.

It had begun innocently enough, saving her from a fall, but he'd held on too long. Then, overwhelmed by the feel of her in his arms, he'd considered kissing her. Louise's long eyelashes swept to her eyebrows, and her gray eyes, which could be severe, had softened to the color of a gentle rain. She'd drawn in her breath, and her cheeks turned the most delightful shade of pink.

Her reaction was so unexpected that it had caught him off guard. She'd been the one woman who didn't sigh and stare at him. She'd seemed completely unaffected until that moment. Maybe that was what had tempted him. The immoveable had become irresistible.

Why had he succumbed to temptation?

That prissy girl with the blond curls had noted the near-embrace with a smug grin of triumph.

Jesse had stepped back the moment Louise leapt from his arms. Her explanation might have succeeded if she wasn't blushing the entire time. Then she demanded the girl leave them.

This would not end well.

"Perhaps I should go," he offered. "We could discuss the lecture another day. Or not at all."

"Are you suggesting I don't know enough about the subject to even assist you? I'll have you know that I could give that lecture."

Jesse put up his hands in surrender. "I'm sure you could. I'm just offering to step away if it'll make matters better for you."

"Things will go just fine, no thanks to you."

Jesse wasn't used to receiving reprimands from a feminine quarter. His sister, Beatrice, had been more interested in her own trials than in disciplining her little brother. His father…well, he'd never quite been himself after Ma's death. "Forgive me. Next time I'll let you fall."

Louise flushed even more furiously. "That's not what I meant. I was referring to…to…well, you know." She brushed at her hair, though it was in perfect order. "Priscilla probably got the wrong impression."

No doubt she had. Jesse's lips had brushed against Louise's forehead. Preventing her fall could be explained away, but not holding her in such an intimate way. "I will talk to Mrs. Evans."

For a brief second, she looked hopeful, and then a shadow clouded her eyes. "That won't be necessary." Yet she stepped a little farther away. Her gaze drifted downward and then she exclaimed, "The book!"

She bent to pick up the fallen volume.

Jesse hurried to lift the heavy tome first. His hand collided with hers.

"Oh!" She jumped back and rubbed her hand as if it had been stung.

"I'm sorry." He seemed to be saying that a lot. "Maybe I'd better leave."

"Yes, perhaps you should." Yet that admission came with surprising wistfulness.

"I can cancel the lecture." Had those words really come from his mouth? Yet it was the perfect solution. "Since you are very knowledgeable about the weather, I'll leave the lecture to you."

Something like a smile flashed across her lips, only to vanish the next instant. "Thank you for your confidence, but Mrs. Evans asked you to give the lecture. I am only here to answer your questions and offer support."

Jesse ignored the irony. Moments before they'd argued bitterly over just that.

"I might like to hear what your Captain Elder told you," he suggested.

The smile returned, this time to stay.

"He was well-read and experienced, a dear man, and highly acquainted with the sea."

"I have no doubt," he murmured.

She gave him a sharp look.

"As you said," he added, "ship masters need to understand the weather."

Again she beamed, and he had to admit it felt good. He would much rather be on Louise Smythe's good side than endure her scathing tongue. Not that he was interested in courting her. Not at all.

"It was completely innocent." Louise reported to Fiona Evans just after the midday meal. "I slipped, and he—Mr. Hammond—caught me. I tried to explain that to Priscilla, but I don't think she believed me. I'm afraid that this time she will make trouble."

Fiona arched an eyebrow. "I would never dismiss you."

"Thank you." It was the other possibility that had made it impossible for Louise to eat more than a few spoonfuls of soup. "I'm worried that she will disparage the school. Priscilla could tell her parents that the school allows improper behavior." That could then force Louise's dismissal. Since her purse was empty, she would be in a terrible predicament.

"How exactly is a gentleman coming to your rescue improper?" Fiona brushed back a red curl. "I'd call it gallant."

"I, uh, might have lingered too long after he steadied me. Priscilla could have interpreted that as…attraction." Heat flooded Louise's cheeks.

"Oh?" The single word clearly carried an additional inference.

"It's not what you're thinking." Actually, it probably was exactly what Fiona was thinking. That man had a way of taking away Louise's good sense. "I—I was too flustered to think clearly. The point is, Priscilla doubtless thought there was more to the situation."

"Is there?"

"No!" Yet Louise's burning cheeks refuted her statement. "I don't know. I just met him." She squared her shoulders and looked Fiona in the eye. "But I can tell you that Jesse Hammond is the last man I would let court me."

Fiona's eyebrow lifted again. "Why is that?"

It was so difficult to explain. Or was it? "He reminds me too much of my late husband."

"Oh. I see."

Last spring, Louise had shared with Fiona a little of what she'd endured during her marriage, but she didn't care to explain further.

"That's neither here nor there." Louise tried her best to sound cheerful. "What matters now is how to address the situation with Priscilla. I don't want the school to suffer.

The Benningtons are influential enough to drive away prospective students."

Fiona sighed. "I'm afraid this is a problem she's had at the other schools she attended."

Though that news was not surprising, Louise wished her friend had passed that along before now. "What did the schools do?"

"Sent Priscilla home and refunded her entire tuition. Do you recommend we do that too?"

Louise blanched. That solution would surely shut down the school; Priscilla would doubtless take the other girls with her, for the parents were all acquainted.

"No," Louise said slowly. "She shouldn't pay for my mistake. I should have been more careful. I hope we can convince her not to turn this incident into a complaint."

"How would you suggest doing that?"

Louise hadn't expected to have this tossed back at her, but an idea rushed into her mind. "I don't think she wants to leave. Not deep down. I've known girls like her, and what they want most of all is attention."

"You could be right." Still, Fiona shook her head. "I've known girls like Priscilla. They could never get enough attention and would take down everyone around them in the effort."

"But I must try," Louise whispered. "I just don't know how."

"Try encouraging her more. Give her praise when she deserves it."

That would be difficult. Priscilla seldom did anything praiseworthy. "I'll try."

Fiona rose. "If there is nothing else, I would like to speak with my husband before voice lessons."

"Thank you for understanding."

Fiona cast her a knowing smile. "Don't worry so much

about reputation. It's perfectly natural for a woman to find Mr. Hammond attractive. You do want to marry, after all."

Louise hadn't the heart to tell her friend that she no longer wished for marriage. The kind of gentleman she sought could only be found in novels. The men of real life never measured up. Mrs. Evans's School for Ladies had given her a means to support herself without the assistance of a husband. That was far safer than risking marriage, especially to a man whose strength and need for control was just like that of her late husband.

Jesse had expected Louise Smythe to accept his offer to step aside from the lecture. Her refusal left him unsteady, as if trying to get footing on the heaving deck of a ship. He'd offered exactly what she wanted. Why turn it down? Was she trying to force him into something? If she considered her reputation compromised, would she expect marriage? Blackthorn had mentioned she came to Singapore to marry, but the groom chose another woman. Perhaps she was desperate. Had he just stepped into her snare?

He couldn't marry Louise Smythe. Even if she came from a privileged background, which her education indicated she did, a lumber town wouldn't care about a woman's reputation.

The memory of Louise in his arms flitted through his mind.

He shook it away. A momentary feeling had no bearing on choosing a lifetime partner. Jesse must select wisely. He would not make the mistake his father had made in marrying a woman unable to bear the rigors of the life she'd married into.

Etta Webber had been born into society with all its

manners and protectiveness. The fragile girl had fallen in love with his father and, ignoring her family's protests, wed him and moved to Chicago. Pa worked the wharves. Life was rough. Ma had to make do in a tiny apartment with no servants. First came Beatrice and then ten years later Jesse. But it was the stillborn baby that sent her into that dark place from which she never returned.

Intense sorrow threatened to flood in, but Jesse pushed it away. He'd been just seven when his mother died. Died! Bitterness twisted a soul worse than the deepest grief. Etta Hammond hadn't just died. She'd walked out of the house and into the path of an oncoming train.

No, Jesse would choose a sturdy, solid woman for a wife. Preferably without emotional attachment. That ruled out Louise Smythe.

As he polished brass filling pitchers, funnels and measuring cans at the little table at the base of the tower staircase, he considered how best to get out of this lecture. Approaching Louise wouldn't work. He couldn't think straight around her. He would tell Mrs. Evans that he needed to withdraw from the lecture and recommend Louise give it instead. Louise wouldn't be able to refuse her employer.

If that didn't work… Jesse blew out his breath. It had to work.

Blackthorn pushed open the door. "Done with that pitcher? It's time to fill the lamps." He rotated his shoulder with a groan. "Gets heavier every day."

Jesse gave the pitcher a final swipe. "I could haul the first batch of oil up the stairs." Best to give up his quest to refine procedure until Blackthorn was more receptive. "You carry the pitcher and funnel."

Blackthorn hesitated. For a moment he looked ready to agree, but then he shook his head. "I've got it."

Jesse suddenly realized what an opportunity stood before him. Blackthorn was the answer. If Louise refused to give the lecture, maybe the light keeper would. He had complained about not being asked. If Jesse did this right, he could learn a little about preparing the light at the same time.

"Actually, I'd like your advice…on a personal matter." Jesse nodded his head toward the house. "Away from female ears."

"Oh?" That definitely caught Blackthorn's attention. "In that case, why don't you carry the oil while I bring the rest of the stuff? You can bring the large can up to the lantern."

"Yes, sir." Jesse bit back the impulse to point out that this was exactly what he'd just suggested.

He lifted the large transfer can. It could hold up to five gallons, but Blackthorn had only filled it halfway. Jesse could easily carry double the weight, but Blackthorn wasn't young anymore. No wonder he preferred to pour the oil into the smaller cans and make multiple trips up the tower staircase. Maybe he let his sons help when they were home from school.

A son. What a blessing that would be! An intense longing sprang up in Jesse. He would do things differently from his father. No threats. Jesse would be there for his sons. He could imagine skipping stones across the waves, tossing a ball and teaching his boys all the duties of a lighthouse keeper. At meals, the large family would settle around the table as his wife…

Jesse shook his head. Why on earth had he pictured Louise carrying a roast to the table? She was completely unsuited to be a keeper's wife, and no amount of bravado could compensate for her slight frame.

By the last turn of the circular staircase, Jesse was

panting from the exertion. He'd switched hands several times, but they still burned from hefting the weight. No wonder Blackthorn favored the smaller cans. Jesse had been wrong, but he didn't care to admit it. Not yet. The last segment of the climb was a nearly vertical ladder.

"Let me go first," Blackthorn said, "and then hand me the oil can."

It was a sensible solution. When Blackthorn took the can from Jesse's hands at the top of the ladder, Jesse rolled his shoulders to loosen the tight muscles. He then climbed into the lantern.

By the time Jesse stepped into the glass-enclosed room, Blackthorn had already begun filling the pitcher. Apparently that duty couldn't be entrusted to Jesse yet.

"What's bothering you?" Blackthorn asked.

Jesse blew out his breath. He would begin with the personal situation as the reason why he needed Blackthorn to give the lecture. "A situation came up when I was at the school this morning."

Blackthorn peered at him. "Speak plainly, son."

Jesse warmed to the familiar appellation. Blackthorn hadn't used that term before.

"All right." Still, he had to say this carefully. "Mrs. Smythe slipped off a step stool, and I caught her before she got hurt."

"That doesn't sound like a problem to me."

"One of the students saw us while I was still holding on to Mrs. Smythe."

"And the girl thought the worst."

"I'm afraid so. Mrs. Smythe explained the situation, but the girl didn't look like she believed it." Jesse gathered his courage. "I need to know if Singapore's the kind of town that would hold something like that against a lady's reputation."

Blackthorn shook his head. "Not likely to cause even a ripple. Unless Mabel Calloway gets ahold of it."

"Mabel Calloway?"

"Runs the boardinghouse. Louise Smythe used to stay there, so they're well-acquainted. Ain't never seen a bigger matchmaker in my life."

Jesse's heart sank. "Surely coming to a woman's aid isn't a crime."

Blackthorn chuckled. "Mabel Calloway saw three women married this year. You can be sure she's set her mind to marrying off Louise Smythe. Seems to me, you're the most likely candidate, even if you hadn't caught her during a fall."

"Then I need to break off all contact."

Blackthorn positioned the funnel in the lamp. "Or you could court her."

"I'm not courting her. I have no interest in Mrs. Smythe."

"Don't care for the lady, eh?"

Jesse recalled the feeling of her in his arms, the softness of her skin when his lips had accidentally brushed across her forehead. He did care, and that was the problem. She was entirely unsuitable, just like his mother hadn't been suited to the harshness of life without servants. Jesse had learned one truth well. The people you cared about most always left you. His mother. Fellow soldiers. Even Clarice, the only woman he'd seriously courted. That's why a mail-order marriage was the perfect solution.

"Not my type," he answered simply. "I sent an advertisement for a wife to the Chicago newspapers."

"You don't say." Blackthorn scratched his jaw. "Better a woman you've never seen than one you've met?"

"Yes. But in case Mrs. Smythe gets any ideas, I need

to stay away. It'll help squash any rumors too." This was the moment of truth. "That means not giving that lecture on the weather. Would you be willing to do it?"

Blackthorn stared. "Speak to a bunch of girls?"

"You did say you should have been asked."

The keeper muttered something about fools, laced with a little colorful language.

"You'll do it then?" Jesse said as confidently as he could.

"Too busy for such nonsense." Blackthorn pointed a finger at him. "You got yourself into this. A true lighthouse keeper don't go back on his promises."

Jesse stifled a groan. If Mrs. Evans didn't let him out of the lecture, he was stuck spending more time with Louise Smythe. That was a definite problem.

The afternoon's class had left Louise exhausted.

For a change of pace, she had brought her favorite novel, *Pride and Prejudice*, and asked each girl to read a page aloud. Dinah burst into tears when it was her turn. That led Priscilla to comment that "someone" clearly couldn't read, followed by snickers from her cohorts.

Louise had been livid and made Priscilla stay in the classroom after the remainder of the class was dismissed.

Now she faced the girl, who gazed steadily at her without a trace of remorse.

"I expect you to encourage those who haven't had the same privileges as you," Louise began, growing more and more uncomfortable under Priscilla's unblinking stare. "Do you understand?"

The girl tilted her head slightly, her lips pinched into a smirk. "Of course I understand. *I* am not illiterate."

Louise gritted her teeth. Every instinct prompted her to chide the girl, but Fiona's advice came to mind. Encourage and praise her. Impossible. The girl did nothing worthy of either praise or encouragement. If anything, she'd been even more troublesome after seeing Louise in Jesse Hammond's arms. That smirk was intended to convey that if Louise threatened to punish her, she would tell tales destined to end Louise's employment.

A cold chill shook her. She had nowhere else to go, but she would not let a spoiled girl dictate her life. Not this time.

"You were fortunate enough to be born to wealth," Louise said slowly. "Few are."

"That's the way God ordained it should be."

The girl's answer raised Louise's hackles. Compassion, not privilege, was a cornerstone of Christian life. Though a retort rose to her lips, she took a deep breath and offered a silent prayer for restraint and understanding. Christ acted in truth *and* love. Louise must attempt to emulate that. Only then did she realize that Priscilla's words sounded too pat, as if she was just repeating what her mother had told her. That gave Louise an idea.

"America is a land of opportunity. Everyone deserves a chance to make a new life."

"Like you?" Priscilla asked without batting an eyelash.

Louise felt vulnerable. Just how much did the girl know about her? Though born to slightly less privilege than Priscilla, her past had its ugly chapters, with wounds that had just begun to heal. Priscilla couldn't possibly know what had happened in New York. Even though the Benningtons ran in the same sphere as Warren's parents, the Smythes were intensely private and protective. Anything they might have communicated would disparage Louise, not reveal the truth.

She took a shaky breath and redirected the conversation. "You have much to offer Dinah. Instead of pointing out her deficiencies, you could help her."

Priscilla stared. "That's what you're supposed to do, isn't it? You are the teacher."

Louise wanted to wipe the smirk off the girl's face, but that would only increase the animosity. No, to gain Priscilla's confidence, she would have to give her a role that she would relish. She quickly went through the possibilities.

"Until next week, then." The booming masculine voice in the hallway could only belong to Jesse Hammond. "Good evening, Mrs. Evans."

Priscilla's attention shifted to the doorway and its closed door. No doubt the girl would have sought out Jesse. He was by far the most handsome bachelor in Singapore. In spite of the difference in their ages, the girls clearly thought him attractive. It was a good thing she hadn't begun reading Jane Austen's *Emma*, which described just such a romance between a much younger woman and an experienced man.

Louise shook herself. Jealousy was not only wrong, it did no good for anyone. To show she could not be held in its bonds, Louise addressed her student.

"You are gifted in literature." She hoped the compliment helped. "Are you willing to assist Dinah with her reading?"

Priscilla glanced at the closed door before blinking her impossibly long lashes. "Yes, Mrs. Smythe."

Was it Louise's imagination or had the girl stressed *Mrs.*?

"Very well, you may go then."

Priscilla scrambled from her seat and rushed out the door.

Unwelcome disappointment flooded into Louise. To

counter it, she whistled a cheerful tune, the first that came to her, the carol "We Three Kings." She then began entering the day's marks into her record book.

"Isn't it a little early for Christmas carols?" Jesse's deep voice knifed through her.

She didn't dare look up, lest she lose her composure again. "It's never too early to celebrate the Savior's birth."

Though distracted, she managed to place Adeline's arithmetic score in the proper column.

"Mrs. Evans would like me to give the lecture next Monday," he said. "If that's all right with you, that is."

Naturally it would be on Monday, her usual day for a class on the sciences. At least it would only be once.

"If she approved it, then it's fine with me." She began to place another score in the record book but forgot whose it was. "If you don't mind, I am busy."

"I can see that."

Yet he didn't leave.

Louise looked up, prepared to scold him. He cast a sheepish grin her way, and her irritation evaporated. She shook herself. This sympathy for him was dangerous. It had gotten her into all sorts of trouble. She resumed entering grades.

"She asked me to do five more lectures," he said.

"Five!" Louise's blood boiled. Five additional lectures would eliminate her science lessons for the entire month of October and half of November. By then, they would no longer be able to go outdoors to examine plant life.

"She insisted."

Louise swallowed her anger. It wasn't Jesse's fault that Fiona was trying to match him to her, just as it wasn't Priscilla's fault that Louise had lingered too long in Jesse's arms. Oh, dear. How was she going to manage six lectures with him?

"I didn't realize there was that much information to reveal about the weather."

He looked even more sheepish. "Mrs. Evans suggested I tell your students about the working of the lighthouse."

Wonderful. Fiona thought science was too obscure for the girls. It had taken all of Louise's persuasive abilities to convince her to allow a single class each week. Now she was throwing an entire period to Jesse, and for what? Talking about the lighthouse? What possible good would that do the students?

"I thought you didn't want to lecture," she pointed out. "You did offer to withdraw and let me do it."

"Mrs. Evans has a way of persuading a person. She did say we wouldn't have to work together. You can simply introduce me and monitor from the back of the classroom."

Didn't he know how difficult that would be? She could only get rid of these unwanted feelings by distancing herself from Jesse, not putting herself in his path each week.

A piercing scream sent Louise to her feet and Jesse into the hallway.

"One of the girls," she cried, rushing past him.

He followed and soon ran past her. Then, when he reached the parlor, he halted. Right in the doorway. Louise skidded on the wood floor and nearly bumped into him. Only the door frame spared her from another embarrassing encounter.

Then she spotted Priscilla, who lay at the base of the staircase, moaning and grasping her ankle.

"Mr. Hammond," Priscilla sobbed. "Help me."

He hurried toward her and knelt.

Louise wrestled with unseemly thoughts—that Priscilla hadn't fallen at all and that this was all a ruse to attract Jesse. The jealousy welling within was wrong.

Fiona pushed past Louise. "What happened?"

"I tripped and fell," Priscilla cried. "My ankle."

Fiona took charge. "Louise, fetch Mrs. Calloway. She'll know whether or not to get the doctor from Saugatuck. Mr. Hammond, let's get Priscilla to the sofa."

Jesse didn't need Fiona's help. While Louise donned her hat, he scooped up Priscilla, who draped both arms around his neck and leaned her head against his shoulder. Whether or not Priscilla had really tripped and hurt her ankle, she was definitely taking advantage of the situation.

Louise yanked open the door and stepped outside. She would not battle an eighteen-year-old for the attentions of a man. She took a deep breath of the late afternoon air.

Louise Smythe was a teacher. She could stand on her own. No man was required.

Chapter Four

From the look on Louise's face, Jesse had the distinct impression that he'd done something wrong. Yet he'd just gone to the aid of an injured student. Yes, it was the same girl who could make trouble for Louise, but he didn't see how setting her on the sofa was a problem.

Even so, Louise had stormed out of the school. True, she'd gone for help, but that didn't explain the look of fury she'd cast his way. It was a good thing she didn't see him carry the girl upstairs to her bedroom under the guidance of Mrs. Evans. Though he'd retreated to the parlor at once, the sense that he'd done something wrong still gnawed at him. Trouble was, he couldn't figure out exactly what that was.

True, the girl had given him the sort of coy smile that debutantes had cast his way before the war. Her thanks were overly profuse, and she'd hung on to his neck far too intimately, but she was just a girl. Louise knew that. Besides, she was gone for most of that. No, her irritation had begun while they were still in the classroom. She'd been somewhat cool but cordial until he'd mentioned the additional lectures.

He raked a hand through his hair. He must have offended her by agreeing not only to the lecture on the weather but to five more. Yet hadn't Louise refused his offer to step down? It wasn't as if he'd asked to give more lectures. Mrs. Evans had proposed them and then refused to accept his no. He'd only accepted when she agreed that Louise did not have to be involved in the lectures—and when he realized they gave him the perfect opportunity to get Blackthorn to show him the workings of the light. He'd been about to tell her that when the screams interrupted them.

The sound of footsteps on the staircase drew his gaze upward.

Mrs. Evans descended a few steps. "Thank you, Mr. Hammond, that will be all."

Jesse gripped his hat between his hands. "Is she hurt badly?"

"I suspect it's nothing more than a sprain. Mrs. Calloway will help me examine her."

"The doctor is far?"

"Less than a mile upriver."

Jesse hadn't taken time to explore the area yet. "The town's that close?" From what he'd seen, when two towns sprang up next to each other, they either merged into one or the smaller one died out. Fortunately, the lighthouse location wouldn't change. It marked the entrance to a port that saw a decent amount of traffic, thanks to both the lumber trade and the produce that was still being shipped out this time of year.

"Peculiar, isn't it, when Singapore holds the river mouth. Sawyer—that's my husband—says all incoming ships stop here. That virtually ensures Singapore will outlast Saugatuck, even after the timber runs out."

Jesse didn't comment. His thoughts still ranged over

Louise's departure. "If a doctor is needed, I can fetch him. I assume there's a road between the towns."

"Of course, though you'll need to walk it unless you have a mount."

Jesse did not. It seemed virtually no one here did. He'd seen only the wagon horses at work on the wharf.

"I can walk. I'll be at the lighthouse if needed."

Jesse stepped toward the front door at the moment it burst open. Louise flew inside, almost running into him. She hopped aside at the last minute.

"Oh! Excuse me." She then focused on Mrs. Evans. "Is Priscilla any worse? I checked everywhere, but no one has any ice left."

An older woman bustled in after Louise. "Too late in the season." She tugged a bonnet off and headed for the staircase. "I assume she's upstairs?"

"Of course." Mrs. Evans extended a hand. "I'm glad you came, Mrs. Calloway. I'll tell you what happened the best I can."

The two ladies ascended the staircase, talking the entire way. That left him with Louise.

"Well, I suppose that's that," she said.

For a woman of words, that statement was unusually vague, but Jesse was more drawn by the flush of her cheeks and brightness of her gray eyes. At this hour, they ought to be dark, but they sparkled with life and drew him irresistibly toward her.

"I hope she's not injured badly," he said softly.

"I doubt it." The uncharacteristic statement sent another flush of red to her cheeks. "I'm sorry, that was uncalled for."

Jesse couldn't help but come to her defense, even though the only battle she fought was with herself. "I suspect you're right. A break would have caused a great deal more pain."

Louise gave him a grateful smile, just for a moment. Then the wall went back up between them. "Well, I should check in on the patient. Good evening, Mr. Hammond."

"Mister? Maybe we should move beyond formality if we are working together."

Her lips moved, as if she was about to say his given name and then thought better of it. "I must go upstairs. Good night."

"Good night."

But she hadn't waited for his answer. She hurried up the stairs, her gaze averted. A moment later, Jesse stood alone in the parlor. Any hint of affection died in the coolness of her response.

Best concentrate on the opportunity set before him. Tonight he would convince Blackthorn to show him how to work the light. Thanks to Mrs. Evans, he had the perfect reason.

Naturally nothing was wrong with Priscilla. Louise lingered outside the girl's room long enough to learn that. Under the crowded supervision of Fiona and the other four students, Mrs. Calloway had declared there was no swelling or bruising. Priscilla would be up and about by Monday. However, she would miss tonight's church supper.

Louise and Fiona stood in the parlor after Mrs. Calloway departed and the girls returned to their rooms to freshen up before walking to the church.

"I will stay with Priscilla," Louise volunteered.

As combative as her relationship was with the girl, she preferred an evening with Priscilla to the gossip and matchmaking that took place at all community functions. Her position as a widow who'd arrived in town hoping to marry opened the gate for constant suggestions of a suitable match. Not a one of them came close to the type of husband she craved. That included the latest resident, Jesse Hammond. Yes, his handsome features and the way he looked at her made her blush, but that was purely a biological reaction without one iota of sense, common or otherwise.

Naturally, Fiona objected to Louise's offer. "You go to the supper. I will stay with Priscilla."

"Nonsense. You need to be with your family. This school consumes too much of your time. This is a chance for you all to do something together." She added the crowning blow. "I'm sure Mary Clare would love to go."

Fiona looked like she was going to protest, but the thought of pleasing her niece, whom she was raising, ended the matchmaking effort. A sigh of resignation issued from her lips.

Louise took advantage. "I insist."

At that moment, the four girls descended the staircase, giving Louise the opportunity she needed. She hurried upstairs before Fiona could summon a protest.

Priscilla's bedroom door was closed. Though the rest of the girls doubled up in a room, the Benningtons had insisted on a private room for their daughter. At the time, Louise had viewed that request as arrogant, but perhaps it was intended to protect the other girls from Priscilla's manipulations. Perhaps her parents had tired of retrieving their daughter from school after school. Then again, at eighteen—even though just barely that age—Priscilla ought to be receiving suitors at home. Louise could not imagine why her parents insisted on sending their daughter to a ladies' school against her wishes.

Louise rapped lightly on the door, not wanting to wake Priscilla if she was dozing. Mrs. Calloway had insisted on giving the girl a dose of laudanum. Louise didn't think that wise, especially before supper, but Mrs. Calloway brushed away her objections.

When Priscilla did not answer, Louise quietly turned the door handle.

"Mr. Hammond?" The somewhat slurred words trailed off.

The poor girl was dreaming. She must be. Jesse wouldn't have promised to return that evening. Surely he had duties to perform at the lighthouse. Dusk was the crucial hour when the light began its daily vigil. Then again, perhaps he intended to go to the church supper after the light was lit. Between Mr. Blackthorn and Jesse, they could take turns tending the light. That would explain Fiona's insistence that Louise attend but not Priscilla calling out Jesse's name.

Louise gently pushed open the door to the girl's room. The hinges creaked slightly, something that a little oil would remedy. She must tell Fiona's husband, Sawyer, the next time she saw him.

Priscilla lay atop the bed, the bedclothes disheveled, as if she had tossed and turned through a night of terrors, yet she could have slept but a few minutes. The girl's eyes were closed, and her face was flushed.

Louise caught her breath. Something truly was wrong with Priscilla. She crossed the room and placed a hand on the girl's forehead. It was warm but not overly hot. Still, something had caused this thrashing about. Louise poured water from the pitcher into the basin on the washstand and then dipped a cloth in it. A cool compress wouldn't hurt. After wringing out the excess water, she placed it on Priscilla's forehead. The girl moved her head from side to side and murmured something unintelligible, but she didn't wake.

Louise then took the chair from the table that had been intended as a writing desk but had been transformed into a vanity. She set it beside the bed and sat down. Priscilla's uneaten supper lay on a table opposite. Her glass of water was also untouched. Louise watched the girl intently, but she did not thrash about again. Perhaps the compress was helping. The delirium might be caused by the laudanum, or it might be the beginning of a fever. Either way, someone must watch Priscilla carefully.

She would hold vigil tonight and as long as necessary.

Outside, dusk had settled into the early gloom of night. A beam of light flooded the room. The lighthouse! Louise hadn't realized the light's beam reached these windows. Her room faced opposite. The other girls had rooms that faced toward the river. Only Priscilla's room had this vantage.

Louise hurried to close the blinds. The room ought to have shutters. She grasped the thick velvet curtains, ready to pull them shut, when she noticed a figure on the dune opposite, the dune where she'd first encountered Jesse. From the size of this figure, it must be the assistant lighthouse keeper. Mr. Blackthorn was considerably smaller. Pearl Decker said Jesse had been in town nearly a week. Priscilla might have seen him many times before their encounter on the dune. That was more than enough time for a lonely girl to fantasize about a handsome man walking across the dune outside her window.

Jesse headed downhill toward the hotel side of the building that housed both the school and the hotel. Priscilla's delirious mutterings echoed in Louise's mind. Had she expected Jesse to return? Was that the reason for the fall or feigned fall? That awful twinge of jealousy returned. What was wrong with her? She had no interest in Jesse beyond the professional. One way or another, she must gain control of her emotions.

So she began to close the drapes. Then she spotted Jesse moving past the hotel in the direction of the church. He must be going to the supper. Late, certainly, but there would still be food. There was always more than enough. Nothing else was located in that direction—except the saloons.

She drew in a sharp breath and pushed the curtain open again.

What if he frequented drinking establishments? The terrible thought gave her pause. Jesse didn't seem like that sort, but what did she truly know of him? She had only seen him on the dune and in school. He hadn't attended the worship service last Sunday. He might well be a drinking man. Many in town were.

She shifted so she could watch his progress. He would not see her, since she had not lit a lamp in the room, and the door was closed. In the light from the waxing half-moon, she could make him out. He stepped onto the boardwalk beyond the hotel. From there he could cross the street to the saloon or walk up Oak Street to go to the church building. Granted, he could also get to the church by staying on Cedar, but it was less direct. If he crossed at the intersection, it would prove he wasn't going to a saloon.

She held her breath.

He looked toward the wharf and then crossed the street right where the saloon was located.

She let the curtains drop even as memories of Warren crashed into her mind. The drunken binges. The inevitable fights. The torrent of painful blows to face and body. The terror that he would go too far.

It wasn't fair to put Jesse in that category. He might have had a perfectly good reason to cross at that particular point. Maybe someone called out to him. He might be going elsewhere, though the store would be closed and he had no business at the boardinghouse that she knew about. No, try as she might, she could find no reason he would head in that direction.

A strangled sound drew her away from the window. Priscilla thrashed wildly.

Louise ran to the bedside. The compress was gone. She pressed her hand to the girl's forehead. It was on fire.

Louise panicked. Guilt followed on its heels. Why had she let Jesse's movements draw her from her charge? She must help Priscilla, but how? No one else was at the school. They'd all gone to the church supper. She couldn't leave Priscilla, yet to get help she must leave. What if a doctor was needed? What if time was crucial?

She started for the door, but the girl's murmuring changed her mind. First she must calm Priscilla.

Louise found another cloth and dampened it in the cool water. She placed it on the feverish girl's forehead with little hope that it would remain.

Lord, watch over Priscilla. Heal her of this fever. And show me what to do.

The distant bang of a door woke her from the panic.

Of course. She would go to the hotel. Whoever was on duty would be able to fetch help.

Louise took Priscilla's hand. "I must leave for a few minutes so I can send for the doctor, but I'll be right back."

The girl gripped her hand with desperation. Her eyes opened a slit. "Don't!"

The plea reached deep in Louise's heart, but there was no other way. She pried Priscilla's fingers from her hand.

"I'll be right back."

Priscilla's wail followed her out of the room and down the stairs.

Though Jesse was hungry, he was not going to attend the church supper. Mrs. Blackthorn had insisted too strongly that he attend. Every excuse he could devise—didn't have a dish to pass, wouldn't know anyone, didn't want to deprive the Blackthorns—was met with an answer. She had sent a dish ahead with her daughter. Mr. Blackthorn must attend the light. Jesse would know Mrs. Evans and Roland at the very least, and it would give him an opportunity to get to know others in the community.

He knew perfectly well who she had in mind. Louise Smythe.

So he headed in the direction of the church but cut back toward town when he was out of sight of the keeper's quarters. First he headed for the hotel. The dining room should be serving. Yet it looked dark when he stepped into the lobby.

"Closed," said the lad at the desk. "Everyone's gone to the church supper."

Everyone likely meant the Evans family. Had the entire town conspired against him? Jesse put up his collar against the cool evening breeze and stepped back out on the porch. Darkness had set in. A few buildings had a light or two, and the hotel burned a lamp outside the door, but to make his way along the boardwalks without stumbling, he needed to let his eyes adjust to the darkness.

With the hotel dining room closed, that left the boardinghouse or no supper at all. His stomach growled. Jesse could go without. He had often enough during the war, but hunger had a way of eating at the mind as well as the body. He loped down the steps and nearly ran into a woman hurrying toward the hotel with her head down.

"Oh!" She started and jumped backward, losing her footing.

Jesse grabbed the petite woman's shoulders to steady her, and knew at once that all the matchmaking efforts in the world couldn't have planned this better. Once again he'd ended up holding on to Louise Smythe.

"I'm fine," she snapped, stepping out of his grasp. "But I need to get help."

She rushed up the steps and flew across the wooden porch. Before he'd turned around, she burst through the doorway and entered the lobby.

Jesse shook his head. She was likely looking for Mrs. Evans. She wouldn't find her here. Though getting entangled with Louise once more was not at all in his plans, she seemed unusually agitated. Perhaps this wasn't just a momentary crisis, like where to find a clean blanket. Maybe the girl who had fallen earlier needed a doctor.

So he climbed the stairs and entered the lobby.

"But I need help," Louise was pleading.

The lad of perhaps fourteen or fifteen shook his head. "Mr. Evans said I wasn't to leave my post for any reason."

Louise blew out her breath and rubbed her forehead, eyes closed. "I need someone to fetch a doctor."

Just as he'd thought.

Jesse stepped forward. "I'll go."

Louise lifted her gaze. Concern melted into relief. "Thank you. It's Priscilla. She has a fever."

Jesse racked his memory for what Mrs. Evans had said and, surprisingly, came up with the peculiar town name. "Where in Saugatuck can I find the doctor?"

He must have pronounced it reasonably well, for Louise didn't give him an odd look.

"Mrs. Calloway will know." Louise paced before him. "I will run over there and ask. She can send her husband to fetch the doctor."

"They might be at the church supper too."

"Not with guests at the boardinghouse." Louise pushed past him, all business once again.

Yet Jesse could only see delays. He looked to the lad. "Do you know where to find the doctor?"

Louise paused at the door.

The lad hesitated. "Aye, but I'm not supposed to leave the hotel."

"How about if I take over for you here, and you run to get the doctor?"

Jesse could see the tension release from Louise's shoulders.

"A perfect solution. Will you, Charlie?" She gave Jesse a grateful look before stepping toward the registration desk. "It would save a lot of time and could save Priscilla's life."

Charlie looked uncertain. "But Mr. Evans—"

Louise had regained her confidence. "If Mr. Evans gives you any trouble, you tell him to talk to me."

Instead of continuing to resist, Charlie grabbed his jacket and was out the door before Jesse could say anything.

Louise then turned to him. "Thank you, Mr. Hammond. That was an excellent idea."

He warmed in her smile of gratitude. It had been a while since a woman looked at him with such appreciation. It felt good. It felt almost normal. Maybe the nightmares wouldn't return tonight.

"Glad to help. But please call me Jesse. We are going to work together, after all."

The familiarity made her blush. "I thought I only

needed to take attendance and monitor from the back of the room." She brushed a hand over her hair, though it was perfectly in place, still pulled back in that dour bun. What he wouldn't give to see it loose. But a widow, especially one like Louise Smythe, would never wear her hair down.

Now he was at a loss for words. "I, uh, suppose I should get to work." He eyed the registration desk.

"Can you handle things here?"

"How difficult can it be? There don't appear to be many guests."

"I suppose you're right." She glanced toward the door but didn't move. "I suppose I should get back to Priscilla."

"Is there anything else I can help you with?"

"No." She backed away, her cheeks aglow. "Not at all."

"I'll let Mrs. Evans know what happened the moment she and her husband return."

"Thank you." She lifted her face then and offered a grateful smile that made him feel like the noblest man alive. As if he had solved the problem. As if he was somehow a hero.

In the quiet emptiness that followed after she walked out the door, he knew without a doubt that he was not that man.

Chapter Five

Though the fever lessened by Sunday morning, thanks
to the doctor's ministrations, Priscilla was still too weak
to leave untended. Louise volunteered to remain.

"You have been here since Friday night," Fiona pointed
out. "At least attend worship this morning."

"It's Sunday?" Louise rubbed her swollen eyes. "So
it is. You go with Sawyer and Mary Clare. I will read
the Bible right here. Perhaps Priscilla will wake, and I
can read aloud."

Fiona shook her head. "When I return, you will rest.
No debate."

Louise conceded and sometime later watched her
friend and employer walk out of the hotel with her husband and niece and head toward the church. Movement
on the dune caught the corner of her eye. She looked, expecting to see Jesse, but it was the Blackthorn family. The
parents and the three children still at home trailed along
the surface of the dune, with Mr. Blackthorn bringing up
the rear. For a moment she wondered why Jesse wasn't
with them, but he might have gone ahead of the family.

Perhaps she had misjudged him again. Earlier she had
assumed he wanted the attention that would be lavished

upon him as a lecturer, but he had tried to step aside. Then again, he'd let Fiona talk him into more lectures. Fiona could be persuasive—intimidating even—but Jesse was too substantial a man to let any woman boss him around.

Goose bumps dusted her arms.

"Jesse is not Warren," she said softly to herself.

Priscilla murmured, and Louise drew her attention from the window to her patient. Surely she had not heard what Louise had just whispered. No, the girl looked sound asleep, her chest rising and falling regularly now.

Did the girl realize that the teacher she despised had spent nearly two days at her side? Though Louise's eyelids had dropped many a time during the quiet hours, she had jolted awake at each sound or movement. Even though she'd never had children of her own, she suspected that was how a mother would react when her daughter ailed. Concern and love kept her ever vigilant, like the wise virgins tending their lamps in Jesus' parable.

She leafed through the book of Matthew until she located that passage. All ten virgins waited for the bridegroom to appear, yet only five were prepared and vigilant. Was Louise prepared? She had leapt into teaching as a means to support herself after failing to marry a man who had advertised for a wife. She was educated beyond most women, but prepared to teach? Certainly not.

Though she possessed knowledge on many subjects, she knew little about young women. Their wildly fluctuating emotions left her at a loss. She could recall clinging to foolish dreams only to be forced to discard them, but not with the rapidity of these girls. They seemed to pine for something one day and consider it inconsequential the next.

Louise sighed. A mother brought love to the equation.

Louise had only affection for her students. And not for all. Priscilla. The girl slept peacefully now, but soon she would wake and Louise must again face the girl's opposition and manipulation. She struggled to muster love for someone who worked against her.

She turned back to the reading, but the words swam before her eyes and she felt herself drifting off to sleep...

She was in the parlor. Five young ladies stood before her, each with a lamp. None were lit, and they all looked to her for a match, but Louise didn't have any. She searched her apron pockets and the fireplace mantle. None could be found. The fireplace was cold, so they could not light a taper in it. There was no flame anywhere. How could she tell them that they wouldn't be able to light their lamps and thus would miss the bridegroom?

"Mrs. Smythe?"

The faint words pierced through the heavy fog. Louise started. She'd fallen asleep. Blinking her eyes, she took in the surroundings. Not the parlor. A bedchamber. Priscilla!

The girl was awake and looking intently at her.

Louise closed her Bible. "Are you thirsty?" With shaking hands she poured a glass of water.

"Why are you here?"

"You were feverish." Louise handed her the water and then felt her forehead.

The girl pulled away. "I feel fine."

"Your color is better, but you should still rest." She fought the defensive wall that tried to rise against Priscilla's obvious displeasure. "Your ankle swelled badly Friday night, and the doctor said you need to rest at least a week."

"The doctor?"

Was that a flash of calculation that Louise spotted in

the girl's expression? Her sleep-deprived senses couldn't be certain. "We called in a doctor Friday evening. He visited again yesterday and will check on you later today."

"Three days?"

Louise nodded. "Almost."

"Where is everyone?"

"At church. I'm sure they'll all want to see you when they return." Louise didn't bother to mention that Fiona would take over then. Priscilla had never shown the slightest inclination to annoy Fiona the way she'd attempted to ruffle her.

"Did Mr. Hammond visit?"

Why did that question set Louise on edge? Jealousy was sinful and very inappropriate.

Louise took a deep breath. "He asked about you and was instrumental in bringing the doctor here."

Priscilla turned her attention to the glass of water, but not before a coy smile tugged at the corners of her mouth.

After Sunday dinner with the traditional roasted chicken, potatoes and gravy, Jesse was ready to escape the confines of the lighthouse. Blackthorn took over the watch after a short nap, freeing Jesse to take a walk.

The winds were stiff but the day had warmed to an almost summery temperature. He left his coat behind. Jesse trekked north along the top of the dune. To his left, waves crashed ashore after their long trip across Lake Michigan. To his right, the town of Singapore nestled between dunes. Most of the buildings lined the waterfront. Away from the river, the buildings dwindled to a cabin here and there. Sun glinted off the sand, making him squint. He didn't have a destination. He just needed some time to himself.

Ordinarily a lighthouse afforded plenty of quiet, but

the Blackthorn family brought plenty of lively discussion to daily life there. When the children, ranging from thirteen to sixteen, weren't in school, the house got noisy. Jesse had grown up in a quiet home. With no mother, his father working, and his sister much older, he often had the house to himself, other than the housekeeper. He undertook quiet pursuits.

The war brought noise. Too much noise. The cries of the dying still rang in his ears. Maybe here, alone on the dunes, he could find some relief from the voices of the past.

He plodded on, seeing little beyond his thoughts. A sand cherry here. A patch of dune grass there. He skirted around a juniper with its blue berries that were too bitter for his taste.

Then he saw Louise, bent over a wiry plant with that old journal of hers.

From twenty feet away, he could see the dune lily she was sketching. Like the rest of the plant life, its growth was stunted, making it no more than a foot tall, when the flower could rise to three times that height in a good year. Oddly enough, this one still bloomed.

He moved closer.

She didn't notice.

He cleared his throat, not wanting to startle her.

She still didn't seem to hear him. Why not?

Then he realized the wind worked against him. It blew the sounds he made away from her. He could either shout out a greeting or climb above her and let the wind bring the sounds of his movement to her attention.

He opted for the former. "Mrs. Smythe!"

She didn't so much as lift her head. In fact, she set down the journal, grasped the lily's flower between two fingers and bent until her lips grazed it.

"No! Stop!" He hollered at the top of his lungs as he ran toward her. "Don't eat it!"

At last she heard him. Lifting her head, she stared at him as if he was mad.

Jesse covered the distance between them in seconds. Though slightly out of breath, he managed to finish his caution. "That's Death Camas, highly poisonous if eaten."

Her gray eyes lightened, as if reflecting the sun. "I know that."

"Then why are you putting your lips to it?"

"I'm sniffing the bloom. That is one of the items I note in my journal." She gathered that journal and rose, brushing the sand from her skirt. "I don't make a habit of eating plants that might harm me."

He felt the heat creep up his neck. "I didn't know if you realized it was *zigadenus glaucus*."

Her eyebrows lifted, revealing the depth of her gray eyes. "I didn't realize you knew the scientific names of the local flora."

"I did study botany in my youth."

"Oh." She looked away, and he had the distinct impression she had not been given the same opportunity.

"You are so knowledgeable that I assumed you attended school."

"Naturally I was sent to school."

He wondered if it was the sort that many ladies from wealthy families attended, where scholarly pursuits were frowned upon. "You are self-taught?"

She jutted out her chin. "I have received instruction."

He didn't pry further. Her defensiveness meant she didn't judge her education on a par with his. That was nonsense, of course. His father had given him the best he could, but Jesse couldn't afford to attend school beyond the eighth grade. Further education came from befriending the professor who lived in the same building. After working all day, Jesse would spend long nights soaking in everything Professor Windley taught him.

In spite of teaching in a lumber boom town, Louise came from quality. Her clothing shouted that out. Something had happened to force her to leave home in answer to an advertisement for a bride. What a shock this town must be for an educated woman.

"You know as much as even the finest botanist, say, William Saunders."

"William Saunders," she gasped, her eyes wide. "He designed the Gettysburg cemetery, among many achievements. I am hardly in that class."

He pointed to her journal. "If you're noting the scent of each flower, your records must be very comprehensive."

A pleasing pink flushed her cheeks. "It's an avocation I greatly enjoy. That is all."

"An avocation." He let the word settle on his tongue. Few women of his acquaintance would know the word, least of all use it. Louise Smythe continually surprised him.

"I'm sorry. An avocation is a pastime. In this case, most people view it as a bit of a hobby."

Jesse struggled to hide a grin. Even though he'd admitted to studying botany, she still thought him as uneducated as the lumberjacks and sawyers passing through the village. What fun it would be when she discovered just how wrong she was. "Thank you for the explanation, but I only repeated your wording from surprise. It's unusual to find both a scientist and a lover of words in a lumber town."

She sucked in her breath and lowered her gaze. "I—I find few care for such a virtue in a woman."

Virtue was an odd word to use, as if she was embarrassed by her intellect and needed to justify it.

"I happen to enjoy the company of an educated woman."

She lifted bright eyes to meet his gaze, and Jesse could have bit his tongue. What had possessed him to blurt that out? Now she looked upon him with a hopefulness that would do neither of them any good. She wanted to marry. He had no intention of marrying a war widow.

He rephrased his statement. "I meant that I enjoy the *friendship* of an educated woman."

She blinked several times before looking away.

Once again his tongue had gotten him in trouble.

Louise could not figure out Jesse Hammond. One moment he showered compliments and understanding her way. The next he made it painfully clear that she could not expect a relationship beyond friendship. Fine. That was all she wanted too.

Then why the sinking disappointment?

She squared her shoulders. "Of course. Friendship is all I'm seeking now as well."

That was true. Then why did it feel like a lie?

Even so, his expression relaxed, and he returned to the friendly demeanor he'd had before she'd somehow given him the impression she was sweet on him. "What did you learn about your specimen?"

Botany provided a safe harbor for both of them. By focusing on the plant, she could almost forget how close Jesse stood and how gentle were his words.

She kept her gaze on the lily. "It is stunted this year, just like the tall wormwood. Last year it stood at least double this size. I've been watching it all year for growth, but after the burst in the spring and early summer, it stopped entirely."

"Yet it bloomed."

She had to admit that, even as her heart raced from his nearness. What was wrong with her? She was not in the market for a husband, especially not one whose size reminded her too much of her late husband. She could only account for this irrational reaction as a result of some unknown biological reaction. That meant it would fade soon enough. She must simply press on until the first flush of attraction ran its course. Since avoidance had proven impossible, she would rely on strict regulation of her emotions. Focusing on the practical was a start.

"The bloom came later than normal and is smaller in size."

He nodded. "And the leaves?"

"They are wiry and tough, like the grasses that grow in the sands. In my estimation that makes it better able to withstand the harsh climate."

"Especially when rainfall is lacking. I gather from the dryness of the plants and bushes that it hasn't rained much this summer."

She couldn't help but sigh. "Barely at all. Those who attempted to grow vegetables in town have given up the effort. I understand the harvest inland is greatly reduced also. It will be difficult and expensive to get fresh vegetables and fruits."

"We could resort to juniper berries."

She could not help but give him a sharp look.

"Forgive me. They're pretty unpalatable." Jesse looked toward the lake. "The sun has set. It grows dark quickly this time of year."

Louise looked west. "I didn't realize how late it had gotten."

"Please allow me to walk you back to the school."

She hesitated. He could not know how this would confirm the speculation already running wild around town. On the other hand, a misstep alone and this far from town would mean spending the night on the dune. That could prove dangerous, if not fatal.

"As friends," he added. "No gentleman would leave a lady alone so far from town."

She allowed a brief smile. "Very well, then. You may walk me to town."

He extended an arm.

She hesitated, knowing what his touch had done to her in the past. Maintaining control of her emotions would not be easy if she was constantly close to him. Moreover, once they drew near the school, they would be in full view of Priscilla's room.

"If you don't mind, I prefer to walk on my own." At his look of shock, she added, "It allows me to make notes if anything should catch my eye on the way."

It was a pitiful excuse, but he seemed to accept it.

So they walked side by side. His presence was still powerful, sending her emotions swirling and her imagination dreaming of dances and all the foolishness of her girlhood. Stop! She was widowed, a woman experienced in both the joys and heartache of marriage. That experience should erase any feelings toward a man, but it did not. It most certainly did not.

Lest a stumble force him to come to her rescue yet again, she carefully placed each step. Her short strides already made her twice as slow as him. Yet he slowed for her, pausing and watching to ensure she did not fall.

"How is the young lady who turned her ankle?" he asked.

Only then did she realize how quickly Priscilla had

slipped from her mind. She counted the fact that he did not mention Priscilla's name a clear indication that although the girl might find him appealing, he had no such interest. "She is much improved."

"Good." They walked a few steps in silence.

"Though unable to attend classes for another few days."

"I'm sorry. Perhaps I should postpone the lecture on the weather."

Louise had forgotten about Jesse's lecture, scheduled for tomorrow. "Perhaps you should."

"Gladly."

He sounded a bit too ready to put off the lecture. Then again, she was terribly tired and might be misinterpreting his intent. "Thank you for your assistance."

"Assistance?"

"Getting the doctor."

"Oh. Anyone would have done the same."

She supposed they would. People here cared about each other. The sand slid beneath her left foot and his hand shot out to steady her, but she brushed away his assistance and hurried forward to more stable ground.

"It's a beautiful sunset," he said moments later.

"Yes." Pink stained the undersides of the clouds. "God's creation always makes me pause in awestruck wonder."

He stopped then. "You do not subscribe to scientific explanations?"

She had not considered that their walk might lead to a debate. "I believe God created the heavens and the earth. Don't you?"

"I agree." But his brow was creased.

"Then why do you look so concerned?"

He pointed toward the lighthouse. "Mr. Blackthorn should have lit the light by now."

She caught her breath. "I've kept you out here too long. Go. I can make my way home from here."

He looked unwilling to leave her.

"Go," she urged. "He might need you. Ships rely on the light. I will be fine. I simply need to descend the dune and walk through town to the school."

He shook his head, stubborn to the last. "You might slide again and fall. Come with me to the lighthouse. One of the boys can walk you home."

It was a sensible solution. Then why did she feel as if she was walking into trouble?

Chapter Six

Jesse found Blackthorn at the kitchen table while his wife rubbed a smelly ointment into his shoulder.

He stopped at the doorway, preventing Louise from walking into the room and seeing a man with his shoulder exposed. "What happened?"

"Pulled something lugging the oil up to the lantern." Blackthorn glared at him. "Tried takin' it all at once, like you've been pestering me to do."

Jesse swallowed a trace of guilt. He should have told the keeper that he'd rethought that idea. "Where is the oil can?"

"Where I left it. Where else would it be?"

Jesse supposed he deserved the surly response. After all, it was somewhat his fault. "I'll fill the lamps."

The keeper's gaze narrowed. "Tryin' to take my job?"

"No, sir. Assisting you." Jesse could feel Louise at his back.

"I'll go now," she said quietly.

Mrs. Blackthorn stopped rubbing the ointment. "Who's that? Did you bring a lady caller?"

Blackthorn hastily stuck his arm through the sleeve of this shirt and buttoned it.

"You just hold on, Samuel," Mrs. Blackthorn said. "I'm not quite done." She then turned her attention back to Jesse, calling out, "You tell her to wait in the parlor, and I'll be out presently."

Jesse gritted his teeth. This was getting more and more out of hand.

"I'm not staying," Louise said a bit more forcefully.

"Nonsense. Jesse, you tell your lady friend that I will be done here soon."

"It's not a lady friend," Jesse explained. "I merely walked Mrs. Smythe here since it was getting dark."

"Mrs. Smythe! Why didn't you say so?"

"I'm heading back to the school," Louise called out from behind him. "We can talk later."

"No, no," Jane Blackthorn called out. "Let's have a nice chat."

Jesse heard Louise step back just before Mrs. Blackthorn wiped the ointment from her hands and headed his way. He stood aside to let her pass. Better the women get together than Louise walk down the slope to the school in the dark. Mrs. Blackthorn would insist on sending one of her sons with her. That left him free to assist Blackthorn.

"I'd—that is, *we* had better get the light lit. Could be a long night," Jesse added for the sake of the women.

Blackthorn breezed past him, muttering under his breath.

Jesse let the man lead. He'd tried to be diplomatic. He'd tried to take into account the man's feelings. But the man barged ahead with the subtlety of a bull. Blackthorn couldn't possibly carry the oil transfer can up the circular staircase, not with a lame shoulder.

"Don't think I don't know what you're doing," Blackthorn snapped. "You're not gettin' my job anytime soon."

It would be a lie to claim he didn't want it. "I'm here to assist you."

"Assist. Humph."

Blackthorn didn't even glance at him as he opened the door to the small room between the quarters and the tower.

Jesse hated that he felt like a child begging to show his father that he could do the task. It was demeaning. Had Louise witnessed the exchange? If so, her opinion of him must have suffered a blow. She would rightly assume that he wasn't qualified to lecture about lighthouse tending if he wasn't even allowed to carry a can of oil.

Speaking of Louise, where was the woman anyway? He should have run into her and Mrs. Blackthorn between the kitchen and the small room connecting the quarters to the tower. But he'd neither seen nor heard anything. He glanced back. Neither woman was anywhere to be seen.

"Louise? Um, Mrs. Smythe?"

He didn't receive an answer. What had that independent-minded woman gone and done now?

Blackthorn threw open the door to the tower and grimaced. The man would seriously injure himself if Jesse didn't step in.

"I'm right behind you." Jesse crossed the distance in seconds.

Blackthorn grunted and, at the base of the circular staircase, paused.

This was Jesse's chance. He needed to make the most of it. "Why don't I go first? I can carry the transfer can, and you can tell me what to do."

It wasn't ideal, but the solution seemed to appease Blackthorn.

"All right, but ain't you gonna miss spending time with your lady caller?"

Jesse gritted his teeth. There was no sense correcting Blackthorn. The man had already made up his mind, no doubt spurred by his wife. But this time Blackthorn could not talk him out of tending the light.

"Duty first." Jesse stared down the keeper. "That means lighting the lamps, not chatting with callers."

Louise did not care to get caught by Jane Blackthorn. The woman was doubtless lonely, tied as she was to the lighthouse, but she was also known to promote matches nearly as much as Mrs. Calloway.

Each of the women felt it their duty to see her married. Even Fiona, who knew some of the circumstances of Louise's first marriage, saw fit to promote likely candidates. No doubt Jane Blackthorn would join the growing chorus extolling the virtues of Jesse Hammond.

They needn't bother. Louise was beginning to see that her first impression of the man had been a little off. Jesse wasn't an ignorant lout. He could be surprisingly pleasant when not fixated on rules and regulations.

Approaching footsteps meant Louise had little time to escape. Never having been inside the keeper's quarters, she made for what she assumed was the front doorway only to find herself in a cold and unlit room.

"Louise! It is you!" Jane Blackthorn hurried toward her, cutting off all avenues of escape.

"I seem to have gotten lost."

Jane brushed off the mistake. "We seldom use the parlor. Let's have a chat back in the kitchen."

"I should get back to the school, so Fiona—Mrs. Evans—can return home to her husband and niece."

"Why, it's pitch-black outside. You shouldn't walk alone in the dark. Anything might happen."

Louise recalled Jesse's suggestion. "Perhaps one of your sons could escort me?"

"Oh, they're off visiting friends." Jane took her arm. "Let's sit a spell until the men are done, and then Jesse can walk you to the school."

"But he said it would be a long night."

"Nonsense. The wind's died down, and there isn't a storm cloud to be seen."

They entered the kitchen to the smell of camphor, undoubtedly from the ointment Mrs. Blackthorn had used for her husband's injury. Louise fought the urge to cover her nose. The astringent odor burned with each breath. A cup of tea amid such lingering scent would not be pleasant.

Jane had already placed tea leaves in a strainer and was pouring steaming water from the stove kettle through it and into two cups.

"I don't want you to go to so much trouble."

"It's no trouble at all," Jane said. "As a matter of fact, there happens to be something I've been wanting to ask you. You being at the hotel and all, I thought you might know what's going on."

"What's going on?" Louise frowned and shook her head. "I don't know what you mean."

Yet fears surged. Had the Benningtons responded already to their daughter's illness? A wire might have been sent from Holland. The man who brought mail south from that community was willing to send cables upon his return for a small fee.

Jane Blackthorn patted the caned hardwood chair beside her.

Louise couldn't bear to sit, not if her livelihood and that of her friend were at stake.

"Have a bit of tea, Louise."

Since Jane apparently wouldn't say anything until she sipped her tea, Louise sat and obliged her with a tiny sip. It tasted of camphor.

Jane leaned close. "Well, Mabel Calloway said that she'd heard the hotel was going to close."

Louise's heart thudded to a stop. Surely that wasn't possible. Fiona would have told her. Then she recalled her friend's strained expression and the way she rubbed her temples when she was looking at the ledgers for the school. Since the hotel and the school were inextricably linked financially, the failure of one meant the end of the other.

"I told her that was impossible," Jane said in a low voice, as if there was anyone near to overhear. "Why, Sawyer's family is enormously wealthy. He could simply borrow from them."

Louise knew her friend well enough to see through that solution. Sawyer's father had besmirched Fiona's reputation back in New York. The repercussions had driven Fiona here to Singapore, only to fall in love with the dastardly man's son. It had been a tangle that had seemed solved, thanks to the generosity of Sawyer's mother. But a woman has only so much influence in her marriage. Men invariably found a way to seize back control. Louise knew that lesson all too well. She had brought home a stray dog, Falstaff, named for his comical large ears and clown-like spots of white around his eyes. For a while, Warren tried to train Falstaff, but when the dog went to Louise instead, Warren grew to hate it.

Though years ago, her heart still ached for her poor pup. She blinked back a tear and took another tiny sip of the tea while drawing her thoughts back to the present.

If the hotel was suffering financially, Sawyer would

let it close before he took one penny from his father. If Louise had been in his situation, she would do the same.

Jane squeezed her hand. "Oh, dear. Then it is true."

Louise must have let her fears show. She mustered a smile, pitiful though it must be. "In truth, I'm not privy to such matters. Fiona said nothing to me of any problems."

"But it's possible."

"Anything is possible, but surely Fiona would have told me. We are friends."

Jane gave her a pitying look. "Some things are difficult to say, even to a friend."

Louise was spared further discussion by the men's reappearance.

"The light is lit," Mr. Blackthorn announced.

Jesse halted just inside the door. His scowl changed to surprise when he saw her. "You're still here."

Louise struggled to find something that would pull Jesse Hammond from the silence that enveloped him.

She brushed off his offer of his arm, still conscious that Priscilla might be watching for them. "Not necessary."

Instead of debating her, as he had on the walk to the lighthouse, he maintained a respectable distance, close enough to assist if she stumbled and far enough away not to cause any gossip.

The descent to town took place in silence, so she dwelled on the possibility that the hotel might close. Alas, she could think of nothing to improve business. Though many cargo ships called on the port, the town had few visitors. Most who came ashore were passing through on their way to the lumber camps.

She sighed.

"What's wrong?" Jesse said.

He sounded genuinely interested. Rather than radiating tension, he seemed much more relaxed. Louise, on the other hand, had gone in the reverse direction.

"Oh, nothing," she said automatically. "Just thinking."

"That sigh sounded more like a problem."

"It could be," she admitted. "Mrs. Blackthorn said she heard the hotel is not doing well. Sawyer and Fiona Evans own both the hotel and the school."

"So if the hotel closes, you're afraid the school will too."

She didn't want to admit that fear. "One shouldn't affect the other."

"You don't sound very confident."

"It doesn't matter if I'm confident or not. I have no control over the situation."

"A person always has some control, and an intelligent woman like you has more than you think."

She was glad that darkness hid the heat that rose to her cheeks. "My intelligence has nothing to do with the situation. Neither the hotel nor the school belong to me."

"But their stability affects you. If the school fails, you could lose your position."

That sounded terribly selfish. "Fiona is my friend. I want her and her husband to succeed, not because of my teaching position but because I care about her."

"Of course you do."

"I don't know how to help."

He didn't say anything for several steps. Then he halted, making her come to a stop. She waited, but he said nothing.

She peered into the darkness, unable to make out his expression, even in the moonlight. "What is it?"

He shook his head. "I don't know anything about running a school, but I do know that a business succeeds when the income outweighs the expenses."

"I know that." Then, realizing she'd sounded arrogant, she added, "I meant to say that I would like to find a way to help increase receipts, but thus far I fear I've only hurt them."

She resumed walking.

This time he joined her. "In what way have you hurt receipts? Has one of the students left?"

"No." Louise didn't care to mention her struggles with Priscilla, especially since the girl had honed in on Jesse as a way to irritate her. "But as an employee I draw wages."

"Rightfully so. I'm sure Mrs. Evans doesn't regret one cent paid to such an invaluable employee."

How could that man infuriate her one moment and touch her heart the next? "Thank you for the compliment, but kind words don't bring in more students." Especially with Priscilla working against her.

"Maybe it's not a question of bringing in students. Maybe you could bring in more people who need a place to stay."

"The hotel?"

"You said they're owned by the same people."

She nodded. "But they're entirely different institutions."

"Naturally, but we can apply similar principles. Though I've never had anything to do with running a hotel, I have frequented my share, enough to know they are a business like any other. In any business you first need to discover what people need and then find a way to meet that need."

"They need a place to stay."

"That's a start," he continued, "but now figure out what else they need."

"Clean linens? Heat? Meals? They can get all that at the hotel."

"Is there competition?"

That didn't take much thought. "The boardinghouse."

"What can the hotel offer that the boardinghouse can't in order to meet the needs of their clientele?"

They'd reached the school. She climbed the porch stairs, Jesse's words tumbling around in her head. His suggestion was all well and good, but lumberjacks wanted inexpensive housing and little more. They weren't about to spend their last dollars on an elegant hotel when for a lot less they could get a room and meals.

"I'm afraid the hotel is too fancy for the average man coming into Singapore," she sighed.

"Then they will need to find other clientele."

"Find other…" A steamship's horn interrupted her thoughts. One must have just arrived or was ready to depart. Ships did arrive in port regularly. Many came to haul out lumber and produce, but others brought needed supplies. Some also carried passengers on their way to Holland or Detroit or Chicago. What if those passengers got off here instead? What if Singapore could become a destination?

"That might be the answer," she mused.

"What might?"

Louise began to answer him but was interrupted by the front door of the school opening.

Fiona stood in the doorway. Her color was high, and she looked agitated. "I thought I heard someone arrive, and I hoped it was you." Then she noticed Jesse. "Oh, Mr. Hammond! I'd invite you in, but I need to speak to Louise right away."

The delight of puzzling out a problem with Jesse vanished under Fiona's jangled nerves. Louise had seldom seen her friend in this state, and past instances had only been under extreme duress. Had something terrible happened? She hurried to the door, forgetting Jesse in her rush to discover the source of Fiona's agitation.

"Thank you, Mrs. Evans, but I can't stay." Jesse tipped a finger to his hat. "I need to get back to the lighthouse. Good night."

"Good night to you also."

Louise turned to face him before entering the school. The light from the doorway cast his face in a golden hue. "Thank you for walking me here."

"My pleasure." Jesse nodded farewell and clattered down the stairs before disappearing into the night.

After Louise entered the school, Fiona closed the front door and leaned against it with evident exhaustion. "I'm glad you're here."

"What happened?" Louise removed her hat and stuck the pins in the hatband, hoping that she was not about to learn that what Jane Blackthorn had suggested was indeed happening to the hotel. "Has Priscilla taken a turn for the worse?"

"No! Not that, though it does relate to our patient." Fiona took a deep breath. "They have arrived."

That was not what Louise had expected to hear. "Who has?"

"Mr. and Mrs. Bennington. They've seen their daughter, and now they're waiting to speak with us."

Louise knew at once what that meant. Trouble had landed.

Chapter Seven

❧

"This is the teacher in question?" Mrs. Cecilia Bennington peered down her patrician nose at Louise before sniffing with disdain. "There is no accounting for the lower class's taste." She then directed her attention back at Fiona.

Louise had no idea if Mrs. Bennington viewed her as lower class or if she was referring to Jesse and thus measured Louise as beneath lower class. In either case, the woman had clearly meant to insult her. She had silently endured similar treatment from women like Cecilia Bennington during her marriage and widowhood, but a year in Singapore had shown her that she did indeed have value. She was not merely an oddity to be examined and then pushed into a corner. Her opinions counted for something. Hadn't Jesse said as much?

She could bear disdain, snubs and even false accusations from the likes of Cecilia Bennington, but she could not and would not allow her or anyone else to disparage another person, especially when that individual happened to be an intelligent man who had valiantly served the Union during the recent conflict.

"Mr. Hammond is a credit to his country."

Mrs. Bennington snapped her head toward her at the unexpected comment. "One would expect the unprincipled one to defend the other."

Louise was livid. She could no longer sit quietly and endure blatant insults. She was about to respond when she caught Fiona's warning glare out of the corner of her eye. Her friend clearly wanted to handle this herself, but Fiona wasn't the one being disparaged.

"Mrs. Bennington. Mr. Bennington." Fiona fluttered between the two the way she did amongst patrons at one of her concerts. "Surely we can sit and discuss this over tea like civilized people."

She motioned to the two stuffed chairs that someone—probably Sawyer—had dragged into her office.

"Would you care for tea?" Fiona managed gracious hospitality even when facing the insufferable. She must have been a fine actress as well as singer.

If only Louise could exude such grace. Instead, she stood stiff as a wooden doll.

Fiona swept a hand toward the desk. "Allow me."

That's when Louise noticed the tea service. My! She took pride in her powers of observation, but temper had narrowed her vision to the extent that she could not see the details. Fiona's warning glance had spared her from an ugly confrontation and deep regret.

"I will serve." Louise brushed past Fiona to get to the tea service. She needed to do something. Being useful had kept her out of the eye of the wealthier women in the past. Serving seemed to make her invisible, as if she became no more than a maid.

"Milk and sugar for me," Mr. Bennington said with a consoling smile as he settled into one of the chairs.

He was definitely the more companionable of the pair, though clearly not the one in charge. His top hat and overcoat hung from a coat tree in the corner. Expensive silk and quality fabric. Louise remembered it well, though she would never again be able to afford such luxuries.

"I take mine black," Mrs. Bennington said without looking in her direction. "Now, where were we?"

Fiona sat in the chair beside the desk. "We are going to discuss the matter in a civilized manner."

"What is there to discuss?" Cecilia Bennington said with a swish of her silk skirts. "When we received the wire, we rushed to our dear Priscilla's side only to find she has suffered greatly under the tutelage of a woman of questionable virtue." Her glare in Louise's direction made it perfectly clear who that woman was.

"It's a simple misunderstanding." Fiona's voice took on a soft, comforting tone, quite different from usual. "Your daughter happened to walk past the classroom precisely when Mr. Hammond rescued Mrs. Smythe from a precipitous fall."

"So that woman says." Cecelia Bennington didn't so much as look at Louise. "It's her word against my daughter's."

Louise lifted the full teapot and poured into the first cup, but her shaking hand caused the liquid to slosh onto the saucer. After setting down the pot, she took a deep breath. Best give this one to Mr. Bennington. His wife would criticize her pouring. Now, what had he wanted? Milk and sugar? She hoped so.

"Mr. Hammond concurred with Mrs. Smythe's account," Fiona said calmly.

Louise poured the second cup, spilling even more of the liquid on the saucer. Perhaps Louise should have had her friend serve the tea after all.

"Of course he did," Cecilia Bennington said. "They are in this together, after all."

Louise gritted her teeth. "For your information, we did not like each other at the time."

Cecilia stared at her as if she'd just realized Louise was still in the room. "Which is as good as admitting that you are enamored by the man now. I understand you are a widow, Mrs. Smythe. As such, you must take extra care with your reputation, even if you weren't instructing young ladies. My daughter informed me that you have been walking with him alone after dark."

Fiona let out a dramatic sigh and closed her eyes, followed by a shake of the head. This was not heading in a good direction, but Louise would not allow this woman to destroy her. She had kept quiet about Warren's drinking and violent temper to preserve his reputation. She had given excuses, taking the blame onto herself. No more, especially since nothing improper had occurred.

"Mr. Hammond was escorting me home for my safety. Perhaps your daughter also told you that I kept a respectable distance from him while he watched only to ensure I did not lose my footing. Mr. Hammond should be praised, not accused."

"Now, now, no one said they were accusing the man of anything," Mr. Bennington said. "Come, Cecilia. Have a seat." He stood and repositioned the other chair nearer to his.

Mrs. Bennington ignored her husband in favor of continuing the attack. "That is your version of events, Mrs. Smythe." Her attention shifted to Fiona. "It wouldn't do your fledgling school any good to have news of these incidents reach the ears of prospective students."

Louise shut her eyes. Why hadn't she kept her mouth closed? If the hotel truly was suffering, this only added to Fiona's woes.

"Come, dear." Mr. Bennington shoved the chair nearly to the back of his wife's knees. "Do sit."

Mrs. Bennington at last sank into the chair. After adjusting her skirts, she returned her attention to Louise. "Are you going to wait until the tea is cold to serve it?"

In the past, a comment like that would have unnerved Louise and sent her to her books, where she could retreat from the harshness of reality. Today Louise carried the cups to the Benningtons without spilling a single drop.

Wouldn't Elizabeth Bennett, the heroine of *Pride and Prejudice*, be proud? That character would have known how to handle such a woman. At the very least she would roll her eyes and whisper her observations to her dear sister, Jane, or her friend, Charlotte Lucas. Louise would have to wait for such comfort from her friend, though given the way events were unfurling, Louise might have to give the comfort.

Fiona and her husband could well be standing on the precipice of ruin if Fiona's strained expression was any indication. Louise's defense of her actions had done nothing to help the situation. If anything, it had harmed the school.

The choice was simple. Only one thing would appease the Benningtons. It was a difficult gift to give, but one Louise owed the dear friend who had given her a new lease on life.

She stepped before the Benningtons. "I will resign my position."

Fiona rose. Cecilia Bennington smiled in triumph.

"A sensible solution," the woman said before sipping the tea.

"A hasty one." Fiona frowned at Louise but shifted to a placating tone for the Benningtons. "There is no reason to rush to a decision. You are welcome to stay at the hotel as my guests. If you have not yet eaten, I will ask the cook to make a light supper for you." Even as she spoke, she ushered the Benningtons from her office.

Mr. Bennington voiced no objection. In fact, he seemed to take the entire matter with a bit of humor. He even gave Louise a wink when passing and his wife wasn't looking, as if to say that Louise shouldn't take his wife's complaints to heart.

Louise couldn't muster any confidence in Mr. Bennington's ability to change his wife's mind. With Priscilla's goading, Cecilia Bennington would have Louise out the door before sunrise.

Jesse flung off the bedclothes and rolled onto his right side. His toes smashed into the wall, waking him further. He growled to himself. This bed was too small and the room far too hot. The assistant keeper should have his own quarters, not the smallest bedroom in the peak of the roof. It wasn't large enough for a child, not to mention a full-grown man.

He groaned and rolled onto his back. Silvery light from the three-quarter moon streamed through the tiny window, landing right in his face. He turned toward the wall. A breath of air fluttered the curtains and raced across his prone body, raising a few goose pimples. He reached for the bedclothes and thought better of it. Perspiration drenched his nightshirt. The momentary chill was a relief.

Much like the icy water that had enveloped him in the dream.

Jesse sat up with a start. The dream. It had returned.

This time the chill went to the bone. Memory was stronger than any dream. The cries and screams got louder and louder until he pressed his hands to his ears and squeezed his eyes shut. The people were dying, and he could do nothing about it. His heart pounded. His lungs screamed for air, but there was only water. It dulled the cries but not the thrashing, the desperate clawing for life. The orange light flickered and died, plunging them into darkness. That's when he knew all was lost.

Panic raced like a steam locomotive, growing stronger and stronger until he couldn't fight it. Nothing could stop the cries for help. Nothing could wash away the guilt. Nothing could ease the pain in the center of his chest, feeling like a sharp stake driven clear through him.

"Take me, Lord," he whispered. "Why didn't You take me?"

As always, no answer came. Only the pain remained. He knew what to do, what the kindly druggist advised after refusing to give him the dulling laudanum he had sought. Breathe slowly and deeply, counting to four. Then hold that breath an equal time before slowly letting it out. Repeat until the heart calms. Think of something pleasant. Louise. Her gray eyes could soothe any tempest.

Gradually the pounding slowed and the panic went away, leaving him exhausted but too awake to sleep. Jesse's hand trembled as he fumbled to light a match and then the candle at his bedside. It took more than slowing his breathing to calm the panic. He had to do something with his hands.

Soon the warm glow of the candle filled the room, vanquishing the shadows of the past to the corners. Then he took up his penknife and one of the bits of wood he'd scavenged from the shoreline. The sharp blade cut through the wood easily. He glanced at the small table that served as a desk where all manner of whittled creatures waited in a long line. By morning's first light, he would have another. Judging from the shape of this bit of wood, a seagull waited inside, ready to be freed.

Louise packed her carpetbag that night. Unlike her years as Mrs. Warren Smythe, she didn't own enough to fill a trunk, nor did she have a trunk to fill. Warren's family had seen fit to disinherit her of everything but the clothes on her back, a Sunday gown, her Bible, her journal and three books. They'd taken the jewelry, except the wedding ring, which would no longer slide off her finger.

Oh, the bitter irony! That unadorned band of gold brought nothing but painful memories and, when the weather was hot, uncomfortable swelling of her finger. For a long time, she'd seen it as a symbol of Warren's grip, but now she viewed it as a reminder of what she would never endure again.

If only a paying position was that tenacious. Instead, each had disappeared due to circumstance. Her first, working for Captain and Mrs. Elder as a companion to the ailing lady, had been a delight. Both enjoyed literature, science and debating the latest discoveries. She and the captain had disagreed on Mr. Darwin's theory on the origin of the species, with her arguing for God's infallible Word and Captain Elder eager to grasp the new theory. Many a debate lasted until the wee hours of the morning, and they'd ended up agreeing to disagree for the sake of Mrs. Elder, who put a stop to the discord by stating that only God knew the truth.

Alas, Mrs. Elder's health took a turn for the worse this past winter, and the captain packed their belongings, closed the house and sailed for Chicago, where she would be under the care of knowledgeable physicians.

Until Fiona gave her this teaching position at the beginning of September, Louise had worked at the boardinghouse for her room and board. There she learned to change bed linens and cook meals. Mrs. Calloway had guided her through those tasks, and Louise had thanked God for placing the kindly woman in her path. For with every bit of instruction came a sense of accomplishment and worth.

The teaching position had been a gift from God, bestowing independence, but for the sake of her friend, Fiona, she must relinquish it.

Louise fought back a tear as she shut her carpetbag. With a final look around her room, the bed linens neatly stripped and ready for laundering, she left.

Each step of the staircase creaked under her feet. The scent of the oil used to polish the wood would always remain with her. Mrs. Calloway used a different preparation at the boardinghouse. Louise hoped the woman would take her back under the old arrangement of room and board in exchange for labor. She had only a few coins to her name, not enough to let a room, least of all pay passage to the closest port.

The parlor carpet was new, part of the refurbishing that had been generously provided for by Sawyer Evans's mother. Its thick nap cushioned her feet, sore inside the shoes whose soles had worn through under the ball of each foot. Layers of newspaper kept out the largest stones but would be of no use once the snow fell.

Louise sighed. She couldn't afford new shoes, and the town hadn't a cobbler. She turned toward Fiona's office.

Her friend stood in the hallway. "Where are you going?"

Louise had worked out her speech. "The students' welfare must come before everything else."

Fiona propped her hands on her hips. "And that welfare includes getting a good education. How are they supposed to do that without a teacher?"

"There are others who are qualified. Pearl, for instance."

Fiona rolled her eyes. "Pearl is plenty busy teaching the children at the one-room schoolhouse and helping out her husband at the general store."

"You could teach literature and mathematics until you can hire another teacher."

"I don't know anything about literature or mathematics. If you'll recall, I grew up in the tenements."

Louise had forgotten this sore point of Fiona's past. "You know far more than you think."

"And how am I supposed to help with the hotel and raise Mary Clare while teaching full-time? Moreover, who will stay with the girls and ensure they are safe throughout the day and night?"

Louise blanched. She'd been so focused on sparing the school's reputation that she'd neglected to consider the repercussions of leaving. "But Mrs. Bennington—"

"—has changed her mind."

"She has?" Louise found that difficult to believe.

Fiona grinned. "A few butter rolls can go a long way toward smoothing ruffled feathers."

"You made your rolls?"

Fiona was famed for her baking, but she seldom had the time or inclination to do it since marrying and opening the school. While still seeking a husband, she had used those rolls to encourage prospects to give her a second look.

"That and a little persuasion," Fiona said.

"What sort of persuasion?" Louise was half afraid to hear the answer.

"I merely pointed out that you had saved her daughter's life when she lay ill with fever."

"Me? I didn't do anything." In fact, Louise had felt terribly helpless. "I had to run to the hotel to get help."

"If you hadn't done that, she might have died."

"But the doctor said—"

"She might have died," Fiona repeated. "I will not hear any more of your attempts to discount what you have done. The girls need you. I need you. Please stay."

Louise's spirits buoyed. She wouldn't have to find work elsewhere or even move away. She would see Jesse again.

That shouldn't have mattered as much as it did.

Chapter Eight

News spreads quickly in small towns, even more so in a company town like Singapore. By the midday meal, Jesse learned what had happened at Mrs. Evans's school last night.

"Jimmy says Mrs. Smythe quit," Joe, the youngest Blackthorn boy, said at the dinner table.

Jesse steeled his expression so the family didn't see how much this news affected him.

"What does he know? He only works at the store," the daughter chimed in. "But I heard that Mrs. Evans wouldn't let Mrs. Smythe go. They're friends, you see." Her smug look was meant to inform her brothers that she had access to information they could never get, since they were boys.

Jesse let out a silent breath of relief. He shouldn't care, not since he had advertised for a wife, but Louise had become a friend.

"Isn't that something," Mrs. Blackthorn mused, forgoing a forkful of her chicken pie to join the conversation. "I wonder why Mrs. Smythe would do a thing like that."

"Jimmy says she's jealous of Priscilla Bennington," Joe said.

"Not so," Isabel countered. "Who would ever be jealous of that snob? No one can stand her."

"Then why does she always have those two friends of hers with her?"

Jesse tuned out the childish argument. The hotel and school must be in decent financial condition if Mrs. Evans insisted Louise remain in her position. The woman didn't strike Jesse as one who hired a person and then didn't pay.

The news elevated his spirits enough to shake off the ill effects of poor sleep and Blackthorn's relegating him to whitewashing duty. While he brushed the white paint on the slats of the fence, his mind drifted to the pleasures of the small town below. Though it boasted very few businesses, there was a closeness between the people living here that he hadn't experienced since the army.

That recollection brought both pleasure and pain.

His unit had been close. They joked, sang songs, told stories. He knew the names of each man's sisters, brothers and sweethearts. They'd become brothers. Then came the ambush. The men scattered. More than half lost their lives. Jesse and a handful of others had escaped into the swamp and sank so deep in the muck that the Confederate soldiers either refused to go after them or figured they'd die. Most of the rest were captured and probably ended up in a prisoner camp. Of course, none of them knew how bad things were in the camps at that time. Jesse hadn't known until the soldiers came through Vicksburg on their way home.

He escaped the swamp but nearly died. The subsequent illness left him weak and unfit for any service but working under the quartermaster. That job kept him out of harm's way and opened the door for guilt. He should have died. He should have gone to the prisoner camps.

He should have come back a mere skeleton of his former self. He should have spoken up when the steamboat captains overloaded their boats with veterans.

Not one bit of it could be taken back.

He slapped a brush full of paint on the next slat.

"Oh!" cried a female voice. "You nearly splattered paint all over my skirt."

Jesse looked up to see Louise standing on the other side of the fence. He stood, paintbrush in hand. "I'm sorry. I didn't realize you were there."

"I called out to you. Didn't you hear me?"

"My thoughts were elsewhere." But he wasn't about to explain where. "What brings you here?"

"Next Monday's lecture. Or do you prefer a different day of the week?"

"No, no. That will be fine." He turned the conversation. "I understand your fears about the school's future were unwarranted."

Her brow furrowed. "For the time being, but I'm not certain how long that will last." She heaved a sigh. "Fiona admitted that the hotel is not doing as well as they'd hoped."

"And thus the school. Were the well-dressed couple parents of a prospective student? I saw them leaving the school this afternoon."

Her expression made it clear she did not care for the couple. "The Benningtons wanted to make sure their daughter is fully recovered."

"The young lady who hurt her ankle?"

"Yes. Though Priscilla is still a bit weak, she is back to her old self." The accompanying sigh meant that wasn't necessarily a good thing.

Jesse could calculate the potential repercussions. "The loss of even one student could be a problem."

"Precipitous." Again the sigh. Then a little smile. "Nearly the same word as precipitation. Isn't that fascinating? What with you giving a lecture on the subject."

Jesse could see she was trying to divert attention from the situation at school, which apparently wasn't as settled as the Blackthorn daughter had made it sound. He needed to lift her spirits.

"Even if something should happen to the school, you will do well. I've never met a woman who knows as much about botany as you do."

She blushed. "Thank you, but there isn't much need for botany instruction here."

"I'm sure you're equally capable in other subjects. There must be a public schoolhouse here."

"There is, and my friend, Pearl, is the teacher."

That eliminated the best option. Jesse could see only one other solution, but it wasn't one he much liked. Still, he must think of Louise, not his own selfish desire to continue their friendship. After all, he expected to receive answers to his advertisements for a wife in the near future.

"You could go to the city," he reluctantly suggested. "Chicago. Or New York."

Her spine stiffened, and he wondered why.

"You don't like the city?" he asked.

"I prefer it here." She brushed a loose strand of hair from her face and tucked it behind an ear, a gesture that made him long to see her hair undone from its severe bun. "I've come to love the fresh breezes and simpler life. Moreover, I can examine specimens here. That's impossible from the inside of a city school."

He loved her practicality, but even more so the sudden burst of longing that danced in her eyes. She truly did love exploring the flora of the area. How much more would she enjoy seeing the unique specimens in other climes. Though her departure would hurt, she deserved every happiness.

"You should travel, see other parts of this country and then the world."

Her expression clouded. "That is not possible, even for a daring woman, without the support of great wealth."

Jesse could have kicked himself. Naturally she did not have the funds for such adventures. If she had, she would not be worried about losing her teaching position. Nor could he help her, even if he wanted to do so. He had no store of riches to draw upon. No inheritance awaited. Neither did he have more than a pittance in savings. He could sympathize, but he could not help.

"It's nice to dream, though," he said.

She nodded. "Sometimes dreams are all we have."

There was meaning behind that, meaning that he desperately wanted to decipher, but she quickly moved on.

"Do you need to borrow Captain Elder's book? I brought it with me."

Only then did he notice she carried the tome in the crook of her arm.

"Thank you, but I think I have all that I need."

She nodded. "Well, then. I should let you get back to your work."

The sadness in her voice touched him. He wanted to bring back the smile and the hope. He wanted her to be able to dream of one day finding a new species or even becoming a scientist. But what could he say to change the fact that her livelihood hung by a thread?

"Goodbye," she said.

He began to wave when the answer came. They had begun the conversation last night, but he'd never finished.

"If the hotel thrives, so will the school," he blurted out.

She halted and turned back to look at him. "What do you mean?"

"Last night you said that the hotel was too fancy for its current clientele, and I suggested getting different clientele."

She stepped back to the fence. "So you did, and an idea came to me, but I forgot, what with the Benningtons' arrival and all."

"Can you tell me your idea?"

That delightful smile returned to her lips. "A way to bring people like the Benningtons to Singapore." She hugged the book to her chest. "It just might work."

"What will?"

She shook her head with a tinkling laugh. "I have to talk to Fiona first. If she agrees, then you will be the next to know about it."

With that she hurried off, a lilt in her step. Jesse looked down at the fence, which he was transforming from dingy gray to sparkling white. He dipped his brush and resumed painting, this time whistling as he worked.

The following Monday morning, Louise watched Jesse from the back of the classroom. He paced nervously from side to side, completely ignoring the podium and the copious notes he'd brought to his first lecture. Few of those words ended up being spoken. His sentences were brief and to the point. After describing each type of cloud with little elaboration, he moved on to precipitation.

"Cirrus clouds don't bring rain. Nimbus clouds do."

Louise's attention drifted back to her talk with Fiona last Tuesday. After taking in Louise's idea to promote the hotel, Fiona had initially turned down the suggestion. A day later, she asked several questions and then agreed that a Christmas Festival was just the thing this town needed.

"It's never been done before," Fiona had said, "but that doesn't mean we can't be the first to try. It won't cost much, and it will benefit the other businesses as well as the hotel. I can't see any reason they wouldn't want to join the effort."

Fiona's enthusiasm had sparked dozens more ideas in the next couple days. Louise had grown more and more excited until Fiona's last suggestion.

"You should be in charge of making the wreaths and garlands," Fiona had declared. "Your knowledge of plants makes you the perfect choice to lead that part of the festivities. You'll know which ones will work best. We will want to decorate the hotel and the other businesses."

Though Louise had held her tongue, she wondered if it was possible to find that much greenery within a ready distance. The last nearby timber stand had been leveled. Young pines had shot up past Saugatuck, the nearest town, but that was quite a hike from Singapore. She would have trouble dragging back more than a few small boughs without assistance and a cart or, if the snow fell, a sleigh.

Fiona must have thought of that objection, because her next suggestion married the festival preparations to her matchmaking efforts. "Ask Mr. Hammond to help you gather what you need."

Louise had been too stunned to counter the suggestion at the time. A night of thinking had given her a viable alternative, but Fiona had shot down the suggestion of sending word up to the lumber camps to send boughs downriver on the mail boat. Her objections made sense. Too expensive to pay for transport. Too difficult to get word to the camps. Too risky to rely on rough lumberjacks to save the right types of boughs.

Louise would have to ask Jesse for help. Naturally,

Fiona had refused to handle that part, insisting that teaching classes, watching over the girls and attending to the Benningtons during their stay had kept her busy. Louise had looked for Jesse at yesterday's church service, but he had tended the lighthouse, allowing the entire Blackthorn family to go to church. That left this morning.

Louise drew her attention back to Jesse's lecture.

He had stopped pacing and now faced the girls. "Any questions?"

Other than an audible sigh, not one girl moved.

Seconds passed.

Jesse started shuffling from foot to foot, his neck growing redder by the moment.

Then Priscilla raised her hand. "Can a whirlwind strike here?"

"Th-that's an excellent question," Jesse stammered, clearly uncertain of the answer.

Louise felt for him. Every instinct told her to rise and give the answer Captain Elder had given her when she asked the very same question, but to do so would undermine Jesse's authority and do nothing to raise Louise in Priscilla's esteem.

Yet, as the seconds ticked on in silence, she must do something to rescue him. "I believe a waterspout was once spotted offshore."

His gaze shot to her. Was that a look of relief?

A couple of the girls glanced back at her, but most kept their attention riveted to Jesse's every move.

"Waterspouts are whirlwinds over water," he said, his confidence growing with each word. "They can come ashore. Then they would be whirlwinds."

Esther's hand shot up. "What do we do if we see one?"

Jesse was visibly relieved, and the rest of the class proceeded smoothly. To Louise's surprise, the girls listened to everything he said, and they asked good questions. Jesse relaxed to the point that he sat atop her desk, one foot on the seat of her chair, while he answered them. Louise wondered how much sand and grime she'd have to clean off her chair once the class ended, but it was good to see Jesse so animated. He even smiled at her, probably in gratitude, but it sent her pulse racing.

After the class ended, and the girls left—albeit reluctantly and with a great many personal exclamations of gratitude—Louise gave him a nod of approval.

"That went well."

He blew out his breath. "It was terrifying."

She chuckled at the memory of his frightened look when he first entered the classroom. "At least there are only five of them."

"Five *girls*."

Though Louise saw no reason why girls should be more difficult than boys, she couldn't help but be delighted that he'd used a term that highlighted their tender years rather than extolling them as young women or ladies. "Five attentive girls. I will give you credit. You held their attention." Better than he'd held hers, alas.

He raked a hand through his hair. "I wish I hadn't agreed to the other five lectures. I'm not sure I'll survive."

"You will."

"As long as you're there."

His gaze met hers, and those sparkling blue eyes drew her in the same way that a brilliant blue sky made her spirits soar. No sunny day could compare to the humble gratitude and approval he'd just showered on her. She swallowed, all too aware of everything about him. From the sandy blond curls to the strong cut of his jaw to the dimple in the center of his chin, she saw it all. His breath.

The rise and fall of his chest. The bit of whiskers that had escaped the blade at the corner of jaw.

"I will be here," she managed to breathe out.

"Good."

His smile warmed her to her toes and muddled her mind.

"I, uh," she began. There was something she wanted to tell him, but couldn't remember what it was.

"You what?"

My stars, she was acting worse than the girls. Except that she should know better. She'd been married and widowed. That marriage had brought pain and heartache. Why should she think marriage to anyone else, even a man like Jesse, would be any better?

She licked her parched lips. "I seem to have forgotten what I was going to say."

His eyes twinkled. "Why would that be?"

Was he jesting with her? "My mind was elsewhere, like yours was the other day while painting the fence."

He stiffened slightly.

Oh, dear. She should have known better. He'd been defensive about it then. Memories of Warren flooded in. Whenever she asked about something he'd done, he would accuse her of trying to control his life or not trusting him, as if the problem was hers. But it wasn't. She hadn't seen it at the time. She'd foolishly believed him, but now that she was removed from his influence she could see how he had manipulated her.

The thrill of Jesse's regard vanished before the harsh memories of her late husband.

"Don't feel badly," Jesse was saying. "It's easy for the mind to drift. If you later recall what you wanted to tell me, you can stop by the lighthouse."

"Or talk to you after church one Sunday."

"I keep watch so the Blackthorns can attend as a family."

That explained why she hadn't seen him there. Her relief was great. "That's kind of you."

"I study the Bible during that time."

That news quickened her heart, even though he had made it clear they were to be no more than friends.

"I might be able to attend on Christmas," Jesse added. "Mr. Blackthorn tells me that shipping is pretty much over by then."

"Christmas! That's it! That's what I wanted to ask you."

"About Christmas?" He looked so uncomfortable that she almost burst out laughing.

"No, what I was trying to remember. It's about Christmas, in a way. I need your help." She then explained what she and Fiona had decided to attempt for the Christmas Festival. "We need to locate evergreen boughs that will make long-lasting wreaths and garlands. Yews are out of the question, but we might find some willow for the framework."

His brow had furrowed more and more with each word. "I don't know how to make wreaths."

"I do." Louise hated remembering the reason. "Back in New York, I made several funeral wreaths for the fallen."

He stiffened.

His reaction made her wonder again if he had served in the war. He was the right age to be a veteran of the conflict. Few of them wanted to talk about what they'd seen. Jesse would be no exception. Fiona had mentioned that Sawyer had fought for the Union. He never talked about the war, preferring to dwell on the present. So would she.

"This will be a festive, cheerful time. People will want to come here, especially if we make it known in Chicago what is happening here." Then she made her plea. "Your knowledge of plants will be invaluable."

That brought back the smile. "Are you sure you don't just want me along to carry the boughs?"

"Oh, dear. You deciphered my real purpose." Louise immediately regretted the playful jab. He didn't appear to understand her humor, judging from the look on his face. She braced herself.

Instead of chastising her, he roared with laughter. "Of course I'll help. Anything for a friend who speaks her mind."

A friend. He'd called her a friend. She should be glad. Yet, in spite of all she'd endured in her marriage to Warren, deep down she wanted more.

The sparkle left Louise's eyes at the word *friend*. Jesse regretted causing her dismay, but he had to make sure she understood that there could be nothing more between them. Any day now he could receive an answer to his advertisement. As much as he liked Louise, selecting a wife required far more than a pleasant temperament, comely face and an unnerving ability to capture his attention.

No, he'd accepted this task of hers for a much more practical reason. Ever since Blackthorn learned Jesse would be talking to the students about the lighthouse service, he'd shown him more of the operation. The keeper still urged Jesse to fit in with the community. Helping with the Christmas Festival would show the man that Jesse wanted to belong. Consequently, Blackthorn would let him take over more and more of the daily duties.

"Thank you," Louise said with considerably less animation than a moment before. "We appreciate the help."

"We?"

"Fiona and I."

Jesse couldn't picture the redhead traipsing across the countryside. "Will Mrs. Evans help us cut boughs?"

That brought a laugh and the smile he regretted stifling. "I doubt it. She will leave that to me. To us." Louise sobered. "I'm afraid that you will have to do the cutting. I have no experience with a saw."

Few women did. Even fewer expected to wield a saw under such circumstances. He couldn't resist poking fun at her comment. "I can show you how to use one."

"You would do that? Thank you."

That wasn't the response he'd expected. For a moment his jaw went slack. He blinked. "You *want* to learn how to use a saw?"

"It is a useful skill."

Louise Smythe continually amazed him.

"I've never met a woman who wanted to learn how to saw anything." He raked a hand through his hair, uncomfortable with the idea of Louise handling a saw. "Are you sure?"

"They would be twigs and small branches," she said, "not entire trees. Promise we won't cut down whole trees."

Jesse recalled her dismay when he reached to pull out the weed she was examining. She'd begged him not to kill it. Now she didn't want to harm a tree, even for the sake of the festival that would rescue her friend's business and her own livelihood.

He shook his head. "You are a remarkable woman, but you shouldn't be doing something so dangerous."

That lovely shade of pink suffused her cheeks and her jaw jutted out. "If you'd rather not teach me, I can ask Sawyer. He's Fiona's husband. He got his name from his skill with saws. He still helps out at the sawmill when the rush is on. He managed it last spring, until Mr. Stockton's new schooner was launched."

Jesse wondered how Evans could run a hotel and work in a sawmill at the same time. Jesse wasn't opposed to hard work. He'd labored hard himself over the years and already had put in some long days at the lighthouse, but Evans had a family. That changed everything. Jesse thought about Blackthorn. Perhaps there was an advantage to having one's family at the workplace. They could help out and a man would get to see them throughout the day. Visions of Louise and a handful of children crossed his mind. The idea of a large family was a lot more appealing than the way he'd grown up, motherless from the age of seven and with a father who worked the docks.

That he'd thought first of Louise was disconcerting. That he'd envisioned her with a houseful of children was even worse. At her age and after a childless marriage, that wasn't likely.

"The trouble will be finding enough evergreens within easy walking distance," she was saying. "Amanda says there's a large stand upriver from Saugatuck, but we would need a horse and cart to haul them back. I wonder if Roland would loan us the store's cart. Or maybe Garrett could spare the horse and wagon from the sawmill since there's not a rush underway."

He could see her mind working through the problem. She walked about the classroom while deep in thought, not seeing him or anything else. Some of the names she mentioned were unfamiliar to him, but she clearly knew them well.

"Once we have the boughs," she continued, "the girls will help make the wreaths. We can put all sorts of things on them, like ribbon and pinecones and whatever we can find."

A thought crossed Jesse's mind. He dug in his pocket and pulled out the miniature cardinal that he'd almost finished. "Do you think some of these would work?"

She drew in her breath and examined the bird.

He held his breath. Did she like it?

"It's lovely. You made this? Look at all the detail. The cardinal's crest is perfect."

He soaked in her praise. "You know your birds too."

"How many do you have?"

He shrugged. "A couple dozen."

"All cardinals?"

"No, many different types of birds."

She clapped her hands together. "Wonderful! The girls could paint them. Fiona has paints. If we had enough, the schoolchildren might help out too. Pearl and Amanda might want to take part, not to mention Mrs. Calloway. Why, we could even have a contest of sorts."

"A contest? For what?"

"The best wreath." Her eyes sparkled with excitement. "The prize could be something small. I'll ask Pearl what she suggests. Isn't that a wonderful idea?"

He wasn't so certain. "Aren't you getting far ahead of things? It's barely October. Christmas is two and a half months away. Wreaths can't be made until shortly before the event."

"True." Her brow pinched in that particularly appealing way, with a little crease between her finely shaped eyebrows. "But we ought to make a test wreath in order to practice. That will also tell us how long they will last, so we know exactly when to make them. And we can make the bows ahead of time. And of course your birds. How many can you make?"

"In a couple months, maybe a couple dozen, depending on my duties at the lighthouse." Jesse glanced out the window, which faced the dune. Blackthorn would be expecting him soon. If Jesse stayed too long, the keeper would begin curtailing duties, not adding to them. "I need to return to work."

"Oh!" Again she blushed. "I'm terribly sorry. I shouldn't have gone on blathering away and keeping you from your duties. Please, go." She waved him away. "I will locate some pine saplings nearby that can provide enough boughs for a test wreath. Do you have time later this week to help me cut off the branches?"

He had to leave. Duty called. Maybe that's why he agreed so quickly when he ought to be cutting short their time together. Soon enough the responses to his advertisement would begin arriving, and he would select one for a wife. Spending time with Louise now would only create more heartache later. So then why did he tell her that late this afternoon would be the perfect time to find pine boughs?

Chapter Nine

After Louise helped Jesse cut willow saplings on the riverbank for the framing, they left them alongside the road to pick up on their return. Then Louise followed the directions that Garrett Decker's wife, Amanda, had given her earlier. The road was well-established between Singapore and Saugatuck, though so sandy in spots that a heavily-laden wagon could bog down. She would have to remember that if she could get the wagon from the sawmill.

She and Jesse had walked for nearly half an hour already, and they weren't much past Saugatuck. Here the road, which had dwindled to more like a path, was less distinct. More than once she had to stop and puzzle which direction the path went.

Jesse offered nothing beyond toting the saw. He was uncharacteristically quiet, which made the long walk even longer. They had perhaps two hours left of daylight. Fortunately the day was unseasonably warm and the sun shone from a cloudless sky.

"No rain today," she mentioned.

"Yep."

"A few clouds would diminish the heat, though."

He nodded.

What was wrong with him? Had something happened at the lighthouse? The mail boat had come in. Had he received bad news from home?

"All is well at home?" she asked.

He started, as if she'd struck a nerve. "I assume so."

"Your mother and father are well?"

"My mother died when I was seven. My father and I aren't on speaking terms." The words were spoken tersely, with brow drawn and gaze fixed on the ground ahead, as if fearful he might stumble on a root.

"I'm sorry." She walked on a few moments in silence. If she expected him to talk more about his past, she would have to reveal hers first. "My father passed some years ago. My mother lives with my sister." She tried to keep the bitterness from her voice. "They are close."

Mama had always preferred Rachel, whose golden-blond hair resembled her own. Rachel was the beauty, the accomplished pianist and the model of perfection in Mama's eyes. Where Louise took after her papa, Rachel mirrored Mama in height, beauty and elegance. She married well, far above her station, and was beloved and respected throughout Albany, where her husband served as state senator.

"Do you see your family often?" he asked.

Louise thought back to the last time they'd been together. Rachel's house was the only place Louise could retreat after being thrown out of her home by Warren's family. Her sister had taken her in, but only at the urging of her husband, who was a good man. When he was at home, Rachel and Mama treated her with civility. When he was gone, they criticized everything from her hair to her inability to bear children. When they began suggesting she remarry as soon as possible to any man who would have her, Louise began reading the advertisements for a wife. It was a relief to leave—for them and for her. Louise would not return if she could at all avoid it.

"Not since I left over a year ago. This is my home now."

The quiver in her voice drew a glance of pity from him. She had endured enough pity for a lifetime.

"That looks like the new stand of pine that Amanda described." Louise pointed ahead and to their right.

Jesse stopped and put a hand above his eyes to shield from the sun's glare. "They're not very big."

"Hmm. She said there were some larger trees. I wonder if they're farther on."

"Perhaps, but we can get enough here for the test wreath you want to make."

They closed the remaining distance in silence. The trees stood almost to Jesse's shoulder and to the top of Louise's head. They were rather straggly specimens with no sign of this year's growth.

Louise examined a needle. "Soft. This must be a white pine. I'd hate to cut it. Those over there look like red pines. The needles are stronger."

"And more likely to jab you. Are you sure you don't want the white pine?"

"It takes so much longer for the white to grow. With this dry soil, it's already been tested to its limit. We will stick to the red pines."

Jesse shook his head, looking like he couldn't understand her reasoning, but he plodded toward the closest red pine. "How many branches?"

She pointed out which ones.

He began sawing off the slender branches. As the small pile grew, Louise envisioned the wreath. It wouldn't be enough.

"I just need one more branch, shorter and full." She scanned the saplings and spotted one that looked more full. While Jesse sawed off the last branch on the first tree, she headed for the second, fuller one.

"Stop!" Jesse hollered.

The command rooted her to the spot, but only for a second. Who was he to tell her what to do?

"I'm just checking this tree." She resumed trekking toward it.

She heard him running toward her.

"Stop," he panted.

That man had some nerve telling her where she could and could not walk. She increased her pace.

Then, before she even knew what was happening, he scooped her off the ground and swung her around, holding her close.

"What are you doing?" After recovering from the surprise, she pushed against his chest. "Let me go."

"Trap," he panted. "You were about to step in a trap."

"A what?"

He set her down and pointed to the gaping jaws of an iron trap. "It's set. If you'd stepped in it, it would rip the flesh from your ankle and might even break bones."

Shivers raced over her arms. She stepped back. "Who would do such a thing?"

"A trapper. They're trying to get fox, most likely."

"Fox?" The thought of the beautiful animals getting caught in those horrible metal jaws made her sick. "It would hurt the animal but not kill it."

"Eventually it would die from bloodshed or starvation."

Tears rose to her eyes. "Get rid of it."

"What?"

"Get rid of that horrible thing."

Jesse took her by the shoulders. "Now Louise, this is a man's livelihood. We can't go tampering with it."

But the tears wouldn't stop at the thought of the pain the poor creature would suffer. "The man could farm. Or lumber. Or any of a million other things. Why does he have to kill foxes?"

"For the fur coats that keep you warm in the winter."

"I don't have fur." Then she thought of Fiona's fur-trimmed cape, and the tears flowed. "I didn't know."

Strong arms cradled her while she wept. Her tears dampened his shirt, but she couldn't stop. Every time she thought of the poor foxes, a worse memory surfaced. Her beloved Falstaff, an exuberant beagle mix, would bark incessantly whenever he thought his mistress was in harm's way. Warren hated that dog. One night, during an argument after a drinking binge, Falstaff was unusually loud. Infuriated, Warren grabbed the dog and left. She never saw Falstaff again.

She could not hold back the sobs, for she kept seeing Falstaff's fear, kept hearing her pup's whining, kept imagining him stuck in a trap, struggling to break free.

"Shh, shh. It's all right." Jesse rubbed her back while she drenched his shirt.

Desperately she tried to regain control as she stepped away. "I'm sorry." The words came out thick and garbled.

"It's not about the fox, is it?"

She could only shake her head. "My handkerchief. I forgot it."

He pulled a clean handkerchief from his pocket and handed it to her. She dabbed her eyes. The handkerchief hadn't any dainty embroidery or initials. She supposed that was because he hadn't a mother.

"Your father never remarried?"

His jaw tensed. "No."

She blotted yet another tear. "I'm sorry. I don't know what came over me."

His steady gaze told her he didn't believe one word she'd just said.

She sighed. Perhaps she could reveal some of what had happened. "Warren—that's my late husband—he got rid of my dog. For barking too much."

The words stood there, vulnerable, saying so much yet not revealing enough.

"Before or after he went to war?"

The question surprised her.

"Before," she whispered.

He simply nodded. "I'm sorry."

What more was there to say?

Jesse began to understand Louise's reactions. What sort of husband got rid of his wife's dog for barking too much? A lunatic. A fiend. He hoped there was more to the story, that the dog was suffering in some way, but deep down he suspected that wasn't the case.

He tried to bolster her. "You're a strong woman."

"I rely on the Lord's strength. That's sufficient."

Yet she had been badly shaken. So he used the cut end of one of the boughs and sprung the trap.

Louise jumped and looked away.

"No fox is going to get caught in that today." He didn't mention that the trapper probably had dozens of traps set throughout the area. A city dweller like her wouldn't know.

"Thank you," she breathed, still sounding shaky.

She held out the handkerchief.

"Keep it," he insisted.

"I'll wash and return it."

He had a dozen and wouldn't miss one, but he knew

better than to debate something so trivial. He glanced at the southwestern sky. "The sun's getting low. Do we have enough boughs to make your wreath?"

"Yes. I'm sorry for the delay. You have work to do. The light must be lit."

"Mr. Blackthorn will handle that. I'll man the overnight watch."

"Then we should get going. We do still need to pick up the willow branches on the way."

He gathered up the boughs, and they began the long walk. Silence reigned as the sun sank lower. It would be dusk before they reached town.

"Where do you want me to take the boughs when we get back?" he asked.

"To the school. I'm going to make the test wreath tonight. When we get there, could you show me how to cut the twigs off the main branch?"

Though Louise would be eager to wield a pruning saw, he couldn't let her do that, especially in dim light. Doing it himself would cut short the nap he needed before the midnight watch, but he couldn't put off her request. "I will do it."

"You are already late—"

He anticipated and cut off her protest. "It won't take long. I insist."

After quieting a few more of her protests, they walked again in silence. Gradually his thoughts drifted to marriage. True, he hadn't received any responses to his advertisement yet, but it couldn't have appeared in the newspaper too many days ago. It was a little ridiculous to think he would receive a letter so soon. Then his thoughts centered on Louise, as they often had these last few days.

Was God telling him that the answer to his need for a wife was standing right here?

He couldn't deny she felt good in his arms. An intense desire to protect her had settled in. She was isolated here, far from the reach of family, though her expression when talking of her mother and sister told him they were not close. As for her marriage…the pain of that union was obvious. A dark shadow passed over whenever she mentioned it.

Though he wanted to know more, she appeared lost in her thoughts. He couldn't blame her. The pain of the past was a heavy burden to carry. A lout like Smythe didn't deserve a woman like Louise. He'd seen the type in the army. In fact, his direct supervisor in Vicksburg had been just such a man, interested only in twisting each situation to his own advantage. It would never have crossed the man's mind that others might have needs too. To him, they were just hurdles blocking his path to success. No doubt Smythe saw his wife that way too. She was either a support or an obstacle. The dog? If Louise had poured her love on it instead of directing her affection to Smythe's every whim, the man would have destroyed it.

Jesse gripped the boughs tightly, ignoring the prickly needles and sap.

"Such men don't deserve a wife," he growled.

Louise halted. "What men?"

"Sorry. I must have been thinking aloud."

She slowly nodded, though her countenance was pensive. "I don't believe there is any requirement that a man must deserve the woman he marries. She simply must agree." She sighed. "I agreed." A wry smile twisted her lips. "We are foolish when young."

"You married young?"

"When seventeen."

Jesse did the calculations quickly. That meant she'd

been married from four to eight years before her husband died, depending on when he joined the war effort.

"Your husband enlisted early in the conflict?"

She shook her head. "He wasn't one to rush into anything unless it profited him. He joined mere months before the war ended."

Then, nearly eight years of married life without children. A fertile woman would have borne four or more children during that time. Unless they lived separate lives. If the marriage was arranged and they realized they were incompatible…if he was in the city, away from their house in the country…the reasons for childlessness flooded into his mind.

Maybe that sense of belonging that she alone had given him wasn't a sign from God. Not when he deeply desired children.

He must be careful not to give her the wrong impression. Unfortunately, consoling her while she wept had probably convinced her that he was considering her for a wife. Somehow he had to tell her that was not the case, but he didn't have the heart to do it today. Sorrow still lingered on her expression. No, he would wait for the next opportunity.

Chapter Ten

Two days after making the test wreath, the needles had already begun to drop. By the third day, there were more bare twigs than green. Louise gingerly picked up the prickly wreath from its perch on the porch railing, sending a shower of needles to the floor.

"What am I going to do?" Louise asked Dinah, who had helped her add the pine twigs to the willow frame and was now surveying the results. "We can't make all the wreaths the day before the festival. Why, we'll need upwards of twenty. You know how long it took to make this one." She hung the bedraggled wreath back on its hook. "I don't know what to do."

The girl shrugged. "Maybe ask Mr. Hammond. He knows a lot about things like that."

Louise inwardly growled. She knew a fair amount about plant life also. "Mr. Hammond is not here."

"Sure, he is." Dinah nodded toward the boardwalk.

Sure enough, Jesse was striding straight toward them, the breeze ruffling the sandy blond curls that peeked out from under his hat.

"Good afternoon, ladies." He touched a finger to his hat. "How's our project coming along?"

"Badly," Louise admitted. "The needles are already falling. That shouldn't happen. The garlands and wreaths I made in the past would last weeks. Is it the warm weather or did we cut them at the wrong time? Or is it because we took branches from saplings?"

Jesse bounded up the porch steps and passed Dinah with a slight nod before coming to Louise's side.

"See?" Louise motioned to the scattered needles on the porch. "It's been less than three days."

Jesse ran a finger lightly over one of the branches. The needles showered down. "I see what you mean."

"This is a problem. I can't imagine how we can cut and make twenty wreaths the day before the festival."

"When exactly is the festival?"

"December 16th. Close to Christmas but with enough time to return home after visiting."

Jesse nodded and stroked his chin. Long seconds passed. Then, all he said was "Hmm."

"What are you thinking?"

"Yes, what're we gonna do?" Dinah echoed.

"We aren't going to make wreaths," Jesse decided.

"No wreaths?" Louise and Dinah said at once.

"Impossible," Louise added. "It's the one task Fiona entrusted to me. We must make the town look festive. That means wreaths."

"Well, not out of pine, you're not. Maybe juniper."

"Juniper!" Louise stared at the man. "Maybe your hands can take the jabbing from those needles but mine can't. And that's not even accounting for the smell."

"Well, it can't be pine. They're just too dried out from the lack of rain."

Louise fought the disappointment. Here she'd come up with a wonderful idea to bring business to the hotel and the store and the boardinghouse, and she couldn't fulfill the smallest task.

"Maybe if it rains between now and December," she suggested. "Maybe then the needles will stay."

Jesse shrugged. "Maybe, but you'd better get rid of that wreath right away and sweep the needles off the porch."

Louise lifted an eyebrow. "Aren't you being a little too fastidious?"

Out of the corner of her eye, she saw Dinah slink away, as if afraid Louise was about to chastise Jesse. Hadn't Louise made it clear that she was teasing?

Jesse's lips twitched. "No one has ever called me fastidious before."

"It simply means that one shows excessive care."

"I know what fastidious means. I'm also aware it can be used to accuse someone of being overly demanding."

Heat flooded her cheeks. "I'm sorry."

He laughed. "Don't be. You probably have a point. I can be fastidious—in all its meanings."

Louise still felt the sting of his overly cautious approach. "Well, it's not as if I wasn't going to do exactly what you said, but there's no need to rush."

"It's a fire hazard." That simple statement came without a trace of mirth.

"A, uh, what?"

"Pine needles are highly flammable. With the dry air and steady wind off the lake, the slightest spark could set the wreath on fire."

Louise crossed her arms. "I do not have any intention of lighting candles near the wreath."

"That's not what I meant." He leaned closer, intriguingly, uncomfortably close.

Louise held her breath. How could this man raise such emotions in her? One moment teasing her into a temper and the next making her heart pound in an entirely different way.

Jesse stood close, no more than a foot separated them.

"It's tinder dry around here," he said in a low voice, as if a secret between the two of them. "Almost everything is made of wood. One spark could set the town ablaze."

A shiver ran through her at the thought. "It wouldn't happen."

"One spark from a steamboat's stack is all it would take."

She started. Last November, a spark from a tugboat had burned down the woods and schoolhouse just east of town. The schoolhouse had been rebuilt, but the woods were gone.

She squared her shoulders. "We've fought fire before and saved all the buildings except the old schoolhouse. Everyone takes great care with fire."

"Good, but accidents happen. So does lightning. Some things are beyond man's control. That's why we have to be careful with anything that could easily catch fire."

"That's why we depend on God. We do our best and give the rest to Him. Everyone knows it's dry out. We will take care with fire. The rest is in God's hands."

Jesse shook his head, apparently discarding her statement of faith in man and God as impractical. She was about to respond when she saw the fear in his eyes. This strong, intelligent man was terrified of fire. Why, even a single burning leaf had made him react unreasonably.

Curiosity bubbled to the surface. What had happened to cause such fear? The question reached her lips, but the set of his jaw kept it locked inside. Whatever had happened, Jesse did not want to discuss it.

Jesse gritted his teeth. She wasn't taking this seriously. True, she looked concerned but not, he suspected, for the reason she should. She'd taken offense, apparently thinking he didn't trust God. It was the first part of her statement that was the issue. No matter how careful people were, mistakes happened. Even if everyone stayed attentive all the time, which was never the case, some things were beyond control.

"It might not even be something you realize is happening," he urged. "The spark could come from lightning or the sunlight reflecting off a lens or pane of glass."

Her lips pressed into a line of displeasure. "Or a magnifying glass. That is what you really mean, isn't it?"

Uh-oh. He shouldn't have brought up that sore spot.

"It was an accident." He hastily retreated. "Accidents happen."

"And people are there to take care of the consequences of those accidents—with God's help."

Jesse believed in God, but he also believed in personal responsibility. He'd seen his share of men say they were leaving matters in God's hands when they should have acted. It had been true in the army. Men shirked duty with all manner of excuse. Or, like his former commander, they twisted circumstance to their own benefit. Jesse set his jaw. He would never forgive the man.

"I did stomp out the burning leaf," Louise pointed out, still appearing affronted.

That failure on his part still stung. He should have leapt into action. Instead he'd stood rooted to the spot while a woman put out the tiny blaze.

"Yes, you did," he said softly.

Maybe it was his tone, because Louise's ire drained away, followed by the gentle smile he'd grown to cherish.

"I only did what I must. Anyone else would have done the same."

Unfortunately, he hadn't. His limbs had frozen. His

heart had nearly stopped. The fear was unreasonable, and it paralyzed him. He wasn't sure what he'd do in the face of a real fire.

A bead of perspiration rolled down his temple. She reached up to brush it off, and in that gesture was all the tenderness he'd craved but in the person of a woman who would never suit the future he'd chosen. He backed away and brushed it off himself.

"You're hot," she said. "Would you like some lemonade? I can fetch some from the hotel kitchen."

He shook his head. "No. It's just the angle of the sun."

That excuse sounded pretty feeble, but she didn't question it.

"We could go indoors. No one is using the parlor at this hour."

The thought of spending time in Louise's company was far too attractive.

He cleared his throat and glanced at the lighthouse. Blackthorn had pushed him away from lighting the lamps yet again. At this rate he would have nothing to lecture about next week, which was why he'd come to the school in the first place, not to check up on Louise's wreath.

"I need to get back to the lighthouse."

"Oh, yes," she exclaimed. "Forgive me. I forgot that you have duties to perform."

"I needed to speak to Mrs. Evans."

"She's with her family."

Jesse fidgeted with the tiny wooden bird in his coat pocket. "Maybe you can tell her then that I won't be able to do any more lectures."

"You won't?"

She looked both surprised and far too disappointed for a woman who had opposed him giving even one lecture. Then she *was* growing attached to him. Coupled with the feelings that he was developing for her, a volatile situation was taking root. Unfortunately, his future required certain elements, including a sturdy wife and large family. He would need both wherever he was posted, but especially if he was assigned to one of the remote lighthouses. He'd dreamed of such a post. There the past couldn't catch up to him. There the day-to-day goings-on of a large family would tire him so much that the nightmares couldn't get a toehold.

He looked to the lighthouse. "You can give the lectures."

"I know nothing about the running of a lighthouse."

He couldn't mention that he knew little more than she did. Well, he'd memorized the manual, so he knew what should happen, but Blackthorn didn't follow the manual, and the keeper wouldn't explain why not.

"Teach them more about the weather or the plants or whatever you want. My place is at the lighthouse."

She nodded slowly. "It was wrong of us to assume you would have time to talk to the girls."

Us. That little word changed everything. Louise had used the plural, meaning she had been in on the offer from the start. Maybe she and her friend had plotted that whole lecture series as a way to snare a husband for her.

He stepped back. "My future is set. I plan to be head keeper one day."

She nodded. "A worthy goal."

"Not necessarily here. An island lighthouse would suit me well."

"You wouldn't miss the companionship that can be found in a town?"

"I would have the company of a wife and family. I'd like eight to ten children."

Her jaw dropped. "Ten?"

He'd shocked her. That's what he'd intended, but he hadn't expected the raw pain of her disappointment.

"Yes." It was a necessity. Then why did saying it sting?

She looked away, her voice barely a whisper. "I won't keep you any longer from your duties."

Jesse opened his mouth but then thought better of it. He'd intended to caution her against forming any emotional attachment to him. Now that he'd accomplished that goal, he couldn't allow his feelings for her to change his mind.

So he clapped his hat on his head and walked down the porch steps and away from the woman whose silent pain stretched across the sands like fog.

Chapter Eleven

Louise hoped her disappointment didn't show, but as the days passed without seeing Jesse again, she feared she had chased him away. He had revealed his dream to her, and she had thought only of herself. How wrong! After all, he had already told her that he thought of her only as a friend. Friends ought to encourage and prompt one another to share what troubled them. She had thought only of herself.

Ten children!

That was a lofty goal for any woman but an impossible one for her. Even without knowledge of her infertility, he must have realized that. The freshness of youth no longer graced her cheeks. Simple calculation made it clear a woman her age was incapable of having that large a family. No, she was a widow and likely to remain that way the rest of her life.

Shame on her. Just the other day she had cherished her independence. Now, a single man's rejection had left her as despondent as a schoolgirl. She needed to return Jesse's cleaned and pressed handkerchief, and each day she took it out of her dresser drawer and contemplated walking up to the lighthouse. At the thought of the cold

rejection she would see in his eyes, she put the handkerchief back in the drawer. Perhaps he would come to the
school to fetch it.

Her charges handled disappointment much better than
she had. When she informed them that Mr. Hammond
would not be giving the lectures on the lighthouse, their
dismay didn't last long. Her announcement that those
lectures would be replaced by more botanical trips onto
the dunes, however, elicited a lot of groans and Priscilla's outright refusal to participate in such an unladylike
venture.

Louise had learned not to react at once to Priscilla's
outbursts, but she also didn't know what to do to make
them better. It was one thing to ask the girl to help in the
classroom. Louise could not force her to leave the building against her will. Though she suspected Priscilla's refusal was tied to Jesse's absence—if he had suggested
they climb the dune, every girl would have followed—
she had no idea how to combat the problem.

Later, when approaching the dining room for the midday meal she overheard Priscilla's thoughts on the subject.

"She chased him away with her forwardness," the girl
said none too quietly to her entourage. "The whole town
can see that she's sweet on him. Can you imagine someone like Mr. Hammond being interested in a withered
old widow like her? He's tall and strong and incredibly
handsome."

The three girls giggled and their comments hushed to
whispers, but the blade had been thrust deep into Louise's heart.

She *had* been a fool. Even worse, she'd made a fool of
herself in front of the students. Perhaps the Benningtons
had been right, and she should have been terminated.

Then she felt movement at her elbow.

It was Dinah.

"Don't listen to 'em," Dinah whispered. "They're jess plain mean."

Louise offered the girl a smile of appreciation, though she could not deny the truth beneath their cruel words. She had overstepped her role and her position. From now on, she would stick to teaching and leave romance to the pages of novels.

"Thank you, Dinah, but I'm all right."

The girl didn't look like she believed Louise, but, like all young ladies, got distracted the moment her friend appeared. She dashed off to join Linore, and they entered the dining room arm in arm.

Louise ate alone, as usual, so she could oversee the students and maintain order. As she sipped the chicken soup, the truth became clear. This must be her family. She could never have one of her own. That meant finding a solution to the division Priscilla was causing. She would visit Pearl Decker over the weekend. No doubt the fellow schoolteacher could give her pointers on handling students who subtly opposed her at every turn.

Jesse awoke with a start, his nightshirt and the bedclothes soaked with perspiration. The room wasn't overly hot. No, yet another nightmare had visited.

That made the third night in a row, every night since crushing Louise's hopes.

He lay on his back, exhausted and panting. The ceiling of the small room offered no answers. The white plaster reflected the light of the waning moon that filtered in through the window.

Yes, the nightmares had begun in earnest the night after he informed Louise that he wanted a large family.

She had been crushed. Any fool could see it, for she didn't hide her emotions well. She was developing hopes, and he thought he was smart, perhaps even kind, to break off those hopes before they grew too strong.

He must have caught it early enough. After all, she didn't weep and carry on like other ladies. No, she had kept her composure, and he could admire that.

Then why the nightmares? The images crowded into his mind night after night. The cold water, the dark, the sudden explosion, being thrown into the water, the screams and then finally the silence. He had been among the hundreds who survived, but upwards of 1700 had perished. And he'd done nothing to prevent the disaster.

In his dream, he walked aboard, just as he had in real life, handing his ticket to the crewman assigned to that task. Then he wandered through strange corridors and up a staircase, always pressed on every side by the tide of soldiers. The men laughed and joked. None of them seemed to notice him.

He pushed through the crowd, looking for someplace to stand alone and catch his breath. The hurricane deck sagged perilously, but no one seemed to care. As the miles chugged by, some sought sleep. He crouched on the promenade, unable to doze as towns passed by. The stop in Memphis passed in the blink of an eye. The chugging of the steam engines resumed, and the paddleboat headed upstream. His eyelids drifted downward. Then the explosion.

It rocked him from slumber and sent him flying.

A woman's horrified face then appeared before him, her mouth forming the words, "Don't leave me a widow."

Jesse sat bolt upright.

That had never been part of the dream before. He

rubbed his face. Was it memory or a fancy of his sleeping imagination?

All he recalled after the explosion was hitting the cold water, listening to the cries and wondering if he was truly alive.

After six and a half years, he wasn't certain what was memory and what was dream.

The woman hadn't been there. The huge number of soldiers dwarfed the regular passengers. No, the woman must be in his dreams because of Louise. Even though the dream was fading, he recalled a resemblance to her in the woman's face.

What did it mean?

Was guilt over crushing her hopes driving this dream, or was it fear that he would be drawn into a relationship with her? She had come to Singapore to marry. Moreover, she did seem to find reasons to involve him in projects that included her. She also had a lot of help in that respect. Maybe the dream was a warning to stay clear of her. But they had intensified since he began doing just that.

He groaned and then dressed, unable to sleep any longer. He could escape to the tower and polish brass, or he could consult the Bible for answers.

He opted for lighting a candle and reading his Bible. It opened to the fifth chapter of Ephesians and the passage about how a husband is to love his wife.

"That's not helping," he muttered, for it made him think of Louise and how unsuitable that match would be. Just like his parents.

Had Pa loved Ma? Somehow Wilson Hammond had caught the fancy of Etta Webber. She had softened the rough man. Before her death, Jesse's father had laughed and loved to go to the park for a picnic or to toss a ball. Afterward, drink and despair hardened him. Whenever

Jesse failed, Pa threatened to leave him at the nearest orphanage. That fear clouded every day. Jesse would never
inflict such pain on his children. Ever.

Or would he? Would adherence to some rule or con-
vention unwittingly bring pain to those he loved? Back
in Vicksburg, he'd followed protocol and his own selfish desire to get home instead of listening to intuition.

Then again, he couldn't see the future. If he'd known
the overcrowded steamboat would explode, he might have
risked reprimand or court-martial and warned the soldiers not to board the *Sultana*. But he hadn't. He'd stood
idly by and even boarded himself, just as eager as the
rest to get home.

Jesse buried his face in his hands. Why, Lord?

Saturday morning proved so busy with the students,
that Louise didn't have a chance to talk to Pearl Decker
until that afternoon.

She entered the store to the ringing of the door's bell.
To her dismay, Roland was at the counter, not Pearl.

"May I help you, Mrs. Smythe?" he asked with his
usual beaming smile.

"Is Pearl available?"

"I'm sorry." Roland truly looked dismayed. "She was
feeling poorly, so I insisted she rest."

That threw her plans out the window. No one else
could give her advice on how to handle Priscilla and
her cohorts.

Louise sighed. "Then I will have to speak to her tomorrow, provided she is feeling better."

"I'm sure she will be. She doesn't miss a sermon."

"Unless confined to bed," Louise pointed out. Last November wounds from the fire had kept Pearl bedridden.

"We certainly don't want that again," Roland agreed. "She is not a good patient."

Louise then recalled how Pearl had blamed Roland for the fire and refused to speak to him until she learned he wasn't at fault. Once again Louise had said the wrong thing at the wrong time. "No, of course not."

The relationship between Roland and Pearl had worked out in the end. Louise wasn't as certain about Jesse. Every time they grew closer, he slammed the door in her face. Ten children. She still couldn't believe he'd said that.

"Is there anything else I can do for you?" Roland was peering at her in such a way that Louise must have missed something else he'd said.

"No, no. I don't need anything." Neither should she spend frivolously, not with Priscilla ready to threaten her job at a moment's notice.

"Would you mind taking the school's mail?"

"The school's?"

Roland turned to the cubbyholes where he sorted out the incoming mail. "Mrs. Evans didn't pick it up."

"Oh." How daft could she be? She'd been thinking of the primary school, not the place she was currently employed. That was ridiculous, for Pearl was that school's sole teacher. She would already have any mail directed there. "Of course, I'll take it."

He fetched a stack of mail from one of the cubbyholes. Nothing for Louise, of course. Fiona had received several pieces of mail. Priscilla, Adeline and Esther all had letters. As usual, neither Linore nor Dinah received anything. Being orphans, they had no blood relations, but Dinah's foster parents could have written at least once. Every child deserved love and parents who longed to hear about everything. To have no one?

She sighed. After her father died, Mama had let her

preference for Rachel run unchecked. Louise had been Papa's favorite, something that Mama had seen fit to counter by lavishing her love on her other daughter.

"Mrs. Smythe? Louise?"

The sound of her name pulled her from the sad past. "I'm sorry. I was caught up in my thoughts."

Roland didn't comment on her inattention. "Since you're heading in that direction, would you mind bringing the mail up to the lighthouse? Usually Pearl brings it to school and sends it off with one of the Blackthorn children, but she forgot yesterday. I'm sure they'll want to get it."

"Of course. It's not much farther, and I enjoy hiking the dunes anyway."

She would just avoid Jesse. If she went straight to the keeper's quarters and gave the mail to Jane Blackthorn, she could miss Jesse entirely. It would also give her the perfect opportunity to return his handkerchief.

"Yes. I'll do it."

"Thanks." Roland reached into another cubbyhole and pulled out a huge stack of envelopes.

"All that?" Louise struggled to grab hold of the stack and ended up tucking the smaller amount for the school into her bag before picking up the lighthouse's mail. "There must be a lot of correspondence from the lighthouse service."

"I wouldn't know. Excuse me, I need to wait on Mrs. Calloway." Roland hurried across the store, leaving Louise alone at the counter.

She looked down at the first letter. It was addressed in a flowing script that couldn't be from the lighthouse service. A quick glance at the return address confirmed it. A Miss Miller had written. Then she noticed to whom the letter was addressed. Jesse!

He had never mentioned that he was courting. In fact, his behavior was quite inappropriate for a man who had a sweetheart elsewhere. She glanced again. Miss Miller was from Indiana.

Louise pressed a hand to her midsection. Why hadn't he mentioned this? She had just begun to think him moral and upright. Now this. Unless... He had mentioned a sister. Maybe this was his sister, though she'd gotten the impression his sister was married. Maybe she'd misread, and Miss was actually Mrs. The letters were squeezed together and rather difficult to decipher.

She looked back. Roland was still with Mrs. Calloway in the white goods section.

Looking at just one more envelope wouldn't hurt, and it might exonerate Jesse.

She tucked the first letter on the bottom of the pile only to discover the next and the next and the next were all from women who addressed themselves as Miss. Most were from Chicago, but some hailed from surrounding areas.

She felt sick.

Why, there must be two dozen letters addressed to Jesse, all from different women. What was going on?

Jane Blackthorn answered Louise's knock on the lighthouse door.

Louise let out her breath. At least it wasn't Jesse. Even so, her hands trembled, and she had to clutch the letters tighter so she didn't drop them.

"Louise! What a pleasure to see you." The keeper's wife cheerfully waved her in.

Louise hesitated. She did want to know why all these women had written Jesse, but she didn't dare reveal that she'd examined the address of each one. That was, well, *wrong*.

"Roland asked me to bring you the mail for the lighthouse." She held out the thick bundle of letters.

Thankfully, Jane Blackthorn took them without noticing Louise's shaking hand.

"My, there's a lot," the woman exclaimed. She looked through the envelopes. "Lighthouse Service. Letter from home. Another one from the Service. Oh, my."

She had clearly reached the letters to Jesse, for she riffled through them just long enough to note the name on the return address.

"I should be going," Louise said. "I need to get back to the students."

Jane Blackthorn shook her head. "That man has no idea what he's got himself into."

Louise backed from the open doorway. "I must leave."

Jane looked up, a look of determination setting in. "Now, don't you fret. He'll come to his senses."

Louise managed a wan smile. "I'm sorry but I don't know what or whom you mean."

"Why, Jesse Hammond, of course." Jane waved the stack of letters in her direction. "Men can get some fool ideas, but they usually find their way out of them."

Louise's face ached from holding the smile in place. "I hope there's no trouble."

"Oh, there will be trouble all right. A man's bound to get a boatload full when he advertises for a wife."

Chapter Twelve

The following night, Jesse laid out the envelopes on the small table that served as a desk in his bedroom. By overlapping the edges, he could create a grid four by six with two left over. Twenty-six responses! Hadn't he bemoaned the lack of a response a week or so ago? Now this. Moreover, none other than Louise had delivered them—along with his cleaned and pressed handkerchief. It was more than a man could take in.

The names on the envelopes betrayed heritages ranging from English to Irish to Italian to German. There was even a Polish or Russian-looking name in the lot. He'd never imagined so many women would be interested in an assistant lighthouse keeper bound for life at a remote post.

Where should he begin?

Opening the envelopes, he supposed. The stack had intimidated him yesterday, and he took advantage of the opportunity to hear Mr. and Mrs. Evans give a concert at the hotel rather than deal with them.

Tonight he must figure out what to do with them. He took out his penknife and slit open the first. The scent of lavender erupted from the envelope and made him sneeze. He set it down. The next wasn't perfumed, but the lady's script was so flowery that he couldn't make out many of the words. At this rate he would eliminate a good many of the applicants.

The third letter in the top row, second from the right, was more promising. The penmanship was legible and the grammar acceptable, even if Miss Barnes displayed a rather limited vocabulary. Nothing like Louise with her grandiose words.

He chuckled at the memory of her last one—*presumptuous*—and then cringed. He *had* been just that, telling her he planned to have ten children. A person didn't dictate how many children he would have. God made that decision. Illness, injury and death all played a role. But the number wasn't the problem. The motive behind that declaration was. He'd exaggerated in order to dissuade her from caring for him. It was cowardly, but there was no taking it back.

So he reached for the next letter, the last one on the top row. It was written by a woman of Italian heritage, a Miss Marinaro. The paper was unscented, and the letter short and to the point. She was twenty-five, could cook, and was willing to work hard. Promising, yet he felt no delight.

Before coming to Singapore, Louise had responded to just such an advertisement. What had she written? Had she touted her intelligence and curiosity? Would she have mentioned her quiet beauty? He doubted she'd said any of that. Louise was one to quietly downplay her virtues. She would have mentioned she was widowed and educated, but he doubted she would have expounded on either of those.

Louise Smythe carried herself with godly virtue, something that Jesse found incredibly appealing.

Unfortunately age and stature worked against her, at least in his case. An older gentleman might make the perfect match. He would pray she found that match.

Pausing for a moment in his survey of responses, he said a silent prayer for Louise, that she would receive everything she desired.

That didn't make him feel much better, but he told himself this was the only way. As much as he wished she could be his wife, she had too many strikes against her.

He resumed the survey.

By the time he'd finished the second row of letters, the responses muddled together in his mind. He would have to make notes, or he'd never keep them straight. Perhaps he could read each one and put them in a different sort of grid, one based on the positives and negatives each letter generated.

Yes, that was it.

He would establish four criteria: apparent physical hardiness, age, homemaking capabilities, and education. Each letter could then be judged against those criteria. The responses matching none would be discarded. Those matching one, two, three or four criteria would be separated into different piles. Naturally the ones that met all four would be his target. He would write them back asking for more information. Their responses would further differentiate them. If none of the letters met all four, he would then start with those that met the greatest number of criteria.

It was orderly. It was efficient. It made sense.

A rap on the door was followed by Jane Blackthorn calling out his name. "I saw your light so I figured you were awake. Samuel's asking you to join him up in the tower."

At this hour? Jesse was supposed to be napping before

the midnight watch, but he couldn't sleep with all those letters sitting around. If Blackthorn had called for him, he must need help hauling up more oil, or the equipment had failed and repair required an extra set of hands.

He pushed the letters into a pile. "Tell him I'll be there shortly."

"Good."

Another thought popped into Jesse's head, one having to do with Louise. He pushed his door open just before Jane Blackthorn disappeared downstairs.

"Ma'am?"

She stopped and turned back to him.

"I was wondering," he said. "Were you here when Mrs. Smythe dropped off the mail?"

"Yes, indeed. Quite a lot of letters you got."

"Responses to my advertisement."

"That's what I told Louise." Jane Blackthorn stepped closer. "If you don't mind my saying so, she seemed a bit unnerved by them. I thought it only kind to tell her why so many young women would be writing you. I hope you don't mind."

It was as he'd suspected. "Thank you, that was fine."

Yet he could not account for the sinking feeling in his stomach.

Louise set down her pen and rubbed her forehead. She ought not work on Sunday night, but Jesse's refusal to do any more lectures left her scrambling for lessons. She could fill tomorrow's spot with another foray into the field, this time to examine the *rosa blanca,* or meadow roses, near the river mouth. There the dunes harbored a little pocket of vegetation protected from the harsh winds. A single willow tree, untouched by the saw, offered shade.

Before her evening prayers, she could jot down a few ideas. Completing that much would relax her enough so she could sleep. Otherwise, she was liable to toss and turn while fretting about the matter. After making a few notes, she could turn it over to the Lord and rest easy.

She hoped. Thoughts of Jesse kept creeping in. Why had he advertised for a wife before attempting to see if they were suitable? Didn't he feel the same attraction she felt? At the very least, he should acknowledge their growing friendship, which was often a prelude to marriage. Instead, he'd advertised for a wife.

A peculiar sound from the direction of the window drew her from her thoughts. What was that? It sounded as if something had hit the pane.

She rose to check. Children often threw acorns and other small objects to attract the attention of a friend stuck indoors. Even though she worked in the classroom, that was not the case this evening. No one would attempt to lure one of the girls outdoors. Or would they? Both Linore and Dinah had found beaus amongst the lumbermen in the past.

It was dark outside, and she couldn't see what might have made the noise. Maybe it was rain. Rain! It had been so long since the last rain that she'd forgotten to take that into consideration when making her plans for tomorrow's class. The girls had complained bitterly about going outdoors on a warm and sunny day. She wouldn't convince a one of them to leave the school on a rainy day.

That meant coming up with a classroom lesson for tomorrow.

She headed back for her desk when another sound drew her attention back to the window.

What on earth? If there had been someone outdoors, he or she would have seen her in the lit window. That should have stopped all further attempts. Unless that person wanted to alert her. But who would do that? Only one person came to mind. Jesse.

Surely he wouldn't toss objects at a window like a lovelorn youth. Still, the idea made her pulse race and her heart flutter. Had Jesse realized his mistake and come for her?

She returned to the window and lifted the sash, ushering in a stiff breeze. No rain, though. That meant the objects had been thrown.

She stuck her head out the window. "Hello?"

No answer.

No sound except the rush of the wind. This was no breeze. She could hear the roar of the waves and their crashing on the shore. It was a full gale.

A gale. That was it! She would teach the girls about the wind. They had seemed interested when Jesse mentioned it.

She began to close the window, and a bit of dried-up plant struck her on the wrist. The brown object fell to the floor. She picked it up. A withered, curled leaf. That must have been what was hitting the window. The wind was strong enough to lift light debris and fling it against the side of the building.

No one had thrown it. No one sought her. No love waited for her in the dark.

She paused, tears gathering in the corner of her eyes. Just once. One time in her life she would like to know what love felt like. Not the heady rush of capturing the attention of a man that the other girls coveted, which was what she'd felt when Warren directed his attention to her. That was infatuation, not true love. What did the latter feel like, to know a man thought of her, longed to be with her, and was willing to sacrifice for her sake? And in her turn to give all she had to a man worthy of receiving it.

Slowly she closed the window. Such men dwelt on the pages of novels, but there was no Mr. Darcy in Singapore. None at all.

Only then did she realize that the wind had carried in something else—smoke.

She lifted the sash and sniffed. Yes, that was definitely the smell of smoke, but she couldn't see any sign of fire. Last November the fire could easily be seen from town. Her mind flashed to Jesse and his fear of fire. What if he was right? On a night such as this, a spark could carry far. But there was no telltale glow in the darkness. No one appeared alarmed. She closed the window again. The smoke must have been driven her way from the kitchen chimney. The hotel did use wood in its cookstove.

Yes, that must be it. She settled back at her desk and began jotting notes for a lecture on wind.

The moment Jesse stepped into the base of the tower, he smelled the smoke. Maybe the wind had pushed the stove's smoke back down the chimney. Then again, if that was the case, he should have smelled it in the house, not the tower.

Blackthorn wasn't there. He must be in the lantern.

Jesse lit a lamp and began the climb, taking two steps at a time. Something had happened, and he had a feeling it wasn't a mechanical breakdown. Round and around he went until reaching the short landing. From there, he crawled up the ladder and popped through the open hatch into the lantern.

"There you are," Blackthorn said as Jesse pulled himself onto the lantern floor.

In the light of the lamp, Blackthorn looked worried.

Jesse got to his feet. "What is it?"

"Look there, to the north, when the beam faces opposite." Blackthorn pointed up the coast.

Jesse waited, but even before the beam focused away, he saw the glow in the sky. "What is it?"

"Not only there. Look across the lake and south."

Jesse only had to wait a second, and then his mouth went dry. "The sky. It's…orange."

"Just like Holland way. I've never seen anything like it." Blackthorn shook his head. "Sometimes I can pick out the glow of a city, but it's pretty faint. This? I don't know what to make of it."

Jesse did. He'd seen that glow before, though much closer. He squeezed his eyes shut and told himself to take a breath. Then another and another. It couldn't be. There must be another explanation.

"Street lamps?" It was a feeble explanation.

"That'd take a whole lot of lamps from this distance. Must be sixty, seventy miles away at least. Even Chicago couldn't put out that much light."

Jesse's heart sank as the truth settled in. It was the *Sultana* again, only worse. The steamship had taken 1700 lives and lit the night sky. Folks nearby saw it from their homes. But they weren't sixty miles away. For him to see an orange glow from this distance, the conflagration must be enormous. Moreover, it was burning to the north as well, much closer and thus much more deadly to those living in Singapore.

Louise!

His heart stopped. She slept in a wooden building. So did the students. So did families and workers and children. Everyone. The nightmare he'd feared had begun.

"Fire," he croaked.

Wind rattled the panes of glass encasing the lantern.

On such a night, the keeper had to stay ready to relight the lamps, for the gusts could blow them out.

"We have to warn everyone." Yet Jesse's feet stayed rooted to the spot. Just like in Vicksburg. Just like on the *Sultana*. If the blast hadn't propelled him through the air and into the water, he would have perished with the rest. In a crisis, he froze.

Lord, help us. Help me.

Blackthorn grabbed his arm with a viselike grip. "You're faster than me. Go. We might have just enough time."

God answered Jesse's prayer. His limbs moved. Without any thought but saving Louise, he raced to the ladder and headed down it.

"Take the lamp." Blackthorn handed it to him.

Jesse could have made it down without a light. He thought only of one thing. He had to get Louise out of the school before the fires reached Singapore.

Chapter Thirteen

The distant sound of banging pulled Louise from her thoughts and the chapter on wind in Captain Elder's book.

What was that sound, and how long had it been going on? Groggily, she realized the hour was late. Contrary to her earlier plan, she had spent far too long studying the chapter. She ought to be in bed.

Again the pounding began. Not mere knocking. Whoever it was, he had resorted to banging with his fists. It must be a man. No woman would make such a racket.

Rising, she stretched her stiff back and then took up the lamp she'd been using. The treatise on wind would have to wait.

"I'm coming. I'm coming," she said as the pounding continued.

The individual clearly didn't hear her, since the banging didn't stop.

It took long moments to traverse the hallway and reach the front door. The girls must have heard the pounding, for Dinah, Linore and Adeline waited on the steps.

"What is it?" Linore asked.

"I don't know. Go back to your rooms." Louise had

little hope they would do as she asked. Their curiosity must be as great as hers.

At last she reached the front door, which she unlatched and then opened. The swirling gale blew in more withered bits of leaves along with the smell of smoke. On the porch, fist raised, stood Jesse. His face was flushed, and his eyes looked wild.

"Fire!" he gasped.

Louise looked left and then right. She saw nothing. "Where?"

He pointed along the length of the porch, toward the hotel.

Louise hurried outside, her heart nearly stopped. Surely not the hotel. She pushed past Jesse to get a better view and saw nothing but the warm glow of a lamp in the window of the Evanses' quarters.

"The hotel isn't on fire."

"Not the hotel," Jesse croaked, his voice strangely pinched. "The town. Holland."

"Holland?"

The town was roughly ten miles to the north and the largest within ready distance. Those who hadn't come from a place like New York or Chicago considered it a city.

Jesse was nodding. "And Chicago, if we're not mistaken."

"Chicago?" It was beyond belief. "Surely a large city like that with a fire department would not be ablaze."

Jesse was shaking his head. "The streets are wood, the sidewalks are wood, the buildings are wood—just like here."

"But they would never—"

He grabbed her shoulders, stopping her thoughts midstream. "It doesn't matter what's happening elsewhere.

What matters is what might happen here. Holland is close, and I spotted a glow closer, inland. With this wind, it could reach here. You need to get the students out of the building. Get everyone out. The town has to be notified. People can't die in their beds."

He was panicked, and she had to calm him down.

"It's not here yet," she said slowly, "and the winds are from the southwest. They would blow the flames in the opposite direction."

He shook his head. "You saw the tinder-dry slash on the ground and how dry the pines are. A shift in the wind direction would burn them in an instant."

The urgency in his voice propelled her into action, albeit at a less frantic pace. "I will get the girls onto the porch. Then we'll tell everyone at the hotel. I can get to the Garrett Decker house and the mercantile if you can reach the boardinghouse and the bunkhouses."

"I sent the Blackthorn boys to the farthest bunkhouses. I've got the rest." He clattered down the porch steps and then turned around a brief moment. "Louise? Do what you must to stay safe. Go to the shore, to the river, whatever it takes." Then he was off.

Though panic threatened, need was greater. The girls depended on her. So too did precious families, now asleep in their beds. While running back indoors, Louise prayed that not one soul would perish.

As she began to round up the girls, she took comfort in one concern buried in Jesse's words. He'd come to warn her first.

"We need to be ready with buckets," Jesse said to Roland Decker and the other men crowded around.

They stood near the docks, where water could be drawn and where the half-moon's light shone brightest.

While he spoke, the men had been quiet, but now a murmur, punctuated with the occasional complaint, filled the air. Jesse looked around at the crowd. If he'd paid better attention the few times he'd ventured into town, he would remember names. In the darkness, he barely recognized a face other than Roland.

"There's no fire here yet," Roland said calmly. "Maybe we'd better send out scouts to see how close it is."

"Good idea."

Roland searched the growing crowd. "Jimmy?"

That was the lad who helped at the store. Jesse remembered that much.

The boy appeared with a couple of friends, including Charlie from the hotel, all eager to assist. Roland sent them off in different directions—north toward Holland, inland and south.

"I didn't ask if the town has a fire engine," Jesse said.

"Just a steam tractor to clear away flammable materials like logs and such." Roland still looked around, as if trying to find someone. "But there's not much of that left in the area. Thankfully, the sand won't burn." Again he peered into the darkness.

"Are you looking for someone?"

"Pearl." Roland sounded worried. "She went to visit Amanda."

"Amanda?" Jesse was familiar with Roland's wife, Pearl, but the other name was unfamiliar.

"Garrett's wife."

"Your brother."

Roland nodded.

His concern now made sense. Jesse could ease it. "Louise went to your brother's house. She said she was going there immediately after the hotel."

"Then where is Pearl? She should have been here by

now. It's not like her to delay. I hope she didn't go back to the mercantile."

"Don't worry." Jesse gripped his friend's shoulder. "I'll find her if you organize the bucket brigade."

Roland nodded, though he looked less than thrilled that he wasn't the one looking for his wife.

"You know everyone," Jesse explained. "You know who has buckets and who doesn't. I'll bring Pearl here when I find her." He paused as the hole in his plan became obvious. "Where does your brother live?"

"Down this street, third house on the right."

Jesse took off at a brisk pace. The sooner he could bring husband and wife together, the sooner Roland's attention would focus completely on the task at hand. Jesse trusted the man. He was not like his commander in Vicksburg. He wouldn't put personal desire ahead of the greater good. Still, a man wanted to know his loved ones were safe.

In no time he reached the brother's house. It was the same size as the other family homes but the lit windows revealed frilly curtains and a cheerfulness that made Jesse wish for the home he barely remembered—the one from his childhood, when Ma was still living.

He pushed through the gate in the picket fence and strode the short distance to the front door. One knock brought a response, unlike when he'd gone to the school.

Louise opened the door. "Yes?"

He blinked. For some reason he hadn't expected to see Louise. To avoid the rush of emotion, he looked around her, searching for Roland's wife. The house was full of women. He recognized the girls from the school and several women he'd seen at various places around town, but he didn't see Pearl.

"Jesse?" Louise's voice broke through his thoughts. "What is it? Is something wrong?"

Jesse focused on his mission. "Roland is looking for Pearl. Is she here?"

"She is going from house to house organizing the blanket brigade."

"Of course." The women were soaking blankets that would then be placed on the roofs to protect them from sparks. "Then eventually she'll reach her husband. He is worried."

Louise's expression softened. "They're still newlyweds."

The look on her face unleashed a torrent of emotion. He would be worried about Louise if he didn't know where she was.

"Don't worry." Louise touched his arm, and the spot burnt hot as fire. The moment he looked down, she removed it. "We will be quite safe. Garrett is on his way to his brother as we speak. Roland probably already knows what's going on. Together we will save this town."

He'd heard her confidence on this subject before. He prayed she was right, but to the northeast, an orange glow illuminated the horizon.

"I'll be right back," Louise called out to those gathered inside. She pulled a shawl around her shoulders as she joined him on the porch.

"Where are you going?"

"To the boardinghouse. I'm helping to carry blankets to each of the buildings."

It made perfect sense, but Jesse didn't like the idea of Louise out alone with fire in the air. The smell of smoke had grown more intense.

"I'll be all right," she said, her voice full of compassion. "Make sure Roland knows his bride is safe."

Jesse knew that was what he should do. He knew how independent she could be. Louise Smythe did not like to be coddled. That much he had learned in the time they'd spent together.

He glanced toward the two-story boardinghouse. "It's dark. What if you stumble?"

"The moon is bright."

"I can walk with you."

"Jesse Hammond, I am not a naïve young lady prone to wander. I'm a grown woman, and I've traveled this short distance dozens of times. I will not get lost, neither will I turn an ankle." She lightly touched his arm. "Don't worry about me."

Her words bit deep. Was he being overprotective of a woman he had insisted could be no more than a friend?

Her next sentence sent his emotions soaring in quite another direction. "Your knowledge and skill could save this town. We're depending on you. I'm depending on you."

Louise wished she had never spoken. The refrain that had come out of her mouth whenever Warren complained of something lacking in her homemaking had echoed in her frustration over Jesse's overprotectiveness.

She knew better than he did how to navigate this town. After all, she had lived here for over a year while he had been here less than a month.

Yet the look on his face spiked her guilt. She should not have lashed out. Jesse was not Warren. He didn't realize how safe Singapore was nor how capable she could be on her own. Instead of lashing out, she should have boosted his pride through encouragement.

As she hurried over the boardwalks to the boardinghouse, she felt the sting of self-reproach. Could she ever become the woman of God described so well in the thirty-first chapter of the book of Proverbs?

Thankfully, Mrs. Calloway's delight at her arrival shook away the melancholy thoughts.

"We have much to do," the boardinghouse proprietress said as she led Louise into the kitchen. "The men will need feeding, and there are still more blankets to deliver. Can you send someone to fetch the food when you return with the blankets?"

"Of course."

"And we'll need to make up all the rooms. Tell Fiona to get the hotel ready too. People who've lost their homes will come here. You can count on it." Mrs. Calloway continued issuing instructions, following Louise while she fetched a stack of blankets and headed for the front door.

"I'll be right back," Louise stated as she pushed the door open. "I'll send the girls over. They can make beds." It would also get them out from under her wings.

"Thank you, dear."

Louise hurried across the veranda and down the steps. By this, her third trip, the blankets felt much heavier than they had the first time. Perhaps there were more in this load.

The wind howled off the lake, driving sand through the air. It had pushed her along on her way to the boardinghouse. Now she must press against it. She lowered her head and closed her eyes to slits so the grit didn't get into them. Each step became a labor. The wind sucked the breath from her lungs.

"Oof!" She plowed into something solid and nearly lost her armful of blankets.

"Oh dear, I'm sorry." The unfamiliar voice was laced with tearful emotion. "I wasn't watching where I was walking."

"It's all right, Mother," said a man's voice.

Louise's heart jumped into her throat. The people that Mrs. Calloway predicted had begun to arrive. "You are from outside town?"

"We're farmers from east of Goshorn Lake." The woman's voice trembled. "Do you know where we might get shelter?"

"Mrs. Calloway will look after you at the boarding-house." Louise pointed the woman and her husband in the right direction. Only then did she notice the five children huddled between them. They carried nothing and didn't even have coats.

Louise offered blankets, but the husband refused, saying others needed them more, and they had just a short distance to the boardinghouse.

As she watched them walk away, her own petty concerns fell off, like scales from her eyes. This was where true service lay. These people needed help. The sooner she got to the Decker house, the sooner she could send assistance to the boardinghouse.

She hurried her step, this time able to ignore the stinging sand. When she reached the house, she pounded on the door, and it readily opened. The crowd inside had thinned, but the students were still there.

"Mrs. Calloway needs help at the boardinghouse. The first family from the country has arrived. Girls, would you go with me there?"

Linore and Dinah readily agreed. Priscilla and her friends were less inclined until Pearl mentioned that Mrs. Calloway would have food and hot tea ready. Then they eagerly joined Louise on the walk back.

As before, the wind pushed her along the boardwalk. She kept the girls ahead of her so they wouldn't take a wrong turn. Dinah and Linore were nearly as familiar with the town as Louise was, but Priscilla's group had always refused to go anywhere other than the church. One trip to the store had soured them on further forays to that destination. Priscilla had declared it had nothing of value whatsoever. Thankfully neither Roland nor Pearl had heard her.

They had just reached the boardinghouse steps when Jimmy appeared out of the dark, panting hard. Louise sent the girls inside while he caught his breath.

"What is it, Jimmy?"

"Miz Smythe." He coughed and wheezed.

The poor lad had breathed in too much smoke.

"Take your time, Jimmy. There's no rush."

"Yes." He coughed. "Yes, there is, ma'am. Isaac's missing."

Louise felt her heart pound hard as a sledgehammer. "Isaac Decker? Are you sure? He's with his father."

"No, ma'am." Jimmy shuffled from foot to foot, as if too full of energy to stand still. "He went with me to see how close the fires are to town."

Isaac did look up to the older boy, who worked at the mercantile and was thus a ready role model for the young boy. Isaac couldn't be more than what? Eight? Nine?

"We gotta find him before his ma and pa find out," Jimmy pleaded.

Louise pulled her spinning thoughts into some semblance of order. "Where did you last see him?"

"By the turnoff to Goshorn. I went Goshorn-way and sent him east over the hill."

"You sent him? By himself?" Louise could barely control the emotions spilling through her.

"I told him to stop at the top of the hill. The fire was close there. I could see the smoke in the moonlight. He couldn't have gone more'n a hundred yards before turning back."

"Then maybe he returned to town to report."

Jimmy shook his head violently. "I told him to come back and wait. Isaac would've done whatever I told him. Miz Smythe, shouldn't we be lookin' for him rather'n just standin' here?"

"Yes, but it won't do us any good to hurry off unprepared. We'll need lanterns and an idea where to go." She glanced toward the boardinghouse. "Maybe Mrs. Calloway has a lantern that isn't already in use."

"I could get one from the store."

She caught him by the arm. Surprisingly, he stopped.

"No. That will take too much time." Ideas spun in Louise's head. "We'll get a light of some sort at the boardinghouse as well as some damp cloths to cover our faces. It could be smoky where we're heading."

Jimmy slowly nodded his head.

"While I'm getting all that ready, you can run to the Decker house to make sure he hasn't returned there and check with his father also."

"But then—"

"It's not your fault, Jimmy." Louise took him by the shoulders. "Understand that. It just happened. All that's important now is finding him."

He shook off her hands. "No, ma'am. That's not what I'm tryin' to say. We don't got that kinda time. The fire's movin' fast. We gotta go now."

Driven by Louise's confidence in his abilities, Jesse worked hard organizing the bucket brigade and throwing bucketfuls of water on the buildings. He set ladders against houses and carried wet blankets onto the roof. He helped spread them over the wood shingles. He pulled wiry dune grass away from buildings and sawed down junipers that crowded too close.

Perspiration drenched his shirt even as smoke burned his nostrils.

When Fiona brought water to the men, he downed his cupful with relish. Hours must have passed.

"Fire's gettin' closer," said Ernie Calloway, one of the men helping him haul blankets up the ladders.

"One of the farm families, the Norstrands, arrived an hour ago," Fiona added. "Your wife is putting them up for now."

Calloway nodded. "She said to expect that." He heaved a sigh. "Hope that's all there is." He looked to the sky. "Rain would help."

"Yes, it would," Jesse echoed, though he'd seen no indication that a single drop was on its way. "How close to town is the Norstrand farm?"

"'Bout half a mile," Calloway said.

Fiona nodded. "Their children attend school here, and they come to church when they're able. From what Mrs. Calloway told me, they said small fires are burning all over. Their farm was overrun, and there's fire east and south of here, but it looks even worse toward Holland. We need to keep those people in prayer."

All the more reason to work. Jesse could not let Singapore become another *Sultana.*

"Let's get these blankets on the roof," he called out.

The men scrambled into position, and Jesse hefted another soaking wet blanket to the ladder. Every muscle ached, but he could not watch those he cared about fall victim to the flames. Speaking of which...

"Where is Louise?" he called back to Fiona, who was moving on to the next group of workers.

"Last I knew, she was busy rounding up blankets

and carrying them to the Decker house so they could be brought to the river for soaking."

That was a relief.

Fiona halted. "Come to think of it, I haven't seen her in a while, not since she took the students over to the boardinghouse to help out there. Maybe that's where she is. Or we ran out of blankets."

Jesse peered into the darkness. They'd covered the roofs of the hotel, sawmills, store and several houses.

"What about the new school?" Calloway asked. "Looks like the fire might reach it first."

Jesse's stomach churned. If they were out of blankets, they couldn't save the school. "At least no one's there."

Roland Decker appeared out of the darkness. "Anyone seen Jimmy? He and Isaac and Charlie headed out to scout the fires a couple hours ago. They should have been back long before now."

"Charlie is up on the roof," Calloway said. "Hey, Charlie!"

The boy's face appeared at the edge of the roof, barely visible in the moonlight. "Yes, sir?"

"Where's Jimmy and Isaac?"

The boy hesitated. "It wasn't his fault."

"What wasn't whose fault? Don't hold back information," Roland said. "If Jimmy went somewhere with Isaac, we need to know where."

The boy's reserves crumbled. "Jimmy went to find Isaac. He brought Mrs. Smythe with him."

Jesse thought he was going to be ill.

"Where did they go?" He wanted to shake the boy, who stared at him with wide eyes.

"This could be important, Charlie," Fiona added.

The lad, his lip quivering, whispered words that meant nothing to Jesse. "T'ward the Goshorn cutoff."

Jesse shoved the blanket at the nearest man. "Point the way, and I'll go after them."

"I'll rustle up a search party," Calloway said. "You keep directing things here."

"But—"

"We know the way," Roland added. "It'll be faster."

His point made sense, but Jesse couldn't stand by while others searched for Louise. What if they went the wrong way? What if they didn't see her? "What if she's injured?"

Fiona laid a comforting hand on his arm. "Louise is a strong woman with a level head. She won't walk into danger."

"Except to save someone," Jesse whispered, but Calloway and Roland had already taken off, and Fiona was moving to the next group of workers.

No one heard the dread in his heart. No one could hear the panic in his head. He wanted to run after Roland and Calloway, but they'd vanished into the inky blackness, and he had no idea which way they'd gone.

In Vicksburg he had stood back and let others act. People died because of it, while he, the selfish coward, had survived. He squeezed his eyes shut and begged God not to let tonight repeat that mistake.

Chapter Fourteen

Isaac Decker proved easy to find. The boy stood transfixed on the edge of a blazing field, as if he couldn't tear
himself away from the sight. Louise called his name.
Jimmy called his name. The boy stood motionless, un-
hearing.

Jimmy began to run ahead, but Louise stopped him.
"We don't want to frighten Isaac. Let me talk to him."

"We ain't got much time, Miz Smythe."

"I know, but we have a little." She pressed a handkerchief to her nose and mouth so the smoke didn't over-
whelm her.

Both she and Jimmy had already begun to cough.
Soon it would overcome Isaac. How the boy still stood
amazed her. She pushed forward, twigs snapping beneath
her feet. If Jesse was right, they could catch fire in an
instant, trapping all three of them.

They hadn't taken the time to get damp rags or assistance. Once she reached Isaac, she would give him
her handkerchief and pray she had enough breath and
strength to get him out of harm's way. The boy was several paces away when a twig poked through the hole in
her right shoe and stabbed into her foot. The pain shot

up her leg to her knee. She hopped a bit but pressed on. She had to bring Isaac back. That meant not startling him, though he should have heard her approach. Since he hadn't turned around or given any indication he'd heard her, she must assume he did not.

"Isaac?" She softly called his name when she drew close.

He did not so much as waver.

"Isaac." This time stronger and more forcefully.

Again he did not seem to hear.

She touched his shoulder. "Your papa is looking for you."

Isaac started. "Sadie."

Louise was confused. "Sadie is at home. I saw her just a few minutes ago."

"Sadie went to get her kitten."

Louise didn't understand. "But Cocoa is at home too. I saw her too. With your sister." The smoke made her cough. Why wasn't Isaac coughing? "If you come with me, I'll show you."

"Have to find Sadie." He stepped toward the burning field.

"Sadie's not here. She's perfectly safe." Louise grabbed for his arm and missed, but in that instant she understood. Isaac was lost in the past. In last November's schoolhouse fire, Sadie had left the classroom to find her kitten. According to Pearl, Isaac had felt responsible, because he hadn't told either Pearl or Amanda, who was helping out at the school that day. Amanda believed that guilt still dogged him today, even though his father had tried his best to alleviate it.

She raced after Isaac and this time caught his arm.

He shook violently and struggled to break away. "She's

going to die. She's going to die. Don't you see? If I don't find her, she's going to die."

Isaac *was* caught in the past. He pulled free of Louise's grip and began to run alongside the blazing field. She followed, calling his name. He wouldn't believe the truth. He also wouldn't halt. He was trying to make up for his earlier error. She must find another way to stop him.

She balled her hand in frustration, squeezing the handkerchief. That was it!

"Isaac!" She ran after him. "You need to bring this handkerchief with you to cover Sadie's nose and mouth so she can breathe."

He stopped and turned around. That's when she saw the trembling. He was going to collapse. She motioned for Jimmy as Isaac fell prostrate in her arms.

How was a man supposed to work when the woman he cared for was missing in the midst of raging fires? He'd seen the bodies floating on the surface of the Mississippi when the *Sultana* went down. So many needless deaths. Tonight could bring another.

Jesse threw all his strength into hauling the wet blankets up the ladder and tried not to think of either the *Sultana* or Louise. Such efforts were useless. Soon his thoughts drifted back to Louise. What had she said? That a person could only do his best and leave the rest to God? That offered no consolation. Jesse hadn't done his best in Vicksburg. Neither had he done so here. He should have insisted on joining Roland. The men here could handle the dwindling numbers of blankets and the bucket brigade.

"I have to go," he shouted up to those on the roof. "Could someone take my place at the ladder?"

"I will," said a voice from behind.

Jesse whipped around to see a tall man with the build of a lumberjack. Jesse assumed it was Mrs. Evans's husband since he'd seen the two walking home from church together. "They'll find her." The man clapped him on the shoulder. "Louise is a strong and resourceful woman."

"Yes, she is." But fire could overcome.

"Sawyer Evans." The man stuck out his hand.

Jesse didn't have time for pleasantries. "Do you know which direction Roland and Calloway went?"

"You can trust them. They know the area better than anyone."

It wasn't a matter of trust. "I can't just stand around waiting."

"I understand. It's tough to wait when you love a woman."

Love? Jesse nearly choked. "We're not courting."

After all, more than two dozen letters awaited his reply, and more were sure to arrive on the next mail boat. Many had the right qualifications for a lighthouse keeper's wife. Louise did not.

"All in good time," Evans said. "Give her time and space. She'll come around."

Jesse didn't have the heart to tell him that Louise wasn't the one holding back. Let them think it was her decision. He owed her that much. As a widow, she'd already endured loss, even though her husband was rotten. The man had apparently left her in a poor situation if she had resorted to answering an advertisement for a wife. Just like the women clamoring for his attention. That thought made him grimace.

"You can be sure that Roland won't rest until Louise and the boys are found," Evans was saying. "Isaac is his nephew."

The family connection was meant to console. Jesse

also knew firsthand Roland's diligence, but no assurance could wipe away the fear that he had made a huge mistake. What if he hadn't rousted Louise from the school? That building was so far from the fires that she and the students still wouldn't be in danger there. Had he sent them from comparative safety directly into harm's way?

"Roland helped take care of the boy," Evans continued, "after Garrett lost his first wife. I'm praying they find him soon. I'm praying for them all."

"Last blanket," said a woman as she handed it to Jesse.

Evans grabbed one end of the blanket. "I'll go up behind you. Then we'll look for Louise."

Jesse nodded his thanks. He'd been bringing up the heavier rear all night. It was a relief to let someone else shoulder the load for once and an even bigger relief to go after Louise.

A bobbing lantern caught his eye. He stopped, trying to make out who it was.

Evans figured it out first. "That's Calloway. Hey, Ernie!"

The man veered their way.

Evans said what Jesse couldn't get out. "Did they find Louise and the boys?"

"Not yet. We need reinforcements."

Jesse dropped the blanket. "Show me the way. I have to find Louise."

Louise couldn't stop coughing. Even with her arm pressed over her nose and mouth, the smoke was so thick and acrid that she could barely get a breath. Jimmy was ahead of her, half carrying and half dragging Isaac, who had succumbed to the smoke. With every step they got farther ahead of her.

Her legs felt like lead. Her throat burned, and her head

ached. She could hardly draw a breath. It got difficult to concentrate, and she could barely see the path in front of her, even with the lantern.

Jimmy moved quickly under the light of the moon, dipping in and out of shadows. Gradually the landscape began to blur until Louise struggled to make out the boys. They were so far ahead of her now.

She tried to call out to Jimmy, but only ended up hacking and coughing again. This time the spasms stopped her. She bent over, trying to catch her breath. The wind blew, but it was hot, so hot, singeing the skin on her hands and face.

Where was that path? Where did Jimmy and Isaac go? Her lantern sputtered out. She peered into the blackness. Was that Jesse? In her muddled mind, she saw him loping toward her, exactly the way he'd approached that very first day on the dunes.

In fact, she was on the dunes. How did she get there?

The sand grated between her fingers. It filled her shoes. The sun should be shining, shouldn't it? Mustn't be careless with her magnifying glass. Could start a fire.

"Louise! Louise! Mrs. Smythe!"

Someone was shaking her.

"The boys." Her voice sounded odd, detached.

"Roland and Garrett have them." That man's voice again.

"Jesse?" The word was thick, as if her tongue wouldn't work properly.

"She's delirious. We have to get her into clean air." A man's voice. Not Jesse.

Someone lifted her, but she couldn't see who it was. Nor could she speak a single word. Her lips moved. She felt them. But nothing came out. She pushed against the man's arms.

"Calm down, Louise. You're safe now." That was Jesse.

She laid her head on his strong shoulder. He carried her with ease and tenderness. Secure, she stopped struggling and slipped into unconsciousness.

Chapter Fifteen

Jesse could barely control the desire to rush away from the flames. He wanted to get Louise as far from danger as possible. She was light, heavier than a full five-gallon oil transfer can to be sure, but lighter than anyone he had ever lifted in the past. Of course those had been corpses hauled from the battlefield and from the river after the explosion.

Then her body went limp, and panic raced through him.

"Wake up, Louise. Wake up!" He jostled her. He called to her. "Stay with us. Please, stay with us."

Somewhere in the midst of the walk, his pleas to her turned to pleas to God. *Let her live. Please.*

Though Sawyer Evans lit the trail immediately in front of Jesse, and Roland and Garrett's light was still visible, Jesse lost focus and tripped several times.

"You all right?" Evans asked.

"Fine," Jesse said.

Focus. He had to get Louise safely to the school or boardinghouse or wherever there was a doctor. Evans would take him there. Jesse wasn't one to easily trust another's leading, not after obeying his commander in Vicksburg, but Evans knew the way better than he did.

They'd reached yet another hill. Jesse struggled to the top, his feet sliding backward with each step. That would have happened anyway in the loose sand, but Louise's weight made it worse. Once he dropped to his knees.

Evans rushed toward him. "You all right? I can carry her for a while."

"No!" Jesse struggled to his feet. "I'm fine, but we have to get her to a doctor. She fainted a while ago."

At least he hoped she had only fainted.

Evans stayed close. Ahead, Garrett Decker raced forward with his son, who was now coughing and crying. Why wouldn't Louise wake?

"There's no doctor in town," Evans informed him, "but Mrs. Calloway knows a lot about medicines."

That didn't make Jesse feel any more secure. The town might trust a boardinghouse proprietress's medical judgment, but he would rather have a physician on hand. Mrs. Calloway's preferred remedy might help—or it might cause great harm. Louise had to wake.

"Come back to me," he pleaded again. "Come on, Louise, open your eyes. Cough. Do something." He had to know that she was alive.

At the bottom of the dune, the road turned to the right. After another small rise, they descended into town. The glow of lights had never looked so good. Not one building was ablaze. In fact, he couldn't spot a single fire. If the winds stayed from the current direction or died down, Singapore was safe.

Now if only Louise was.

He gripped her close and stepped onto the boardwalk. The boardinghouse was close now. He could make out its tall roof in the light of the moon.

"Louise." He whispered in her ear, so delicately curved, and his lips brushed the soft skin of her neck.

She was still warm.

The sensation jolted him, but the knowledge was even better. Louise was alive.

He erased the remaining distance in seconds. Even before he knocked, Mrs. Calloway opened the door and led him into the parlor, where he placed Louise on the sofa.

"Dearie," the woman clucked softly, "what were you thinking, headin' off on your own? My Ernie would've gone with you. Half the town would've gone with you." She placed a damp cloth on Louise's head. "Now you've gone and given us all a fright."

Though Jesse felt a crowd press around him, he focused only on Louise. "Will she be all right?"

"Let's see." Mrs. Calloway reached into her medicine box and pulled out a small vial. After unstopping it, she waved the glass vial under Louise's nose.

Louise started and then coughed. A good sign. When she opened her eyes, she searched until her gaze landed on him. Then, between the hacking coughs, she smiled.

Jesse felt the relief course through him. She would live.

"I need to be useful," Louise told Mrs. Calloway two mornings later. "Give me something to do."

The boardinghouse proprietress had just told Louise that she'd slept through yesterday and last night. That was shocking enough, but the fact that Louise had fallen asleep on the sofa and Mrs. Calloway didn't have the heart to move her made her shake her head in disbelief. Apparently the woman had closed the doors and forbade anyone from entering. The poor guests had to make do with the writing room for conversation and handiwork as well as reading and writing. The piano had lain dormant.

"Now, you just rest up until you're yourself," Mrs. Calloway said as she set a breakfast tray on the small table often used for playing cards but now serving as a bedside table.

Louise swung her feet to the floor. "I am myself, except for a raw throat from all that coughing and a touch of grogginess from whatever you gave me for sleep."

"Now, dear, there was no need to give you a thing for sleeping. Once Mr. Jesse told you Isaac was all right, you closed your eyes and dropped right off."

Jesse. She remembered looking for him the moment she awoke. "Did he…that is, was he the one who brought me here?"

Mrs. Calloway stopped arranging the napkin on the breakfast tray. "That he did. I've never seen a man so smitten. Excepting Mr. Roland and Mr. Garrett and Mr. Sawyer, of course. Now, eat up."

Louise surveyed the hearty breakfast of eggs, ham and thick slabs of fresh bread. None of it appealed. "No doubt Mr. Calloway was just like them back in the day."

The woman chuckled, diverted from matchmaking to pleasant memories. "That he was, but I didn't see it at the time. A woman can be blind, you see. I had my eyes on someone I thought was a better catch, but the Lord had other ideas. He knew exactly where He wanted me." She sighed and pulled away from the memory. "And He knows where He wants you too."

"Trouble is, I don't know," Louise muttered softly enough that the partially deaf woman couldn't hear. She wrapped the blanket around her shoulders and stood. For a second, spots formed before her eyes, but it passed quickly. "Please tell me where I can find my clothing and where I might get dressed."

Mrs. Calloway clucked her tongue. "Breakfast first."

"I am not hungry."

"You need to eat if you expect to regain your strength."

Louise was about to protest that her strength was just fine when her legs wobbled. "All right." She sat and managed a few bites under Mrs. Calloway's supervision. "I don't generally eat a large breakfast. Not this early. Perhaps later, after I've accomplished something."

"Accomplished, humph. The Good Book says we are saved by grace not by works alone."

"It also says that faith is dead without works, but I don't want to argue. I simply must be useful, and, from what Linore told me earlier, there's a lot that needs doing."

"Nothing that we're not already handling."

"I need to return to school."

"Miss Fiona canceled classes for the rest of the week. That's why the girls are helping here."

"Then I will help also. I understand there are several families housed here and many more are at the hotel. Surely there is something I can do. If you won't let me do anything strenuous, I might read to someone who is injured or ill."

"Well, there is Mr. Linden. His hands got burnt when he pulled his little one from the fire."

A lump formed in Louise's throat. How blessed she was to have only a raw throat and a nagging cough. "I will read to him. Is there anything else I can do?"

"Do you know much about bandaging burns? I seem to recall you helping out with Pearl after her legs got burnt."

Pearl Lawson Decker suffered burnt legs while rescuing little Sadie Decker from the fire that claimed the schoolhouse. That fire was the one that had haunted Sadie's older brother, Isaac, and nearly cost him his life.

"I did." Louise took a sip of tea. Burns were terribly painful, but the bandages must be changed. "I will help with that."

"Thank you, dearie. Now you eat up that breakfast."

It truly was a great deal more than Louise was accustomed to eating, but Mrs. Calloway hovered over her, apparently unwilling to leave until she was assured Louise would eat.

After a few more bites, Louise asked, "Are all the fires out?"

"Aye. Even Holland, though it's suffered a terrible loss, from what we've heard. The VanderLeuvens have returned. They lost everything."

Louise gasped. The VanderLeuvens had sold the hotel to Sawyer and Fiona just last spring and moved to Holland to be with their children. "What will they do?"

"You know Miss Fiona and Mr. Sawyer. They took them right in and put them in the owner's apartment again." Mrs. Calloway dabbed at her eyes. "Why, from what I heard, Mr. Sawyer even gave them a job. Now, that's good Christian folk."

Louise had to agree. Through all of Louise's ups and downs, Fiona had made sure she had employment and a place to live. "We're fortunate to have them in our town. Once I dress, I will change Mr. Linden's bandages. Just show me where you keep the ointment and clean bandages."

"Thank you, dear. Your things are in my room. You can dress there. Do you need any help?"

Louise shook her head, glad that her underpinnings and gowns allowed her to dress herself. She had left behind the fancy gowns requiring the assistance of a maid, knowing that she would never see the ballroom floor again. She'd intended to become a frontier wife. Instead, she'd become a frontier teacher. After changing Mr. Linden's bandage, she would go to the school and tell Fiona they could resume classes.

Jesse slept fitfully after the midnight watch at the lighthouse. The previous morning, he'd gotten only a few hours of rest after a night of hard work dousing the buildings against fire. And finding Louise. The thought of losing her had shaken him worse than he could have imagined, but he'd pushed aside the thought all day yesterday. Duty awaited, and that duty did not include pondering his growing attachment to Louise.

She was a good woman and stronger than he'd first supposed, but she had made a critical error. Running off without telling a soul was never a good idea. It could have cost her dearly.

When Mrs. Blackthorn had informed him yesterday afternoon that Louise was up and about, the concern that had knotted his shoulders melted away. Louise would recover. He had saved her. Though he'd failed in Vicksburg, he hadn't failed the night of the fires. The town escaped unscathed, and not one person from Singapore suffered lasting ill effects. Isaac had been running around as usual the next day. Louise took longer, but that was to be expected. No one else from town was harmed. Unfortunately, many families arrived from the countryside, their farms and homes burned. But he'd heard of no deaths.

Then why had he tossed and turned? Why the same nightmares? Why had he awoken drenched in sweat yet again?

The dreams should have stopped. This time he'd acted. He'd done all he could. No one was harmed. This right should have reversed the wrong. The guilt should be erased. Instead, it had risen up again.

He donned his clothes and stared at the stacks of letters. Any day now another pile would arrive. According to his plan, he should narrow these down to a few prospects and write, but something was holding him back.

Maybe it was someone.

Louise. His pulse quickened.

He hurriedly buttoned his shirt and combed his hair.

What had she said the last time they talked? That they could only do their best and the rest was up to God. He hadn't believed it then, but when faced with losing Louise he had turned to God. No, he'd pleaded with God, and the Lord had answered. If he'd ever needed a sign of what he was supposed to do, he'd received it then.

The thought of losing Louise had panicked him. When he and Sawyer met up with Roland and Garrett, the Decker brothers had reported that they couldn't find any of the missing three. The smoke was too dense and the night too dark. Jesse and Sawyer had pressed on with the Deckers on their heels. Roland had found Jimmy and Isaac first, but the lad's mutterings couldn't point them to Louise.

So what had? God's hand? Sawyer had rushed ahead while Jesse looked carefully. When he thought about how he'd nearly missed seeing her, it shook him. She lay in the shadow of a juniper bush. Yet a sudden snap, like a twig breaking or a fire crackling, had drawn his attention. Then the moonlight caught the metal eyelets on her shoes. That small glint drew him closer, where he found her murmuring incoherently.

He thought he'd lost her when she passed out, but again he was wrong. She lived. Not only that, she hadn't suffered any harm. No burns. No lasting difficulties. Mrs.

Blackthorn said Louise intended to return to the school later today.

Jesse would catch her before she resumed teaching. He hurried downstairs and bypassed the kitchen, where Mrs. Blackthorn would have a meal for him in the warming oven. He plunged out the door and half slid down the dune toward town.

This couldn't wait.

Louise needed to know. All the letters in the world couldn't compete with the compassion and valor that she possessed. She was the strongest woman he'd ever met, determined, intelligent and persistent. She would not wilt under duress. She could stand up under the hard life of a lighthouse keeper's wife.

Was he ready to offer marriage? The thought made his empty stomach churn. What would she think of his nightmares? Could he tell her about the *Sultana* and what had happened at Vicksburg? Would she understand? Somehow he believed she would. Moreover, his actions during this fire must have redeemed him. She would see that.

He stepped onto the boardwalk and headed for the boardinghouse. Men either nodded or shouted a greeting.

Roland called out, "Stop by the store when you have a moment."

"Later," he called back.

He couldn't be diverted from his purpose. No, he had to do this before he thought too much, before he recalled all the reasons he'd had for not pursuing a relationship with Louise Smythe.

This midday, he would tell her how he felt and pray for a good response.

He bounded up the steps of the boardinghouse.

The draperies in the parlor were pulled open, and through the window he saw the most beautiful woman he'd ever met. True, her physical beauty couldn't compare with some women, but Louise exuded something else that completely overshadowed the physical. Why, even now she took his breath away.

He watched, transfixed, as she moved toward the sofa, leaned over, and then straightened up.

A man rose from that sofa, his attention riveted to her. The man glowed with gratitude, and Louise smiled back at him.

Jesse felt a twinge of jealousy until a handful of children surrounded the man. Judging from their delighted cries, this was their pa. Soon a woman joined them, and the man kissed her. The love between husband and wife touched Jesse. This was what he wanted, but Louise's look of longing reminded him of the hurdle that stood between them.

If he married Louise, Jesse would never have the large family he desired.

He turned and left.

Chapter Sixteen

Louise finished wrapping the bandage around Mr. Linden's forearms and hands. She tried to be as gentle as possible, but she saw him wince and grit his teeth several times.

"There, now. We're done. Pearl Decker—she suffered burns in last fall's fire—told me the pain eases over time."

He sucked in his breath. "Didn't hurt a bit."

Louise had been touched by his story of running back into the burning house to rescue his three-year-old. "At least your entire family is safe, thanks to your valor."

Tears gleamed in his eyes. Mr. Linden wasn't a handsome man by any definition, but his love for his family overcame any deficiencies in appearance.

"By the grace of God," he murmured.

"That it is. And your little one is running around as if nothing happened. She's a dear child."

He nodded, clearly overcome. Then his wife and six children rushed into the parlor to embrace him. Louise stepped back, mesmerized by their joy. This was what she wanted and would never have. The thought brought tears to her eyes.

To keep her thoughts away from the sorrow, she announced, "Mrs. Calloway said dinner will be served shortly in the dining room."

"Thank you," Mrs. Linden said.

He was still shaky after his ordeal, but his wife steadied him. He had saved his youngest from the fire that consumed his house, but it had nearly cost his life. When he'd stumbled coming out of the house, his wife and sons pulled him to safety. Louise wasn't sure she could be so brave. She had found Isaac before the blaze reached him. Could she have dashed through flames for his sake?

Her thoughts drifted to Pearl, who had done just that last fall to save little Sadie. Like Mr. Linden, Pearl had suffered deep burns that scarred her legs. Mr. Linden's burns might make it difficult for him to continue farming. With the eldest son barely in his teens and their farm leveled by fire, the future looked grim for the family.

Tears gathered again in her eyes. There was much to rejoice about, yes. People survived the fires, but lives would be changed forever. Her worries over Jesse's affection and her job seemed so insignificant in comparison. Friends here would help her. She'd seen the community band together. No one would be left to suffer.

The Linden family headed for the dining room first. As Louise left the parlor, a movement outside caught the corner of her eye. She looked just in time to see Jesse leaving the boardinghouse porch.

Odd.

She hadn't heard a knock or his voice, and he hadn't stuck his head in the parlor to greet her. She wondered what he'd wanted, but that thought disappeared the moment she reached the crowded dining room.

All those staying at the boardinghouse waited in

line. Mrs. Calloway had set the food on the sideboard so people could serve themselves. Since the dining room couldn't possibly seat everyone housed at the boarding-house, this was the most practical way to run the meals.

Louise was disappointed to see Priscilla and her friends at the head of the line.

"Potatoes and onions?" the girl questioned. "Is that what you expect us to eat?"

Louise felt her temper rise. She hurried to Priscilla's side. "You will eat whatever is placed in front of you or do without."

Priscilla stared at her as if she had made the most foolish statement ever pronounced. That girl needed the discipline of a structured schedule, not the freedom to run about doing whatever she pleased. No doubt Mrs. Calloway had been too busy to keep an eye on Priscilla and her cohorts.

A giggle behind her meant Linore had heard Louise's sharp comment.

Louise inwardly sighed. Why couldn't she hold her temper around Priscilla? She would have much to confess tonight, but for now, she had to relieve Mrs. Calloway of the responsibility for three spoiled girls.

"I plan to return to school after dinner. Priscilla, Adeline and Esther, I expect you to join me."

"Why not Linore and Dinah?" Adeline protested.

"Because they are on schedule with their homework whereas you are not."

"But there's no school," Priscilla pointed out with marked disdain.

"There will be. I intend to ask Mrs. Evans to resume classes tomorrow."

She hoped Fiona would agree.

* * *

Jesse tried again to sort through the letters, but he just couldn't. None of them measured up. None came close to Louise's virtues. Not one mentioned an interest in science. Though the admirable skills of cooking, sewing and cleaning were mentioned, no lady hinted at the sort of valor that drove a woman to rescue a boy she only knew by acquaintance.

Frustrated, he shoved the letters aside and grabbed his coat.

He needed a walk.

The evening was quiet and calm. The crescent moon offered little light, but the lamplight spilling from houses and businesses was enough to light the way. Above, the lighthouse pulsed its beam across the water. He couldn't walk for long. He needed a nap before taking over at midnight.

The school was dark except for windows on the upper level. The students must have returned. Briefly he wondered if Louise was there. He assumed she lived at the school in order to watch over her charges because she always seemed to be there, but she might be staying at the boardinghouse for now.

"Watch out!" cried a woman as he brushed past, barely missing her.

He turned back but only slowed his progress. "I'm sorry, ma'am."

It was Fiona Evans, and she was not pleased.

He halted, chagrined.

Mrs. Evans didn't hold back. "Mr. Hammond, first you refuse to honor your commitment at my school and now you nearly knock me off the boardwalk."

"I'm sorry," he managed to cough out before she continued. "I will make it up to you."

"You could pay me back by resuming your lectures."

Jesse knew manipulation when he saw it. And her efforts were undoubtedly spurred by her belief that he and Louise were a perfect match. Yet it could not be, not if he wanted a houseful of children.

"Mrs. Smythe will do an excellent job."

"*Mrs.* Smythe? I thought you were on friendlier terms."

"It is proper to refer to all but family and close friends in a more formal manner." He ducked his head. "If you won't be needing me further, I have to be on my way."

"To where?"

Where indeed? Saying he needed to work through the most important decision of his life would only lead to more questions.

He glanced ahead. The store's lights were still on. "To the mercantile."

"Ah. I thought for a moment you were going to the boardinghouse, but Louise moved back to the school this afternoon."

That answered that question. "I'm glad to hear she is well."

Fiona's gaze seemed to pierce through him. "She does owe her well-being to your quick actions. Thank you, Mr. Hammond."

Jesse squirmed. "No thanks are needed. Anyone would have done the same. Moreover, your husband was the one who brought me to the correct location. Greater thanks go to the two of you for opening up the hotel to those who lost their homes." He glanced again at the store. "I'd better hurry before they close."

At last she let him go, and Jesse wasted no time getting to the mercantile. The door was still unlocked. He pushed it open, jangling the bell.

Roland looked up from his position at the counter. "Jesse! What can I get for you?"

"A wife?" Had those words really come out of his mouth? He forced a chuckle, as if to indicate he was joking. "Mr. Blackthorn insists a head keeper has to be married. I figure it'll improve my chances of getting a lighthouse of my own."

"That explains it."

Jesse instinctively went on guard. "Explains what?"

"Why you're getting so many letters from women."

"There's more?" Jesse hated to ask.

"A lot more." Roland pulled two handfuls from the cubbyhole.

Jesse stared. "You're joking."

"Absolute truth. Look yourself."

It took a few minutes for Jesse to examine every return address. He could only set aside one letter from his sister. The rest were written by strangers.

"You placed an advertisement," Roland said.

"How did you know?"

"I've seen it before. More than one man in this town has gone that route."

Jesse held up both stacks of envelopes. "How am I supposed to choose? And there's more back in my room."

"Have you written to any from the first batch?"

"I don't know where to start. What if I make a mistake? It could be a catastrophe."

Roland chuckled. "You sound like Garrett."

"Oh? I thought he was married."

"He is, to one of those mail-order brides like you're going after."

Jesse took it in. "How did he decide?"

"Luckily, all three women showed up in person, thanks to the wording on that fool advertisement."

"Are you saying the advertisement was a bad idea?"

"It wasn't ever intended to be published. Isaac and Sadie got a hold of an ad that I wrote as a joke and had Mrs. Calloway send it to a New York newspaper."

"Oh, no."

"Three women showed up: Amanda, Fiona and Louise."

It was all coming back to Jesse. Mrs. Blackthorn had told him a little about this. "But I thought there were four."

Roland grinned. "Pearl wasn't actually responding to the advertisement. She was hired to teach school, but she talked her friend, Amanda, into answering it."

"Well, at least I don't have to face these women in person. There must be at least as many letters here as I already received. What am I going to do?"

"Eliminate the ones that won't work and write a letter of regret. Then whittle down the remaining candidates by asking for more information."

"I suppose I could do that." Jesse pondered what to ask. Maybe if they liked science. No, that was liable to bring an enthusiastic if untrue yes. He'd have to word it carefully, perhaps ask what topics they most enjoyed in school. Those answers would definitely narrow down the field.

"But if you want my honest opinion," Roland said, "go with the one who stirs your heart, the one you can't stop thinking about, the one who drives you crazy."

"Why would I want to marry a woman who drives me crazy?"

"For variety and spice. Life will never be dull. Trust me on this."

Jesse fingered the letters. By those criteria, not one respondent deserved a positive response. Only one woman fit.

The next two days Louise watched for Jesse, hoping and praying that he'd decided advertising for a bride was a mistake. If he had tried to pay her a call at the boardinghouse but left because she was busy, he would call at the school now that life had settled into more of a normal pattern. Not that routine was like before. How could it be, with the hotel and boardinghouse filled with those who had lost their homes? Every plan was thrown into the air. The festival seemed frivolous. Wreaths were inconsequential. These people needed real help, but Louise didn't know how to do it. With Fiona busy between the hotel and the school, she had hoped to discuss ideas with Jesse.

He never called on her.

She waited in the parlor after supper. She looked out the windows every morning after the lighthouse beam was extinguished, hoping to see him loping down the dune. Each day she was disappointed. What had she done? Considering he had carried her from danger, she'd expected he would call to wish her good health if nothing else. But they had established a deeper bond than mere acquaintance. He might consider her only a friend, but he had grown dear to her.

So she waited. Surely he would come to the school. She could not go to him, since she must stay with the girls at all times. He would know that, wouldn't he?

That evening she settled in the parlor with her favorite book while Priscilla played piano. The girl was talented, but the sonatas jangled Louise's nerves. Why didn't Jesse call on her?

She thrust aside her copy of *Pride and Prejudice*, unable to fathom why Lizzie held such prejudice against a man of obvious good character. In the past those scenes would make her laugh or shake her head knowingly. Now they smacked too much of truth. Had she not judged Jesse incorrectly? According to Matthew's gospel, she wasn't to judge at all. *Judge not, that ye be not judged.* Oh, how easily she failed.

Restless, she hopped up and paced the length of the parlor and back again.

"Is something wrong, Mrs. Smythe?" Priscilla asked pointedly, her bright blue eyes too reminiscent of Jesse's.

"No. Just restless. I can't help thinking about all the displaced families." It wasn't the only thing on her mind, but it was all she could reveal to Priscilla. "Where will they go for the winter? Along with their houses and farm, they must have lost all the food they'd stored up. They don't even have a spare set of clothing."

Priscilla resumed the Mozart concerto.

Louise sat back down and picked up her book. She read the same page three times, while her thoughts drifted between Jesse and those who had lost homes. How selfish to think of romance when people were hurting.

Priscilla completed the piece with a flourish and then turned to Louise. "I suppose they will make do on the charity of others. Father contributes heavily to such funds."

The simplistic, dispassionate response set Louise on edge, and she had to remind herself that Priscilla was only echoing what her parents had taught her. Unfortunately, the money her father gave to Chicago charities would never reach a town like Singapore.

"We shall have to turn to each other," Louise said firmly. "I wonder if Mr. Stockton will allow the families to live in empty bunkhouses when the lumberjacks aren't passing through."

"What's a bunkhouse?" Adeline asked from her perch beside Priscilla, where she turned the pages of the sheet music.

"It's like a dormitory or orphanage," Priscilla sniffed, "with everyone jammed together in one room."

Louise saw Linore stiffen and suspected a retort was on its way. Dinah held her tongue better than the redhead.

"Not exactly," Louise clarified. "It's a cabin that houses several workmen. If you've walked around town, you've seen the vacant buildings."

"Those are cabins?" Adeline's mouth gaped. "They've got holes in them."

"They aren't perfect," Louise admitted, "but it would give families a chance to stay together with some measure of privacy."

"What would?" Fiona breezed into the room, looking somewhat pale and decidedly unhappy.

"We were just contemplating ways to give the displaced families a home until they get back on their feet."

"Oh." Fiona didn't appear to even hear Louise.

"We must do something before winter sets in."

"I suppose." Fiona looked fidgety, something that was completely opposite normal. "Mrs. Smythe, may I speak to you? In private?"

The girls looked at each other and would no doubt speculate once their superiors had left the room. Louise's heart skipped a beat. Had Jesse paid a discreet call, knowing the girls waited in the parlor?

She followed Fiona, who led her to her office.

Odd. There was no reason for Jesse to meet her there unless something bad had happened.

Heart in throat, she waited while Fiona unlocked the door and then lit a lamp. The room was empty.

"Please close the door behind you," Fiona directed. Instead of sitting, she paced to the window and then back, clearly upset.

Louise's mind raced to other possibilities. Had the influx of non-paying guests pushed the hotel into failure? Would the school soon follow?

"What is it?" Her voice wavered, drawing a look from Fiona.

"No one is hurt, if that's what you're thinking."

Louise instinctively breathed out in relief.

Fiona smiled. "I assume your Mr. Hammond is well, though I haven't talked to him other than when he nearly ran into me on his way to the store." Her expression sobered. "We've all been busy. Very busy."

"Is that what's troubling you? You may withhold my wages until business improves at the hotel."

Fiona stared and then shook her head. "No, that's not it. It's simply that I've received unbelievable news, and I don't know what to do."

Her gaze held such an expression of pain and disbelief that Louise instinctively went to her friend. Fiona wasn't overly expressive. A simple touch of Louise's hand to Fiona's arm conveyed support. "Whatever it is, I will help."

"Thank you, but this is nothing that any one person can resolve. And yet it affects so many here." Fiona blinked rapidly. "Sawyer wanted to board the first ship, but I begged him to wait at least until further news arrives."

Now Louise was both confused and alarmed. "Don't keep me in suspense. What happened?"

"The fires here, well, they're not the only fires. Chicago is gone."

"Gone?" Louise stepped back, a hand to her throat at the sheer magnitude of the statement. She recalled the grand Great Central Station and beautiful buildings between the train depot and the ship.

"What do you mean that it's gone? A huge city can't just vanish."

"It burnt."

"Some of it."

Fiona shook her head. "According to the captain and crew of the schooner that just arrived, nearly all of it. There's hardly a building left standing within sight of the main pier. And many perished. No one knows for certain how many or who they are."

It was incomprehensible. "A whole great city? Impossible."

"But true." Fiona grasped Louise's hands with urgency. "And that brings us to the dilemma. The girls are all from Chicago."

"Their parents," Louise gasped.

"As well as homes and siblings for Priscilla, Adeline and Esther. Even Dinah and Linore have friends living there. What do we tell them and when?"

Louise had no difficulty spotting the problem. "If we tell them too soon, they will want to find their families, but there's no way to know if their relations survived or even if the family home is still standing."

"I never dreamed of facing such a thing," Fiona whispered.

The implications settled in. All five girls might be orphans.

Chapter Seventeen

"Is there any way to send back the letters?" Jesse asked Roland on Saturday morning.

The store was busy at this hour, but he had managed to corner the manager while Pearl waited on customers. The two men stood at the counter, where yet another stack of letters awaited him.

"Not a chance. They're all in your hands now."

Jesse blew out his breath. "But they'll keep coming, and this stack will put the total over sixty. I can't believe it."

"What was the last date you were accepting applications?"

"Last date?" Jesse started. "Uh, I didn't think about that."

Roland chuckled. "Seems to be a common problem."

"What do you mean?"

"Both Garrett and Sawyer forgot it too. Garrett was fortunate, but Sawyer had a lot of writing to do. I take it this means you've made your choice?"

He had. A lot of prayer reinforced what he'd felt since the night he'd carried Louise from the fire. Telling her was a huge step, one that could crush his heart worse than

Clarice had when she refused him. He had the letters to fall back on, he told himself, but even he knew that a wife on paper alone was a poor substitute for a woman he greatly admired and cared about already.

Louise occupied his thoughts every day. Her grace, her strength and her calm stood far above everyone else. She had risked her life for a boy she barely knew. Even if their family was smaller, she would love each one with all that was within her. That made her the perfect choice— if Louise accepted his proposition. But he wasn't about to tell that to Roland.

"I'm narrowing it down," he said instead.

"Ah, some good prospects then."

"Perhaps." Jesse had to stay noncommittal.

"Then why ask to send these back? The perfect wife might be in this stack of letters."

"It's too much to sort out." Though Jesse suspected any man would see through that excuse, Roland didn't seem to notice.

"Just figure out a polite refusal and say the same thing to each one," the store manager said. "And be glad you don't have to do it in person."

That thought struck terror in a man's heart.

"Imagine sixty women standing in the store. All sizes and shapes and hair colors." Roland swept a hand from back to front of the store. "One is bound to suit, but which one? A mistake lasts a lifetime."

If Jesse hadn't been nervous before, Roland just made it worse. What if pursuing Louise was the wrong choice? He didn't know her all that well, better than those women who'd written, to be certain, but not well. She hadn't said much about her late husband, other than his cruelty to her dog. Her reactions told him the marriage was not a happy one. The man must not have left her anything if she had to come to Singapore to find a husband. On the other hand, considering the number of responses he'd gotten to his advertisement, there must be a lot of war widows out there.

"Speaking of Sawyer," Roland said loudly as he stepped from behind the counter to greet Mr. Evans, "how are you doing, friend?"

The two men shook hands as if long parted instead of fellow business owners in the same small town.

Jesse scooped up his letters, ready to leave.

"Figured I'd better check in with you once I got the word." Sawyer shook his head. "Dreadful news."

"What news?" Jesse asked.

The two men stared at him.

"Didn't you hear?" Roland asked, looking at Sawyer. He cleared his throat. "Are you from Chicago?"

"On the south side."

"Beyond the river?"

In other words, away from the lakeshore and the wealthy homes, but Jesse sensed Roland wasn't trying to shove him into a social class. "Yes."

Roland breathed out what could only be a sigh of relief. "The city burned, but, from what the ship's crew said, most of the area south of the river was spared."

Jesse shook his head in disbelief. "What do you mean the city? A few buildings?"

"No. The heart of the city. It's gone."

Jesse tried to take it in. The shock was staggering. If only he could talk to Louise. Louise! For a second he wondered if she had family there, but then he remembered she hailed from New York.

Roland was talking to Sawyer. "I'm sure we'll get word from your parents soon."

Sawyer's expression was grim. "If the reports are

right, their home will be gone and the business will suffer. Any word on your extended family?"

Roland shook his head. "Not yet. It's early. I'm just glad my mother and father weren't alive to see this. It would have devastated them."

Jesse couldn't concentrate. If what Sawyer said was right, then Pa's hovel would have been spared but had the shipyards survived? If his father was working at the time, then he could have perished. As great as their differences were, Jesse didn't want his father to burn to death.

"The wharves?" he managed to choke out.

Both Roland and Jesse stared at him. Apparently he'd interrupted.

Sawyer answered. "From what I hear, the fire went out the government pier, but the wharves will be the first thing they get operating." He looked to Roland again. "You know what this means."

Roland nodded. "They'll need lumber. Lots of it."

"I expect Stockton will run both mills full-time and maybe add a third. It'll be a boom like you've never seen before."

Jesse was stuck back on the stunning news about Chicago. "I can't believe it." Again he wished for the comfort that Louise could offer.

"The lighthouse is going to be crucial," Sawyer said. "Every ship available will be carrying wood to rebuild Chicago."

All plans of marriage slipped away in the face of this news. He had to find out if his father was all right, and he had to find out now.

Days slipped past while many waited for word from Chicago. Not only Louise's students, but also Sawyer Evans, the Deckers and half of Singapore had friends and family there. Every incoming ship sent people scrambling to the docks. Every messenger from Holland buoyed hope that a wire had gotten through.

Few could focus on the ordinary when their attention was riveted on the extraordinary happenings. Towns decimated, livelihoods erased, a great city nearly wiped out. At first the girls talked excitedly amongst themselves, as if to reassure each other that nothing had changed. Each sent a letter at first opportunity. Even Linore and Dinah, who had no parents to contact, wrote to someone in that great city whose welfare lay heavy on their hearts.

"Sawyer is beside himself," Fiona confided to Louise as they waited for the latest steamboat to come alongside the wharf. "He can't focus on anything and yet he doesn't want to disappoint anyone. I told him we must cancel the Christmas festival. I hope you aren't upset."

"Of course you must cancel it." Louise clasped her friend's hand. "Family is far more important than business."

Fiona breathed out a sigh of relief. "I told Sawyer that you would understand. Others have been equally understanding, especially Roland and Garrett." She eyed the brothers standing with the rest at the dock.

"They're from Chicago, aren't they?"

"Nearly everyone here knows someone in Chicago."

"Except us," Louise pointed out. "We four all hail from New York."

"Where is Jesse from?"

A flash of fear coursed through Louise. "I don't know." Odd that he had never mentioned where he grew up or lived before coming here. His father was still alive. Considering Jesse wasn't pacing the docks like the rest, maybe he hailed from another town.

Fiona must have noted the same thing. "Maybe he's from elsewhere."

Louise hoped that was the case. Those with relations in Chicago had suffered mightily waiting for word.

A moment of silence passed while neither knew what to say next.

"If Sawyer receives bad news, I will have to go with him to Chicago," Fiona said.

"I understand. You can count on me to keep the school operating." Yet she could not look at her friend, could not bear to see the distress. How it must hurt to see the one you love suffering.

Fiona was strong, though, the strongest woman Louise had ever met. "If the students receive bad news and must leave, I will have to close the school, at least for a while."

This was what Louise feared most, yet what could she say? Maybe the news would be good, and the school could continue as usual.

"We'll pray for good news then."

Fiona nodded, but Louise could see the strain in her expression. She wasn't revealing everything.

"What happened?" Louise asked gently.

Fiona tossed her head, sending her red curls dancing. "Good news, in a way. Mr. Stockton sent word that both mills will be running full steam by the end of the month. Roland expects new lumbering crews to arrive within the week. Sawyer is needed at the sawmill." She hesitated. "It's a good income."

Louise knew what that meant. Fiona and Sawyer needed the money. "Then he should take the job."

Fiona squeezed her hand. "I knew you would understand. But it means I'll have to spend most of my time at the hotel. If the students stay, can you run the school?"

"Of course." It would be a lot of work, but Louise

didn't fear labor. Moreover, it would only be for a short time. Soon winter ice would stop the logs from floating downstream. "It will all work out for the best."

Once the ship was secured, the gangway was extended. The crowd pressed close. Though the store expected merchandise, the rest hoped for word from loved ones or business associates.

"Any mail?" one man shouted, issuing in a chorus of people asking the same question.

Soon no one voice could be distinguished from the rest, all speaking louder and louder to try to overcome the din.

Louise pressed a hand to her right ear, which ached in the cold and from the racket. "This is hopeless. I can't hear a thing."

She began to retreat, but a man elbowed past her, pushing her away from Fiona.

A loud whistle quieted the crowd long enough for Roland to shout out that any mail would be taken to the mercantile.

That only sent the crowd and Fiona in a new direction. A rough man, likely a lumberjack or sawyer, pushed past. Louise stumbled, and the loose sole on her shoe caught in between the dock planks. Down she went, to her hands and knees, while all around her the crowd rushed. A knee jolted her shoulder. A careless hand knocked off her hat. Louise hunched over, protecting her face with her arms, and the terrible memories returned.

Warren had come home drunk and in a rage. When she set the warmed supper plate before him, having dismissed the housekeeper hours before, he threw the plate against the wall and then demanded a different meal. She was no cook and could not even attempt what he wanted. When she told him as much, he pummeled her with his fists until she crouched in the corner in much the same position as now. After flinging hateful slurs at her, he retired to his study and, she did not doubt, more drink.

That time she sobbed in the corner, bruised but alive. Today the unheeding crowds stampeded over and around her.

Then a single voice broke through the fear and the noise.

"Stop! Stop! You're hurting her."

Jesse.

The darkness of the past slipped away, brightened by a man of courage and valor. The crowds heeded him and moved away from her. Then she felt his hand on her shoulder and his presence as he knelt beside her.

"Are you injured?"

His gentle voice brought tears to her eyes. Jesse cared. He had rescued her from the fire. He had carried her to safety. No one else had cared if she lived or died since Papa's death.

She nodded, her throat too constricted to speak.

"I'm sorry about your hat." He handed her the trampled remains of what used to be her good hat.

She took the hat. The ribbon was detached, and the straw brim had been ripped. The crown was flattened, and the blackest dirt ground into the straw. It could not be salvaged. How on earth would she be able to afford another? She blinked furiously to keep back the tears. With tragedy all around, what was a hat? No one would look askance if she appeared in church with her everyday hat.

"Can you stand?" Jesse asked.

She took a deep breath. The crowd had largely gone. Doubtless they now filled the mercantile. "Yes. Yes, I can."

Jesse stood and offered her his hand.

She put her hand in his, ruing for a moment that she wore gloves and could not feel the warmth of his skin against hers. Where had that thought come from? A moment before she had feared for her life, lost in the pain of the past. Now she dreamed of Jesse Hammond holding her hand. Heat dusted her cheeks with what she knew was a rosy glow.

"Thank you," she breathed.

Jesse smiled at her and then brushed at her hair.

She caught her breath, surprised by the tenderness in that gesture.

"A stray lock," he explained.

She couldn't seem to look away from those deep blue eyes. A person could get lost in them. How he could smile at her was a mystery. She must look a lot like that trampled hat. She touched her hair and felt a tangled mess. "Oh, dear. I must look a sight."

"A pretty sight."

Now she truly was blushing. "You're too kind."

But instead of answering her, Jesse started and looked past her. "Pa? What are you doing here?"

After a moment of stunned silence in which Pa looked hurt by his question, Jesse managed to find a better greeting.

"You're safe, Pa! We heard about the fire. Everyone's been worried." Jesse had never been one to reveal his emotions, but relief coursed through his veins, their long-standing differences forgotten.

Pa's weather-beaten face stretched into a smile. "I am. Good to see you, son."

The two men clasped hands and then ended up in a brief welcoming embrace that including clapping each other on the back. Pa's "pat" would've knocked the wind out of a lesser man.

"Still working the wharves?" Jesse asked, wondering why his father had come so far just to let him know he had survived the fires.

"It's gonna be busier'n ever pretty soon. Mason— that's the mayor—is talking rebuilding as fast as they can get stone and lumber to the city."

It was exactly as Roland had predicted.

"Then I'll be busy here at the lighthouse."

Pa glanced at Louise who was still standing near, though she had moved a few steps back.

"That's what I come to talk to you about," Pa said. "Care to introduce me to your lady friend?"

Jesse's chest tightened. Louise wasn't the kind of "lady friend" the men on the wharves talked about. Neither could he let on how much she meant to him, not until he knew where she stood.

"Mrs. Smythe is a friend," he said carefully, sticking to the facts. "She stumbled, and I helped her up."

Louise's expression tightened, and the spark went out of her eyes. She turned to Pa. "It's a pleasure to meet you, Mr. Hammond. I must rejoin my friend."

After a nod at Jesse, she hurried off, leaving him to wonder if he'd thoroughly botched matters. He'd have to explain later. Pa was a rough man. He'd always been that way. Jesse had never understood what his gentle, cultured mother saw in him. Perhaps Pa had been dashing as a younger man. Maybe he'd once spoken of dreams with the starry-eyed hope of youth. Maybe he'd simply been so opposite from her upbringing that she rebelled against her strict parents. Whatever the reason, that gentle woman had wed a man whose rough edges only got sharper after marriage. Life in a two-room flat became reality. Cursing, drinking and frustration followed. Then she died, and Jesse had only his father.

"Got someplace we can talk in private?" Pa said. "This town must have a tavern."

Jesse clenched his fists. "You know I won't go in those."

"Then at your lighthouse?"

"It's not mine," Jesse pointed out while trying to envision where on the property he could get any semblance of privacy. For that matter, the town didn't have any place private either, aside from the hotel dining room. "Are you hungry? We could get supper at the hotel after getting you a room."

"Don't you have a spot for your pa at your place?"

Jesse gritted his teeth. "I only have a single bed. You can sleep while I'm working, but the room's not big enough for two."

"We can make do, son." Pa clapped him on the shoulder again. "We always did."

"I was a boy then." He quickly calculated his father's objection. "I'll pay for the room at the hotel. You'll be more comfortable there, since I work the midnight shift." He eyed his father. "How long are you planning to stay?"

"Tryin' to get rid of me already?"

"No, I'm busy."

He and Pa had never gotten along. Pa considered him too soft, too much like his mother. He insisted Jesse needed toughening up, which meant hard labor, rough language and drinking. Jesse didn't mind the hard work, but he had no use for the rest.

"Don't worry, son. I'll be catching the first lumber boat back to the city." He picked up a canvas sack that had been leaning against a dock post. "Let's get that grub and go over my big news."

Jesse looked around. No one except the ship's crew was near. They'd all gone to the mercantile. He led his father toward the hotel.

Once they were out of earshot of anyone, Jesse said, "This is as alone as we're going to get. What's your big news?"

Pa grinned, revealing crooked teeth and a gap where one had either been pulled or knocked out in a brawl. "I been working for the customs collector lately. He let me know, all confidential-like, that there's an opening comin' up at the South Manitou Island Light."

Jesse halted as the impact hit. "A head keeper position?"

"That it is."

Jesse marveled that his father had come all this way to give him this news when a letter would have sufficed.

"Thank you," he choked out.

Pa grinned. "I kin get your name at the top of the list, if you know what I mean." He jingled some coin in his pocket.

Jesse set his jaw. Bribery. Something very much like that had sent 1700 to their death near Memphis. "I don't pay bribes."

"Who said anythin' about bribin' anyone?" Pa whined. "I'm talkin' a little incentive, is all. You'll never get nowhere if you don't give a man a reason ta choose you over the others."

"I don't have that kind of money."

A wealthy man could easily outspend the paltry amount Jesse could provide.

"It's a good post. Pays plenty since it's one of them island lighthouses you're so keen on."

It was tempting. The dream that had lurked for so long in the fringes of memory could become a reality. Head keeper at a remote lighthouse. There he could escape the world and all its troubles. There he could make his own life, alone. Except no man could operate a lighthouse by himself. He would need an assistant or a wife.

"Is there an assistant there?"

"Don't think so."

"When does the post come available?"

"I heard the man's retirin' next month, at the end o' the shippin' season."

That soon. Jesse drew in a breath, and with it came a flood of excitement. He could begin anew, but to get prime consideration he needed a wife—and soon. That eliminated all those letters and made the path crystal clear.

At last he had something of substance to offer a woman like Louise. As head keeper, he would have more than a room. He would have a house and ample provisions, not to mention a better wage. It might not be all she'd been accustomed to back home, but he hoped it would be enough.

Chapter Eighteen

At the school, the long-anticipated letters arrived, and each brought good news. Priscilla's family had escaped unscathed. The fire had burnt near their home but had not touched it. Adeline and Esther's homes weren't as fortunate, but no one was injured. Adeline's home had suffered damage while Esther's had been leveled. Both families had retreated to their summer cottages.

All three girls begged to return home.

Louise had convinced them to wait until she spoke with Fiona. Her friend was so busy at the hotel that she didn't have an opportunity to speak to her until Sunday evening. They gathered in Fiona's office at the school while Sawyer took over the registration desk at the hotel.

"Are you ready for the week's classes?" Fiona asked, rubbing the bridge of her nose, which she did whenever her head ached or she was tired.

"Would you like a warm compress or a cup of hot tea? I find the vapors help clear the head."

"No, thank you." Fiona offered a wan smile. "Nothing will clear away the fatigue except rest."

"Then I won't keep you long, but I do have a pressing question."

Fiona dropped her hand and lifted an eyebrow. "What happened? Is Priscilla acting up again?"

"No, at least not any more than usual. It's about their letters from home."

"Oh, yes." Fiona sighed. "Forgive me. I should have asked how their families were."

"You were busy, and you must have been very relieved that Sawyer's family all survived the blaze." Louise covered her friend's hand with her own.

"Yes, we are. Though their homes were damaged, it could have been much worse. But you are concerned about the students. Did they receive bad news?"

"All are well."

"That's good news." Fiona relaxed. "I did fear the worst."

"No one suffered injury, but both Adeline's and Esther's family homes were damaged. Their families have gone to their summer cottages for the time being."

"Understandable. And the Benningtons?"

"Unscathed." It didn't seem fair that the most troublesome family had escaped without the slightest effect, but Louise kept that thought to herself. "All three girls have asked to return home through the Christmas holiday."

"So long? That's over two months. If the families are well, what's the hurry?"

Louise hated to reveal this part. "Each girl has shown me her letter. The parents have requested their daughters' return for the remainder of the year."

Fiona's jaw dropped for a moment before she pulled it back and her expression hardened. "The calendar year or the school year?"

"They didn't specify."

Fiona sighed. "This isn't about the fire, is it?"

"I can't be certain. I don't know what the girls wrote to their parents, but it's clear they are all upset."

Fiona slumped, bracing her head with one hand. She looked defeated, and Louise had never seen her that way. Even when she feared what Sawyer's father might do to her, she had fought back. At this moment, the fight was gone.

"It's all right." Louise grasped her friend's hand. "God will provide."

Fiona lifted her head. "I'm sorry."

Louise circled the desk that stood between them and hugged her friend. "It's at times like these that we realize what is most important in our lives. Sawyer and Mary Clare need you most right now. Perhaps this is a blessing, for you won't be torn between the school, the hotel and your family."

"We still have Dinah and Linore's education to consider."

"I can teach them at the boardinghouse. With the displaced families staying there, Mrs. Calloway is delighted to have their help. There's no need to keep the school building heated for just the three of us."

Fiona appeared to accept Louise's explanation. "But where will you stay?"

Louise pushed forth a smile that she didn't feel. "I'm sure Mrs. Calloway will accept my help in exchange for room and board, now that a couple of the families are moving into the vacant cabins. Remember, Roland predicted we'll soon see a lot of lumberjacks coming through to work the camps. After that will come more sawmill workers. We will all be busy, including the hotel."

Fiona managed a weak return smile. "Thank you for being so understanding. I would keep the school open if I could."

"I know you would."

"We will reopen after the New Year," Fiona said with determination.

Louise hoped the paying students would return, but that wasn't something she should voice. Instead, she clasped her friend's hands. "It will all turn out for the best."

Somehow. She didn't know how quite yet, but God would provide. She had to believe it.

Jesse decided to wait to approach Louise until after he received word from his father that the customs collector was considering him for the post. Pa agreed to write, but he didn't have much hope that Jesse would get the post without providing sufficient "incentive." Jesse couldn't stomach the thought of a bribe, not after what he'd witnessed in Vicksburg. Bounties and cuts of bounties had wrought disaster. Call it whatever a person wanted, but it was still wrong.

Pa had snapped and snarled and more or less called him a fool, but Jesse wouldn't budge on that point. Better to continue here than to pay for preference.

As the days passed, he began to doubt that decision. Blackthorn kept him on the midnight watch and withheld the rest of the daily chores. Jesse had memorized the manual by now, but book learning was one thing. Experience was quite another. Midnights he had no chance to see the ebb and flow of the waves and their effect on incoming and outgoing ships. The full pattern of daily operation eluded him thanks to Blackthorn accomplishing even more of the tasks during the hours that Jesse slept.

If Jesse changed his sleeping hours, the timing of the chores changed also. Anyone could see that Blackthorn was deliberately preventing Jesse from learning the full operation. It had gotten even worse since Pa's visit. Had someone overheard their conversation and reported it to the keeper? Even if that was the case, Blackthorn shouldn't have been threatened by the prospect of Jesse leaving…unless the keeper didn't want a different assistant assigned to him.

Jesse wished he could speak with Louise, but he seldom saw her, and when he did, she was either surrounded by friends or hurrying in the opposite direction.

By the time Jesse lay down to sleep each night, he was frustrated and exhausted. Then, a good week later, Pa's letter arrived.

Jesse tore it open before he left the store. Oblivious to customers, he scanned the few scrawled words.

Talked to the collector 'n got you on the list even without no incentive. He said yer chances would improve if'n you had a wife. You kin thank me later. Pa.

After the thrill of knowing the keeper's position could be his came the dread. To guarantee he received it, he needed a wife. Louise. Would she agree? She would be a wonderful companion and a pretty sight every morning. The children would arrive soon enough. Surely that would be the case, even though eight years of her previous marriage had failed to produce any offspring. The memory of her disappointed look when he stated he wanted a large family popped into his mind, but he brushed it away. She had been concerned about the number. He could settle for fewer. Once he made that clear, surely she would agree to marry him.

On the first Friday of the month, he dressed in his Sunday suit and made his way to the boardinghouse. With every step, his throat tightened a little more. Dozens of words ran through his head, but none of them were nearly as eloquent as the speeches he'd made up while lying in bed after his watch.

Would she accept? She came from a more distinguished background than he did. He could offer a decent life, though not as privileged as what she had known as Mrs. Smythe. Would it be enough? He would promise to cherish and care for her the rest of her life. She wouldn't have to work for hire, though a lighthouse keeper's wife would know hard labor.

He paused at the bottom of the boardinghouse steps, where Louise had returned after Mrs. Evans's school closed. There were only five steps up to the porch, but they seemed like twenty. His mouth was dry as dust. His heart pounded faster than the slamming of the pistons on the great saws at the mill.

Mrs. Calloway came out to shake a rug. "Hi, Mr. Jesse. Did you come to see Miss Louise? She's in the writing room givin' lessons to Linore and Dinah."

Oh, no. Louise was busy. "Maybe I'd better come back later."

"Nonsense!" She surveyed him, doubtless noting that he wore his Sunday best. "She'll be right upset if you don't stop in and say hello." She held open the front door. "Go on in, now. Don't want to be lettin' out the heat."

Jesse began to protest, but she cut him off with a cluck of her tongue.

"Hurry on up, now," she added.

Jesse dragged his feet up the steps. Why did his legs feel leaden? Why couldn't he quite get a breath? Fear. That's what it was. No one should have such a hold over a man, but Louise clearly did.

"There you go now," Mrs. Calloway said as she closed

the door behind them. "Now don't you go worryin' about your shoes and coat and all. Go down that hallway to the right."

With Mrs. Calloway prodding him forward and pointing the way, Jesse couldn't very well refuse. He pushed forward, just as he had during his interview with the Lighthouse Board, until Mrs. Calloway held him back at the entrance to the writing room.

"Louise, dear, you have a visitor," the woman called out in a voice loud enough to alert the entire boarding-house if not half the town.

The lovely object of his attention lifted her face from the book she and the two students were examining. Her dark eyelashes curved away from those luminous gray eyes. Her expression was so serene that his nerves vanished in an instant.

"Louise, er, Mrs. Smythe."

"It's all right," she said softly. "We have been study-ing many hours. A break is in order."

The two girls, pretty though obviously less well-off than the three who had returned to Chicago, gave him a second look before darting from the room and disappearing with Mrs. Calloway. That left him alone with Louise.

Jesse took a deep breath. Somehow he'd expected a lot more people to be here.

"I thought the boardinghouse was full with those who lost their homes." The minute he said that he regretted it, for her expression fell.

"You came here to note how many are staying?"

"No." He stared at his boots, embarrassed that he'd forgotten to clean them. "I, uh, wanted to ask you some-thing."

The words stuck in his throat and took a monumental effort to force out.

"I see." She rose and placed the now-closed book on the nearest writing desk. She then motioned to the desk that Linore had abandoned. "Please have a seat."

Jesse started for the dainty chair but changed his mind. Even though his proposal was more of a marriage for convenience's sake, a man should still stand when giving it.

"No, thank you. I, uh, prefer to stand."

"Very well." She continued to stand as well.

That woman could certainly frustrate him. He searched for something to say. "Did you find any unique plants lately?"

Her eyebrow arched. "You want to talk about plants?"

It was preposterous, given he was dressed in his best and only suit. "Small talk." He cleared his throat. "Women like that, I understand."

"I'm not overly fond of that social predilection."

Jesse got more nervous. Her expression told him she was not pleased. He searched his memory. When had he last spoken with her, and what had he said to annoy her? Oh, on the dock. When his father arrived. Perhaps she had not heard.

"My father had important news to give me."

"So I understand."

Jesse took another stab at it. "I'm sorry I couldn't continue our conversation that day."

"Were we conversing? I thought you'd merely helped a *friend* who had stumbled."

His words rushed back to mind. No wonder she was perturbed. "I'm sorry, but my father can be an insensitive man." That sounded better than speaking the truth, that he was a rough dockworker who frequented taverns and never turned down a fight.

"I see." Though the tone of her voice indicated exactly the opposite.

He let out his breath. Louise expected nothing less than the truth, even when it was hard. He supposed he owed her that, if he hoped for her to accept his proposal.

"I have never gotten along with my father. He is a drinking, brawling man and very much unlike my late mother." He bowed his head rather than see her expression.

She didn't speak at first. When she did, each word was laden with compassion. "I understand." Her voice trembled ever so slightly. "I have known men who preferred spirits and violence to reason."

Was that sadness in her voice? Was she speaking of her late husband? He had gotten rid of her dog.

Jesse searched her face but she turned away before he could see how that exchange had affected her. Though he longed to hold her in his arms and promise she need never experience pain again, he didn't have the right, except as her husband. That brought him back to the task at hand.

"I—I have a proposal," he stammered, halting at the pitiful beginning.

"A proposal?" she echoed tentatively.

He licked his lips. "You are—or at least were—looking for a husband. I will need a wife should I be appointed as keeper of the South Manitou Island Light."

She stared, mouth agape.

He was botching this.

"I'm sorry," he said hastily. "I'm not much of a romantic." He glanced at her book. *Pride and Prejudice.* That figured. "But I do care for you. A lot. And we can make a good life there. The island is bound to have unique species of plant life. You would have time to examine it all." He was sounding frantic now, so he halted.

Her mouth moved, but nothing came out. She swallowed, looked away, swallowed again, and then looked back at him.

"I care for you too."

His heart leapt, and he took a step toward her. But she put up her hands, warding him off.

"There is something I need to tell you first, something I should have told you long ago." Her voice cracked with emotion. Then, in the softest voice, she killed his dreams. "I cannot have children."

Louise watched Jesse's hopeful expression fade into shock and then harden. Just like Warren. She instinctively stepped back. Her heart pounded. The urge to flee beat in her mind. But where to go? With a shortage of rooms at the boardinghouse due to the displaced families, she shared a room with Dinah and Linore, both of whom had retreated to give her privacy.

Nowhere to go. He could easily prevent her from leaving the writing room. No escape. She must face him.

His jaw clenched.

She backed away again, this time jostling the table, images of Warren so vivid that she nearly cried out. Only by silently repeating that her husband was dead could she calm the fear blossoming out of control.

"Why didn't you tell me?" Jesse said, the pain evident.

She swallowed, trying to gather some semblance of courage. "Since you insisted we could be only friends, I didn't think it necessary."

"Only friends? Couldn't you tell how things had changed between us?"

Had they? She stared at him. Her heart hadn't changed one bit. If anything the attraction had grown stronger, and, yes, his tender care in lifting her from the dock gave her hope, but then he'd crushed it with his impersonal introduction of her to his father.

"Generally when a man is ready to propose marriage, he is willing to acknowledge his beloved to his parents." Her courage grew with each word, until she spoke the last with force. After all, he *had* acted as if he barely knew who she was. Moreover, he hadn't apologized or explained in the weeks that followed. She hadn't even seen him. "I believe you referred to me as a *friend*."

Jesse cringed at her words. "My father would have picked you apart."

"Then I embarrass you."

"No! My father embarrasses me. Not you. Never you."

"Yet you denied me before him."

"I was protecting you," he protested.

"I don't need that sort of 'protection.' I have encountered rough men in my day. And worse." Such as those, like Warren, who appeared perfectly civilized in public but were monstrous in private. "As you can see, I am still alive."

"Yes, but—"

"But I am unable to have children."

He swallowed and looked away. "I wish you had told me."

"You know now." Though her heart was breaking, she would not allow a tear to fall. "I won't hold you to your proposal."

How those words hurt! Her throat ached from holding back the emotion, and her knees were beginning to tremble.

"If I'd known earlier…" He looked away. "You know how much I want a large family."

"Yes."

His jaw steeled again. "That would have been a good time to tell me."

"But you insisted we were only friends."

Moreover, how does a woman admit she's barren to a man she is growing to love? In Biblical times, it was considered a curse, a sign of the loss of favor. Hannah and Elizabeth had prayed without ceasing for a child. Sarah had laughed when told she would bear a child in her advanced age. God had answered their prayers, but not hers. As Warren's violent tempers grew, she came to consider it a blessing, but now? Her heart ached.

"Friends share important things about each other."

"I thought you would have surmised it," she said as softly and calmly as she could manage. What was the point of arguing over something that could not be changed? "I release you from your offer."

He stared at her for what seemed like an eternity, his expression never softening. Though her knees shook and her insides seemed to split in two, she managed to hold back tears.

Then, when she thought she could bear it no longer, he set his hat on his head and, with a final look at her, left.

Louise slumped against the wall. Warren had beat her, but this was far worse, for she had never truly loved her late husband. Now that Jesse was forever beyond reach, she knew without a doubt how much love could hurt.

Chapter Nineteen

The weeks passed with painful slowness. Autumn warmth gave way to icy mornings and frost glazing the windows. Snowfall couldn't be that far away. Occasionally Louise would see Jesse walking to the mercantile, but he never stopped at the boardinghouse or even looked her way.

Once the additional lumberjacks stopped coming through town on their way to the camps, she worked with the Calloways and Deckers to ready more of the cabins for the displaced families to use over the winter. More than one woman embraced her with such gratitude that Louise felt her heart swell with joy. Families would be together for the winter. It wasn't home, but it was a place to call their own temporarily.

Louise and the women scrubbed and sewed while the men painted and stocked the cabins with cordwood for the stoves. Thankfully, the Deckers had instructed the men to send the limbs downstream by barge. That forethought would spare everyone a cold winter.

After rains cooled the smoldering fires, the men had returned to their farms with a borrowed wagon in order to salvage what they could. They returned with very little. The blade of a hoe, the head of an ax. No clothing. No food. Nothing to sustain them through the winter. It had all been incinerated. Everyone in town pooled their resources to ensure the families had enough to eat and sufficient clothing. The store extended credit.

Church services were so full that people stood along the walls and children sat on their parents' laps. All needed a word to cling to that would get them through the harsh reality of daily life. More than once Louise caught herself scanning the crowd for one face in particular, but he seldom appeared, thus allowing the Blackthorns to attend. When Jesse was there, he stood in the back, far from her, and left the moment the service ended.

The hotel stayed open and did a lively business with the additional lumberjacks and sawyers. With both mills running and the boardinghouse full, many stayed at the hotel. The added business brought great relief to Louise's friend. With the VanderLeuvens helping out at the hotel, Fiona could again turn her thoughts to the other wing of the building. She caught Louise on their way out of the church early in December.

"We need to prepare the school for the next term. I've written to the students to let them know the school will reopen on January 8th. The classrooms need dusting and scrubbing. We also need to discuss the curriculum and what changes need to be made."

"Have you heard from them?" Louise half feared the parents would not send their daughters back, especially if Priscilla got her way.

"I haven't yet, but in the letter I offered the full semester at a third the cost to make up for the students' early departure. That should bring them back."

Louise hoped so, but she was less confident than Fiona.

"As you no doubt figured out," Fiona continued as they strode along the boardwalk, "I fear Sawyer will be busy at the mill for a long time to come."

"Then you will be at the hotel."

"Just to oversee things. The VanderLeuvens are a great help, but we have changed a few procedures, and they tend to forget that."

Louise considered the implications. "Managing both the school and the hotel is a lot for one person to do."

"That's why I would like to hire another teacher, so you can handle more of the administrative duties during the interim."

"Can you find anyone willing to step in for a short period of time?" Louise couldn't think of a single woman in Singapore willing and qualified to teach classes other than Pearl Decker, and she was already teaching the public school students.

"I will place an advertisement. Mr. Farmingham gave me excellent ideas for finding an instructor."

A new teacher meant Louise must manage the school, train a new instructor and teach classes. It was a lot, and not at all the life she had hoped to have during those brief months with Jesse. Still, busyness was a blessing, for it would distract her from the loss.

"Do you have any time tonight to go over a few things?" Fiona asked. "I would also like to give you a key so you can begin preparing while I'm busy at the hotel."

"We could do it now or after Sunday dinner."

"We will go to my office now, but only to get the key. No work. I promise."

As they walked, the sun warmed the frozen earth and gave a dying gasp of autumn smells. The grasses and plants had died long ago, with the first frost. Only the evergreens hung on. The ash tree on lighthouse property had shed its leaves long ago.

Louise looked up at its bare branches and sighed.

"I'm sorry," Fiona said with a squeeze of Louise's hand. "I shouldn't have pushed him toward you so forcefully."

Louise had told her friend about Jesse's proposal and his negative reaction to her admission of barrenness. Fiona had been sympathetic, a true friend, but it didn't ease the pain.

"It's not your fault. It's not anyone's fault that I can't have children."

"I'm sorry." Followed by another sympathetic squeeze. "You could always take in an orphan."

"He wants children of his own." Though he hadn't said it outright, she could see it in the devastation written across his face. She had shed many tears into her pillow, wishing he could consider a path other than the one he'd already decided upon. Clearly he could not. She could not blame him. She had once harbored the same intense desire.

"We're here!" Fiona said with far too much cheer.

She inserted the key in the front door and they stepped into the school's foyer, which opened into the parlor. Icy air greeted Louise along with the musty smell of disuse.

"Brr." Fiona shivered. "I'll have Charlie bring some wood over and light the parlor stove."

Considering how short the wood supply was, it was an unnecessary extravagance. "I can sweep and dust without heat."

"You'll do no such thing. The lumbering crews will keep sending wood our way for burning. Some of it's pretty green, but they're also sending any fallen limbs they find."

"But there is far greater need. The families—"

"Will have plenty." Fiona entered her office. "This will be yours now. Once we hire a teacher, if you would prefer to sleep in the hotel rather than with the girls, I can have Sawyer set aside a room."

"No. That won't be necessary."

Fiona opened a desk drawer and pulled out a set of keys. "Here are the duplicate keys to the front door, this office and the door between the hotel and school. I'll keep the other set for now."

Louise took it and at once felt the mantle of responsibility.

"Once we reopen, I will increase your wages," Fiona said.

"That's not necessary."

"Of course it is." She swept out of the office. "Thank you for taking a moment. I should get back to Sawyer and Mary Clare. Sunday is the only day we have together now that the mill is running six days a week from dawn until after nightfall."

After locking the office, Fiona headed toward the door that connected the two wings of the building. Louise lingered, looking into the classroom that had been her home until the fire. It still looked the way it had when she left. A little dusty, perhaps, but that was it.

"Are you coming?" Fiona asked.

Louise hesitated. "If you don't mind, I would like a moment."

"Take as long as you want, just lock the doors when you're done." Fiona then passed through the door to the hotel and locked it behind her.

After her departure, the school took on the deep silence of an unused building. There was sadness in that silence but also a poignant hope. Louise closed her eyes and could imagine the giggles and whispers of the girls. Even the fights, with Priscilla's group against Linore and Dinah, brought a smile to Louise's lips.

The stool stood in the corner now, far from the spot where it had tilted and sent her into Jesse's arms. Louise walked to the shelves where Captain Elder's books were located. Even by stretching, she could only touch a fingertip to the bottom of the spine. This was the spot where he'd held her oh so long.

She sighed and leaned against the shelving. By closing her eyes, she could relive the entire scene. How strong he was! His arms were as thick as her legs. His eyes had sparkled, with delight she liked to believe. But maybe she'd been wrong. She had certainly erred by not telling him about her inability to bear children. Her desire to prolong the possibility of a deepening relationship had only made the break more severe.

Given such grave errors, how could she manage an entire school?

With the grace of God.

She cast a silent prayer to Him, begging for clarity in what had become a muddled life. An answer could not be expected at once, but she had to trust it would arrive in God's perfect timing.

After another sigh, she opened her eyes and prepared to leave. Then something on a shelf caught the corner of her eye. What was that nestled near the notebooks, half hidden by a dusting rag?

It was small and brown. She sincerely hoped it wasn't a dead mouse.

She pulled the step stool closer and climbed onto the bottom rung. That brought the object to eye level and revealed it to be quite safe. In fact, there were two recognizable objects sitting on the shelf. Jesse's whittled birds.

He had loaned them to her for the wreath oh so long ago. When she'd disassembled the wreath and cast the needleless branches into the fire, she'd saved the birds, intending to return them.

She glanced out the window. There he was!

In the distance, he walked up the dune. That meant he'd been in town, though not at the church service. Had he called on her at the boardinghouse only to discover her missing?

She ran to the window and tried to pull it up. It wouldn't budge. Frantic, she tried the next. It, likewise, was stuck. She moved from window to window until one opened.

Sticking out her head, she yelled, "Jesse!"

He didn't even turn around. Oh, no. She tried again, cupping her hands around her mouth.

Still no response.

Again, she yelled his name.

He simply walked away.

Crushed, she blinked back tears. She wanted to see him, but he clearly didn't want to see her. That's when she noticed that the wind was westerly. It had blown her words away from him.

He had reached the keeper's quarters. Soon he would be inside. What should she do?

Louise lifted the birds into the light. A brave woman would pay him a call. He had once called her brave. She would go.

Later.

Immediately after Louise revealed her secret, Jesse agonized over the news. Deep down he'd suspected something was wrong, but her words confirmed what he'd dreaded. It also cemented his certainty that he could not live without the hope of children to carry on the Hammond name. Moreover, a head lighthouse keeper needed a family, especially for a remote island post.

Once he got past the shock and initial pain, he returned to the letters and narrowed the number of candidates down to three. Even though he should write those three first, over the following days he worked out a polite refusal and copied it onto separate letters, a few each day, until his hand ached. Fifty-eight! The resulting stack was enormous, and would cost a goodly amount to mail.

The three winning letters all shared common elements. The women appeared willing to work, could tolerate solitude and loved children. Their grammar and penmanship led him to believe they were educated enough to guide their future children, for a remote island post likely would not have a school.

It all made sense in his head, but his heart lingered.

Why hadn't Louise told him sooner? Why wait until he proposed? Yes, he'd told her they could be no more than friends, but his actions said otherwise, and actions meant a lot more than words. She must have realized his feelings were changing. After all, she had responded to every touch and look with eagerness.

He went back to the candidates' letters. None of them mentioned stature. Hair color, yes. Weight and height? No. For all he knew they were just as short as Louise. And for all their boasting, he had no proof that reality could match their claims.

These letters were more difficult, for he couldn't work out a one-size-fits-all response. He had to ask tough questions in order to have an idea what he was getting into. After all, marriage was forever. If he chose unwisely, he would be stuck with the consequences the rest of his life. The potential pain weighed heavily against the desire for children.

Why had God made the one woman he loved infertile? It wasn't fair.

He railed at the Creator, stomping around the lighthouse and snapping at anyone who dared talk to him. Weeks passed quickly in the rush to prepare the lighthouse for winter. All work not accomplished during the warmer months now needed to be completed. His days were long, and he fell asleep the minute he sat down on his bed.

That was the excuse he used, anyway, instead of tackling those last three letters. The customs collector wouldn't be in a hurry to nominate anyone, after all. The Board wouldn't put the new keeper in place until the ice broke in the spring and a tender could get to the island. He had months to get to know these ladies, who doubtless were busy with Advent underway and Christmas looming.

So he joined the family for Sunday dinner that first Sunday afternoon in December. The air had a snap to it, but the sun had melted the morning frost. Mrs. Blackthorn's chicken and mashed potatoes with gravy were finer than anything he'd eaten before landing this job. Could the candidates cook? He couldn't remember. Maybe after dinner he'd take a look. He had no idea if Louise could cook. Since she lived at the school and boardinghouse, she had no chance to cook. A woman of her upbringing likely had never learned that skill. She would have had servants to do that.

Yet one more thing she hadn't told him. The bitterness in his heart grew a little harder.

"Ice is startin' to form on the river," Blackthorn mused

between bites of food. "Won't be long now before the ships stop coming."

"Don't you think they'll run as late as they can, considering the demand for lumber in Chicago?" Jesse said.

"Yep, but there comes a time when even the greediest ship owner won't put his vessel on the lake. Once the ice gets thick, everything stops."

"It'll take three times as long to get letters," Mrs. Blackthorn added. "Why, I sent a letter just after Christmas last year, and it didn't reach Philadelphia until spring."

"That was a mix-up somewhere along the way," Blackthorn said, "not because the mail boat stopped running."

"The mail boat stops?" Jesse had not taken that into account. He must write his letters at once if that was true.

"Every year," Blackthorn confirmed.

Once dinner was over and the last bite of butter cake devoured, Jesse excused himself. The Blackthorns assumed he wanted to nap, but he sat down and wrote those letters. There was no time to dally now. He had to get them out in the post while the lake was still ice-free. Only one letter might get through before spring. That meant making a decision now. Two ladies would get the letter declining to meet them. The third—the one most like Louise—would get an acceptance letter. The refusals came easily. The words of acceptance were much more difficult, but he managed to get them on paper.

After tucking the letters into his inner coat pocket, he headed for the store. The wind had picked up, and he hunched his shoulders against its knifing edge. Rather than take the long route from the front of the lighthouse and along the docks, he cut across the dune behind the school and hotel.

He instinctively looked up at the school's windows.

Until the fire, he'd taken comfort in the warm glow emanating from them. Though it was still light out, the sun had already slipped lower, bringing out a few lamps. Not in the school. It stood dark and silent, as if accusing him of making a grave error. He shook it off.

For him, marriage would be a matter of practicality, not emotion. Without sentiment clouding the relationship, he and the one he chose could proceed in a businesslike manner. Things would run on schedule. No surprises. No mistakes.

Had something moved inside the school? He hesitated and squinted against the glare of the afternoon sun against the window panes.

Nothing. He must have been mistaken. Wishful thinking.

After raising his collar, he plunged forward. Those letters would go out today. No looking back.

After Sunday dinner, Louise returned to the school to prepare for her meeting with Fiona that evening. To her surprise, Jesse rapidly descended the dune again half an hour later. He gave the school one prolonged glance before hurrying into town. Not long afterward, he returned. This time his pace was slow, his shoulders bowed and his feet leaden, as if slogging through deep mud.

Her heart went out to him. Whatever had happened during that brief foray, he was greatly disappointed in the result.

Had he gone to the boardinghouse to call on her?

Louise had purposely not told anyone where she was going. If she had, Dinah and Linore would have begged to come along. Today she needed the solitude to consider what Fiona was asking of her. Her friend was certain Louise could do the job. Louise wasn't as sure. She had never been in charge of anything, and she had botched both the relationship with Priscilla and with Jesse. Could either be salvaged?

She looked at the small, whittled birds sitting on her desk at the head of the classroom.

The decision took only an instant. She left the icy school, locked the door and headed for the lighthouse. If nothing else, he would appreciate the return of these birds. She would apologize and not pressure him for something he could not give. She would expect nothing and give all she could.

The sun had dipped low and the breeze cut through her coat when she stepped outside. After locking the door to the school, she began the hike up the dune to the lighthouse. The sun had warmed the sand sufficiently that all frost was gone, leaving the surface soft and as strenuous to traverse as during the summer.

She gave the exertion little consideration, for her thoughts remained on Jesse. She could imagine his smile, so very slight, when she handed him the birds. He might act surprised. Perhaps he had forgotten that he'd given them to her. So much had happened between then and now. The fire. The homeless. His father's visit. Their painful break.

Only when the lighthouse loomed near did her heart begin to pound. What would he say? Would he even welcome her? Or had he gone to bed already, making her miss her opportunity?

She lifted a hand to knock, but the door opened.

"Louise!" Jane Blackthorn stood inside. "Come in. I've been thinking of you ever since the fire. How are things going?"

Louise stood frozen in place. She had completely forgotten that Jane would answer the door and had not prepared for it.

No words came, so she simply followed her hostess to the parlor and answered Jane's questions. Telling her which families had moved to cabins and which ones were still at the boardinghouse and hotel focused her mind on something less fraught with emotion than her rift with Jesse.

"It's a hard thing." Jane shook her head. "Can I take your coat?"

Louise knew that she had said that just to prolong the visit. "Actually, I wanted to see Jesse. Is he still awake?"

Though Jane looked disappointed, a spark also lit in her eyes. So, she was as much a matchmaker as Fiona and Mrs. Calloway.

"I expect he is. He just got back from posting some letters."

Louise immediately thought of the responses to his advertisement. He was going ahead with that, dousing the tiny shred of hope that had resided deep in her heart.

"Have a seat, and I'll fetch him," Jane said.

While she bustled off, Louise tried to sit, but her nerves were too much on edge. She did unbutton her coat, but the parlor wasn't very warm, so she left her coat on and wandered to the windows. The view faced the river rather than the town or the lake. Interesting. She wondered why the builders had chosen that orientation. Perhaps they knew how strongly the winds blew off the lake and were trying to spare the occupants from breezes that could rattle windows.

"Louise. Mrs. Smythe."

Jesse's voice sent her nerves fluttering. She turned, half expecting to see the same scowl he'd worn when he left her weeks ago. Instead, he simply looked puzzled.

"What brings you here?" he asked.

She opened her hand, revealing the two tiny birds. "I found these in the classroom today and wanted to return them."

"You were in the school?"

"Yes." Though why he should question that fact was beyond her comprehension. She'd figured he would wonder why she was returning the birds. "Now that there won't be wreaths, I thought you should have them back."

Since he had not moved, she went to him and held out the birds on her open palm.

He stared and then took them from her hand, his fingers brushing her palm. The sensation was as unnerving and thrilling as it had ever been.

He turned the birds over, examining them. "I forgot about these. No festival then."

"There isn't much reason. We had hoped to draw people from Chicago. That won't happen."

"Of course not." He looked at the birds again before closing his large hand around them. "Thank you."

This next part was a terrible risk, but she had missed their companionship.

"I—I was wondering," she began haltingly.

"Yes?" Those sky-blue eyes pierced through her, as if seeing her every motive.

A quick swallow gave her enough strength to go on. "We began as friends. Could we not continue as friends?"

His gaze lifted until he looked past her entirely. And his expression hardened. "That's not a good idea."

Her heart nearly failed.

But he wasn't done. "I have sent for a wife."

Chapter Twenty

"Have you corresponded then?" It was impertinent to ask, but the words came out of Louise's mouth before she thought them through. "I'm sorry. That is none of my business." But his every word had hurt. Foolish though it was, she had hoped that he would change his mind and not choose one of the women who had written in response to his advertisement. She had hoped time would rekindle what they once had between them.

"I don't know her." He paused. "Yet."

"I—I hope you suit each other." That wasn't true. She hoped nothing of the sort. She hoped he found her offensive, loud and pushy. It was very wrong, but she could not help it.

He nodded curtly. "It will suffice."

It? Suffice? He sounded like he was selecting a plow horse or a new carriage. At least her outrage throttled any possibility of tears. Perhaps she had been fortunate to escape a relationship with Jesse Hammond if that's the way he thought of women.

He shuffled his feet, clearly wanting this conversation to end. She would not give him that satisfaction.

"You must know her name at the very least."

"Ruth. Ruth Pickett."

Then it was settled. He looked resolute, yet something flashed in his eyes. Longing? Or was she seeing the reflection of her own hopes?

He cleared his throat and looked past her. "Well, if there's nothing more, I need to get some sleep before the midnight watch."

"Oh." She had forgotten that he sometimes worked overnight. "Of course. Good night."

For the briefest moment, sorrow crossed his expression. Then he gathered himself and left the room.

Only then did the full impact of his announcement sink in. There was no hope. He might feel something for her, but the issue of children had become an impenetrable barrier between them.

Within seconds Jane Blackthorn appeared. For her to get there that quickly, she must have been listening to the conversation.

"My dear." The woman crossed the room and clasped Louise's hands. "I am so sorry. If I'd known I would never have sent him to you. What a foolish thing to do. Why, I never thought he would turn down someone as wonderful as you in favor of a mail-order bride. Why, if I had, I would never have suggested it."

"You suggested he place an advertisement for a wife?"

"It was an offhand remark. I was trying to point out how much better it was to marry someone you know."

Louise squeezed shut her eyes as the frustration and pain finally summoned the tears.

"Oh, dear," Jane cried out. "I am so sorry. Is there anything I can get you? A cup of tea, perhaps?"

"No. Nothing at all." She didn't want to go over the encounter in fine detail. She didn't want sympathy. She certainly didn't want to weep in Jane's presence. "I am quite all right. We had no understanding. In fact, Jesse already told me that we could never be more than friends."

Oh, each word hurt! As much as she wanted to blame him, he had tried to give her fair warning. She was the one who had disregarded his cautions. If she had heeded them, she wouldn't have been surprised or hurt.

"When do you expect her?" Louise whispered.

"I have no idea. This is the first I've heard of it. Well, I tell you, she will not be welcome in this house."

"Of course she will. You must accept her. I insist." Louise managed a weak smile.

"Oh, my dear, you are so kind. Even in the face of rejection! I wouldn't be so understanding in your place."

Louise wouldn't call herself understanding. She was hurting and wanted to escape to the boardinghouse and her room where she could cry out to God and listen for His comfort. Maybe in familiar verses she could find some purpose to this pain. *Lord, reveal it.*

"I must go home."

"Of course." Jane gave her hands one final squeeze. "Oh, if it's not too much trouble, could you take some clothes with you to give to the families? I went through the attic and found a sack of old clothing from when the boys were younger. They're not in the best condition but not entirely worn out either. Since those poor families have nothing, especially with Christmas coming, I thought it best for them to have the clothing."

"Yes, of course," Louise said absently.

As she followed Jane to the kitchen, a new thought spun through her mind. Christmas. The homeless families couldn't afford to give their children anything on that special day, not even the tiniest practical item. How dreary the holiday would be after losing home and belongings. Most of the children didn't even have a doll or a marble to play with.

Jane pulled a small sack from the back porch. "If it's too heavy, I can have Jesse bring it into town. Are you still at the boardinghouse?"

"For now." She lifted the sack, which was very light. "There's no need to send him. I'm sure I can manage."

Jane gasped. "Oh, dear. I'm so sorry. What a terrible thing to suggest. I can have one of the boys bring it when they go to school."

Louise forced a smile. "I can carry it quite easily. Thank you, Jane. I'm sure these will be put to good use."

Even if worn, Amanda and Mrs. Calloway could patch and repair. The families would appreciate anything, but a grander plan was forming in Louise's mind. Singapore might not have its Christmas Festival anymore, but it could still celebrate Christmas in a new way. Instead of helping the businesses, the town could help those who had lost so much.

A week had passed, each day knotting Jesse's stomach tighter than the last. Rather than look forward to meeting Miss Pickett, he could only see the disappointment etched on Louise's face. Moreover, the nightmares had grown to the point that the images stayed with him into the day. Jesse couldn't eat. He couldn't sleep. He could barely think. More than once Blackthorn had caught him making a mistake. Everything was going wrong.

"You best be going to service this morning," Mrs. Blackthorn stated when he came down from the tower at daybreak.

"I don't want you to miss a Sunday in advent."

"I won't hear a word of protest," she insisted. "Samuel's under the weather and the children are old enough to attend on their own."

"If Mr. Blackthorn is ill, I can't leave the lighthouse."

She waved off that idea. "Who do you think ran the light when he was feelin' poorly in the past? Besides, it's a calm, sunny day." Before he could offer another excuse, she reiterated her insistence. "Not one word of protest, and I'll be expecting you for Sunday dinner."

Jesse hadn't attended a full service in a long time. After the war, he'd stopped attending. Then he attended but didn't understand what the minister was trying to say. Jesse was educated, but that man used words that only the clergy and scholars understood. Since arriving in Singapore, he'd deferred in favor of the Blackthorn family almost every week.

Today he sat stiffly on the rear bench that served as a pew and watched Mr. and Mrs. Evans go straight to the front with their daughter. Louise followed and joined them, but she did not so much as look his way. He deserved that.

Jesse looked around the room and caught Roland's attention. The man grinned and nodded. He then pointed to Pearl, who was readying a group of children to apparently sing or recite Scripture.

A rather dilapidated man in a patched coat and mismatched trousers walked up the aisle. One of the homeless, Jesse supposed. Mrs. Blackthorn said she sent every old item of clothing to the church for helping out those who'd been displaced by the fire. Instead of stopping midway, the beggar walked all the way to the front. In fact, he stood at the lectern that served as a pulpit.

"Welcome, friends," the man said and was rewarded with a hearty response.

"Welcome, Brother John!" the congregation answered with obvious delight.

Brother John? He must be the itinerant preacher that Mrs. Blackthorn mentioned, the one who'd married Roland and Pearl, as well as Garrett and Amanda. Jesse sank a little lower on his pew. He hoped the man wasn't here expecting to marry Jesse to Miss Pickett. For all Jesse knew, the woman might not show.

"It's good to be back," Brother John's voice boomed, filling the room. "It's been too long, since last winter. I got slowed down a bunch when I broke my leg."

The congregation murmured sympathetically.

"Now, now." He motioned for them to quiet. "It wasn't bad, and I knew that there was no need to check up on you, seeing as you'd been meeting together as a church for half a decade already."

"We missed you," came a cry from the other side of the room.

Brother John chuckled. "I missed you too. Today I'll be talking about waiting on the Lord, but first Mrs. Smythe has something to ask all of you."

Louise? Talking in front of the congregation? Jesse's heart pounded. If she hadn't spotted him before, she would surely see him now. Their encounter last week had been awkward. Painful. For both of them. He sank a bit lower in order to hide behind the woman in front of him.

Louise stepped to the front amid a host of whispers and the low rumble of possibilities. Jesse couldn't help but notice that she wasn't all that much shorter than the pastor. That only reminded him of how wrong he'd been to judge her by her size. She was stronger physically and had greater fortitude than any woman he had ever met.

Her voice was clear and unwavering. "I have spoken to several of you this week about an important matter.

I would like to invite every citizen of Singapore to stay after the service for a few minutes to listen to the idea Fiona Evans and I have come up with."

Mrs. Calloway stood up. "I approve of it wholeheartedly, and any man or woman who says otherwise is not welcome at my boardinghouse." She nodded emphatically to drive home the point and then sat down.

"Thank you, Mrs. Calloway," Louise said, though she didn't look especially thankful.

Jesse suspected she did not want to force people to do anything. Maybe that's why she had just accepted his breaking off contact with her. Most of the women he'd considered in the past had sobbed and pleaded. Even Clarice had been all tears and pleas when her family insisted she end the courtship. Louise had done neither. In fact, she had wished him well. He didn't know if he could be that gracious.

Louise thanked everyone in advance and made her way to sit next to the Evans family.

How pretty she was in that deep russet gown. He had never seen her wear anything but the nondescript beige print that did nothing for her complexion or features. This gown brought out the red highlights in her hair and warmed her pale complexion. Rather than small and insignificant, she commanded attention.

He was glad when the opening hymn gave him an excuse to bow his head in order to look at the hymnal. Staring at Louise Smythe was neither proper nor helpful. Ruth Pickett was to be his new bride. The thought made his stomach clench again.

After prayers and several songs, Brother John returned to the pulpit. The humble man who had spoken earlier turned into the most eloquent speaker Jesse had ever heard when preaching the Word. He drove straight to the point, and he might as well have been pointing a finger at Jesse. The gist of the message was impossible to miss. Man makes a mess of things when he doesn't wait on God's answer.

Jesse had waited plenty, but not on the Lord. No, he'd dragged his feet for various reasons, and he'd even posed the question to God, asking Him to bring the right woman into his life, but he had not sought God's answer. He had not waited. When circumstances made a decision necessary, he'd hurried ahead with his own plans. Was that why his stomach had knotted ever since sending that letter?

He closed his eyes right then and there and humbled himself before God, pleading forgiveness for racing on ahead instead of waiting. When he opened his eyes, the congregation was standing and singing the closing hymn. Jesse hastily stood until the hymn was over.

"Could all the children come with me, please? The older ones too," Pearl said. "We are going to do something special outside before you go home."

Once she, Amanda Decker and the children had left, the preacher resumed. First, he asked all the visitors to leave. After they were gone, he turned to Louise.

"Now, Mrs. Smythe." Brother John stepped aside as Louise approached.

She took his place behind the lectern and smiled at the congregation. "Friends, as you know, the businesses in town planned a festival before Christmas that was necessarily canceled."

Her voice was firm and confident. She radiated peace and a joy that amazed him. How could she know peace when he was a mess? Whatever it was, he wanted it too. All his peace had vanished on the river north of Memphis. The guilt that he hadn't done enough to stop the situation wouldn't go away. She seemed to carry no guilt or pain, yet he knew from her brief moments of personal revelation that her marriage had been painful. Even so, she had found peace.

"...so I'm asking for your help," Louise said.

Jesse shook himself from his thoughts. He'd missed the bulk of her speech.

"We need toys for the children, so they can have something new and filled with love for their Christmas. Amanda, Mrs. Calloway and I will sew dolls for the girls. Anyone willing to help can join us at the boardinghouse on Tuesday night. We will have a pattern there that you can follow."

A few women eagerly volunteered and asked questions, each of which Louise said she would answer on Tuesday.

"For the boys," she continued, "I'm looking for small wooden toys. Sailboats, blocks, whistles, anything that can be made in time for Christmas."

Garrett Decker stood. "I'll lead the men's crew. We'll meet tonight at the mercantile."

Several men volunteered to make boats and blocks.

Jesse stood. This was something he could do, something that would take his mind off the mess in his life. "I'll make whistles. I can whittle a dozen by Christmas. They won't be perfect, but they'll work."

Louise beamed at him.

He drank it in, and an unfamiliar feeling of joy welled up from deep inside. Doing something for others. That was it. Helping the needy was the answer, not running away to an island. He could have shouted praises, because in that moment he saw with clarity what had been shrouded in shadow for so very long.

"Thank you," Louise said.

Two simple words, but they soaked and nourished his

soul like nothing had in a very long time. He longed for the friendship they'd once had, for her smile that brightened the gloomiest day, for the gentle understanding that washed away the nightmares. If only...

"Excuse me?" An unfamiliar female voice pierced the air like the sawmill's steam whistle.

Jesse turned toward the doorway along with the rest.

A woman he'd never seen before stood just inside the door. She was tall and robust. Her features were pleasant and her honey-gold hair shone in the sunlight streaming through the windows.

She smiled back at the congregation. "Howdy, folks! I'm lookin' fer a Mr. Jesse Hammond."

She held up a letter. His letter.

His stomach clenched. He wanted to hide, to deny his very name, but he couldn't.

"Miss Pickett?" he managed to squeak out.

"Why, yes I am. Miss Ruth Pickett. Are you Mr. Hammond?"

Why Lord, when everything had just become clear?

There was no avoiding this. He nodded.

She walked to him and stuck out her gloved hand. "I'm plumb tickled ta meet my fiancé."

Chapter Twenty-One

Louise had hurried away after the briefest introduction, but she could not avoid the pain that seared through her every time she thought of Miss Ruth Pickett. Though Jesse had told Louise that he planned to marry this woman, it hadn't seemed real until she heard Ruth declare their engagement.

Louise could not entirely avoid Ruth, who lodged at the boardinghouse, but she did her best by taking on every task and opportunity to go elsewhere. Between coordinating the Christmas festivities and toy construction as well as readying for school next semester, she shouldn't have time to weep. Yet each night when she lay down after saying her prayers and after her roommates, Dinah and Linore, stopped chattering, her thoughts drifted to Jesse and his new bride-to-be. In the darkness with only Linore's light snoring to break the silence, she could not stop the memories and the thoughts.

It didn't just hurt that he'd rejected her, but he'd chosen an impersonal, mail-order bride instead. True, she had come to Singapore in exactly the same manner. Never had she considered that her answering the advertisement might bring heartache to another woman.

She squeezed her eyes shut against the tears. What mattered now was helping those families who were hurting. The children's joy would have to replace the empty place in her heart.

"Lord, if I am destined never to have a family of my own, take away this desire," she prayed softly.

Dinah, who shared the big bed with her, rolled over. "I know I'm young and all, but everyone can tell he loves you, not that Miss Pickett."

Though Louise thrilled at Dinah's words, she chastised herself for whispering the prayer aloud. "I'm sorry I disturbed you. I thought you were asleep."

"It's all right. I been praying for you."

Louise was ashamed. Dinah, who ought to be enjoying the attention of suitors at her age, had the consideration to pray for others. Louise had not been as stalwart in her prayers for the students.

"Thank you. I will pray for you also."

"Maybe you can pray that Donnie Lewis notices me?"

Louise smiled at the girl's hopefulness. "I've learned that it's best to let God bring the right man into our lives." In her case, that man apparently was not Jesse.

"Well then, pray that Donnie's the right man."

Louise didn't push the point. Instead she wished the girl pleasant dreams and turned toward the window. It was bitterly cold with only a crescent moon to cast the tiniest bit of light into the room. No need to pull the curtains. The girls slept soundly. She was the one tormented by lost hopes.

Forgive me, Lord. I must accept what is, as Brother John preached, and wait on Your perfect timing. To arrange things according to my wants and desires is to invite disaster.

Maybe that was what had ruined their relationship. She

hadn't been completely honest with Jesse from the start. If she had, perhaps he would have seen her differently. He certainly would have treated her differently, and no romance would have sprung up between them.

Cold radiated through the thin windowpanes. By morning she would feel a chill almost cold enough to see her breath. She pulled the blanket tighter around her shoulders.

Was it wrong to long for children and a husband? Was it wrong to hope for a family?

If only she knew God's answer.

Trust.

The word came to mind as if from nowhere. It all came down to trust. Did she trust God's plan enough to let Him do the work? Could she pray and trust like the Biblical Hannah instead of taking matters into her own hands like Abraham's wife, Sarah?

In the cold silence of night, she knew that was the only answer. She released her sorrow and her hopes to God. Who was she to guess the Lord's plan? If He had planted the desire in her heart, then He would fulfill it. If not Jesse, then in another way that she could not now imagine. Best of all, it would be the right way.

At last, secure in His hands, she fell asleep.

Jesse knew at once that if he married Ruth Pickett, it would be a mistake, but he had more or less proposed in the letter. He could not go back on a promise. Still, whenever he looked at her, he could only see how different she was from Louise.

Louise's lips were more expressive. Her hair had rich highlights. Her gray eyes calmed his very soul. She could converse on any topic. She was far more secure than

Ruth, who nervously hopped from topic to topic as if afraid of one moment of silence.

"I don't know what to do," he confided to Roland the next time he went to the mercantile. "I can't imagine a lifetime with Miss Pickett, yet that is what I have apparently promised."

His friend mused a moment. "What exactly did you tell her?"

"I wrote that I was seeking a wife and she met the qualifications. That I'd be pleased if she would come to Singapore."

Roland whistled. "And?"

"And what?"

"What did you promise her when she got here?"

"I'm not exactly sure. I didn't write down a copy of the letter, and I sent it in haste. I don't think I formally proposed, but it doesn't matter. The intent was there. I need to stand by my word, even though…"

"Even though?"

This was the hard part. "Even though she's not exactly what I had in mind."

"What did you have in mind?" Roland asked with a grin. "Someone more like Louise?"

Jesse squirmed. He didn't realize his feelings were so obvious. "She has good—no, excellent—qualities, but…"

"But?"

The mercantile door opened, sparing Jesse from finding a believable reason why he couldn't marry Louise. He could never reveal her secret, even to mutual friends. Both he and Roland glanced toward the door. It was Roland's wife.

Pearl Decker unbuttoned her coat and joined them. "A chill is in the air. Perhaps we will have snow for Christmas after all."

"Maybe." Roland took the hat from his wife's hands and then swept that hand to his lips in a lavish kiss. "Mrs. Decker, you look extremely beautiful today."

She blushed with obvious delight and then looked at Jesse. "What happened?"

"Nothing happened," Roland answered. "Jesse's just in a bit of a quandary."

Her attention returned to Jesse. "What sort of quandary?"

It had been difficult telling Roland. It would be impossible to tell his wife.

"I don't want to bother you," he hedged.

"It's no bother," Roland said brightly before turning back to his wife. "You see, Jesse invited Miss Pickett to meet him and apparently led her to believe they are already engaged to marry."

Jesse's face burned. "I don't recall exactly what I wrote."

"You could ask her," Pearl suggested.

That was the last thing Jesse could do. During each of the calls he'd paid on her at the boardinghouse, Ruth had babbled on without letting him get more than a word in here and there. No, his course was set, and there was no getting out of it.

"I must honor any agreement, no matter how unintended."

Pearl's sympathetic look didn't help. "You are a man of honor. It's true that Miss Pickett is nothing like Louise, but companionship will grow over time."

Time. The thought didn't give him much comfort. "She seems to think I already love her. I don't know what to do."

"Tell her how you feel," Pearl said simply. "A woman

wants to know the truth. Then you can start on the foundation of mutual understanding."

At that moment, the door to the mercantile flung open, jangling the bell and ushering in Ruth Pickett.

Jesse's heart sank. He wasn't ready to step forward even though he knew deep down that Pearl's counsel was the correct course.

"Jesse Hammond," Ruth exclaimed. "There you are. I went all the way to the lighthouse lookin' fer you 'n Mrs. Blackthorn said you gone down here."

Jesse gritted his teeth and tried to focus on Ruth's virtues. She had boundless energy and was excited with every new thing. She seemed taken with him and ecstatic over the prospect of marriage. She did indeed fit the qualifications he thought he'd wanted in a wife. She had held up her end of the agreement admirably. It wasn't her fault that he'd leapt forward when he should have placed the matter before God and waited on His answer.

Roland and Pearl tactfully slipped away from the counter.

"Please excuse me," Pearl pleaded. "I have to work on some of the dolls."

"Oh, the Christmas toys," Ruth Pickett cried out as she grabbed onto Jesse's arm. "I wanna help too. Kin I paint them whistles of yours?"

It was too much. He disliked how Ruth was always grabbing his arm and begging to do things with him. He wasn't ready. Why couldn't she be more like Louise? The frustration of the past five days reached a boiling point.

"Lord, help me," he silently pleaded, as he extracted his arm from her grasp. He didn't want to lash out at Ruth. She was the innocent in this whole mess.

He mustered a brief smile. "Thank you for the offer, but I'm not yet certain if I want to paint them."

"Of course they gotta be painted. Children like bright colors."

That was true, but he needed time alone to accept this future he'd made for himself.

He took another stab at it. "I wanted to varnish them."

Her expression fell.

"On the other hand, you might have a point," he admitted.

Ruth beamed at him. "'Course I got a point. I know what little ones like."

Though her words reinforced what Jesse thought he'd wanted—children—they brought no comfort.

"We kin start right now," she added.

"I can't." The words came out too quickly.

"Why not?"

"I have duties to complete at the lighthouse."

She brightened. "I kin help. I gotta learn it all anyway."

"No." He swallowed, again regretting the abrupt response. "There are very specific regulations that govern every aspect of the light keeping process."

She frowned. "Are you sayin' I cain't help?"

"I'm saying, well…it wouldn't be wise."

Her puzzlement evaporated. "Oh! Until we're married, you mean." She giggled. "You're such a stickler fer the rules. Life isn't that orderly."

It sure wasn't. Jesse could tell she was ready to start arguing again that she should help him.

"It has to be this way," he said firmly.

Again her expression fell.

Jesse felt terrible. Maybe Pearl was right, and he should tell her exactly how he felt. But here? In the mercantile? No, that was better said elsewhere. But where? Not at the boardinghouse where Louise might overhear.

Not at the lighthouse. No, this was his best chance. No one was in the store except Roland, who tidied shelves in the rear.

"Listen, Miss Pickett. Ruth." He faced her squarely and looked into her eyes. "I need time to get used to this."

Her expression hardened. "What're you sayin'?"

As much as he wanted to end this, he could not. Ruth was his future. Louise must become a distant memory. Once he moved to another lighthouse, it would get easier. For now, he must honor his commitment.

"Give me time to sort out what you can and cannot do…according to regulation."

"There's that regulation again." She shook her head in disapproval. "Why you so stuck on them?"

"Because they ensure safety for everyone. It's my job, and it's who I am."

"Oh. Guess I'll go help the ladies sew, then." She whisked away, without giving Jesse a second glance.

A man could think Ruth Pickett was only interested in the idea of marriage, not in the man she was marrying. With a rueful shake of the head, Jesse supposed he deserved that, but it didn't solve the problem. To begin their relationship honestly, he must confess his prior attachment to Louise, and he needed to do it at once.

"Forgive me, but I'm struggling to remain cordial around Miss Pickett," Louise said to Amanda Decker after the woman had sashayed past them on her way to the parlor to sew button eyes on the stuffed dolls. Since Mrs. Calloway, Dinah, Linore and Mrs. Wardman were in the parlor already, Ruth would have much company. "Mrs. Calloway and the girls try to keep us apart, but she seems to seek me out. Do you think she knows that Jesse and I were once…friends?"

Amanda didn't comment on the term Louise had chosen to describe her relationship with Jesse. "Maybe he told her."

"Oh, my." If Jesse had revealed that, then he was determined to marry Ruth Pickett. "I suppose he would, wouldn't he?"

Amanda put her hand over Louise's hand. "I'm here for you. So are Pearl and Fiona."

Louise squeezed Amanda's hand, grateful for the offer, but it did nothing to relieve the pain. "I will be glad to return to the school."

"And Miss Bennington?" Amanda completed the stitching on another doll and handed it to her.

Louise turned it right-side out and began stuffing it. "Priscilla will be a welcome change."

"Because she could never have captured Mr. Hammond's attention?"

Hearing her thoughts spoken aloud sent heat to Louise's cheeks. "No, that's not it." But it was, and Louise had vowed to pursue honesty after seeing what withholding the truth had done to her relationship with Jesse. She sighed. "That's not true. I'm ashamed to say that Priscilla's interest in Jesse did make me jealous. But—" Tears rose to her eyes. "Miss Pickett is going to be his wife."

Amanda touched her shoulder. "I'm sorry."

The consolation of a friend was almost too much. Louise turned her face away so Amanda wouldn't see her tears. "I wonder how she'll feel about living on a remote island."

"What do you mean?"

"Jesse expects to get the head keeper's position at a lighthouse on the island of South Manitou. I don't think there's much there."

Amanda thought a moment. "How would you feel about living so far from friends and family?"

"I'm already far from family." She hoped the bitterness didn't show in her voice. Her sister didn't want to see her, and her mother loved only Louise's sister. There was no one else back in New York. "But I would greatly miss my friends here." This time she mustered a smile.

"Then maybe it's for the best."

"Perhaps. I've prayed about it and am trying to accept whatever happens."

"You will, and, as you said, you won't have to be around them for long."

That thought didn't console. "How could he marry someone he doesn't know, someone so completely wrong for him?"

Amanda gave her a brief smile. "Maybe he's afraid."

"Afraid?"

She sighed. "Garrett was terrified of remarrying. He'd been through so much with his first wife, that the thought of marrying someone else was more than he could bear. He wanted to hide away with his children and not let anyone get close to him."

"That sounds like Jesse, except he was never married before. At least he didn't say he was widowed. Surely he would have mentioned that if he was."

"I'm sure he would have."

"But something does weigh heavily on him, and I think it has to do with fire."

"Fire?"

"From the first moment I met him, he has been overly cautious about fire."

Amanda looked off in the distance. "Garrett feared the river, but he overcame that fear. Jesse led the efforts that saved our town, and he braved the flames to rescue you. That shows true courage."

Louise had to agree, but that left just the one immovable problem between them. "Then it's all because of children."

"What children? He's making whistles and helping out a lot."

A lump formed in Louise's throat. The words had been nearly impossible to say to Jesse. It would be easier to tell a woman. "I can't have children."

Amanda stopped stitching shut one of the dolls. "Oh, Louise. Are you certain?"

"As certain as an infertile marriage can be." She managed to shove away the memories of Warren's rough handling of her. "Jesse wants a large family."

"There are other ways," Amanda said softly. "I'm an orphan. So is Pearl. A family took me in. It wasn't a good situation, but at least someone wanted me. No one chose Pearl. We would have given anything to have parents like you and Jesse."

Louise blinked back tears. Jesse had set his mind on children of his own. She doubted he would have considered adoption.

Louise rose, the tears unstoppable. "Forgive me."

Before Amanda could respond, she hurried from the room.

Head down, she skirted the parlor entrance and the joyful camaraderie of women working together for a cause.

"Louise—Mrs. Smythe?"

Jesse's voice made her stop. She stared. He was dressed like normal, with that navy hat on his head. His back was straight, stiff even, and his expression was so stern that he reminded her of the soldiers she had seen marching past the house on their way to war.

"Jesse." It came out in a gasp. Then she remembered herself. "Mr. Hammond."

He removed his hat. "You are well?"

How could she answer? It was not right for her to speak to him at all.

"I—I need to go upstairs." But her legs would not move. She looked away and grasped the banister before her knees gave out.

"Jesse?" Miss Pickett emerged from the parlor. She looked from Louise to Jesse and back again. Her initial puzzlement gave way to understanding. Her lips pressed together, and her arms crossed. "You know each other."

So, he hadn't told her. That left the task up to Louise.

"We once did," she whispered before hurrying up the stairs.

Jesse struggled for words as his future wife glared at him. This was not how things were supposed to happen, but he'd brought it on himself by not telling Ruth about his friendship with Louise.

"We were once friends," he said.

Ruth snorted. "Friends? Friends don't look at each other the way you two do."

"Any relationship between Mrs. Smythe and myself is over." Yet he couldn't help but look at the empty staircase that Louise had just ascended.

"No, it isn't. I'm no fool, Jesse Hammond, and I don't much appreciate bein' treated like one."

The full impact of his error struck home. He had hurt a decent woman—two good women.

"Forgive me." He looked Ruth in the eyes, noticing

for the first time that they were brown. "I should have told you everything at once."

"Yes, you should have."

"Let me try now. Mrs. Smythe and I were friends. I never courted her." At Ruth's skeptical look, he added, "We did…do…care for each other, but a future together is not possible." Not after the way he'd messed up things.

She lowered her arms. "That's not what I saw."

"It's the truth."

She shook her head. "I don't wanna be your second choice."

What could he honestly say in response? Ruth *was* his second choice. He should never have put her in that position.

"I'm sorry."

"Humph." She squared her shoulders and tossed her head defiantly. "I didn't much care for you neither, if truth be told. Yer too set on following yer rules and regulations to pay much attention to anything else. I've been in a mind to call the whole thing off."

"You have?"

She nodded.

Jesse had greatly underestimated Ruth. She not only had a big heart but strength of spirit. "You will make someone a wonderful wife."

Ruth jutted out her chin. "Yes, I will. But not you."

Jesse swallowed the lump in his throat. He'd never experienced such undeserved generosity. "I will pay all your costs for coming here and going home."

"Yes, you will. And then you can patch things up with her." She jerked her head toward the staircase.

Though Jesse naturally looked in that direction, only the empty staircase met his gaze.

"I don't know if that's possible."

"With God, anything's possible," Ruth stated.

It was exactly the sort of thing Louise would say.

Chapter Twenty-Two

Though Mrs. Calloway told Louise that Ruth had broken off the engagement with Jesse, Louise stayed far from him. She felt terrible for Ruth, who not only held up under the constant speculation but made a point to tell Louise that she wished her the best. The woman's graciousness humbled Louise.

When it came time to collect the toys from all the people making them, Mrs. Calloway insisted Louise do it. Louise refused, for it meant gathering the whistles from Jesse. Only after Ruth insisted did Louise agree.

She approached the lighthouse in the morning, hoping Jesse would be sleeping after working the midnight shift. Jane Blackthorn would either know where the whistles were located or could have Jesse bring them to the hotel later. From there, Fiona would make sure they were stored in the school until Christmas Eve, when they would give the toys to the parents while the children prepared the nativity play that Pearl had organized.

Louise didn't need to imagine the reaction they would receive from parents who could provide nothing. She and the town officials, such as they were, had already received much gratitude and many emotion-filled embraces. It had moved her to tears and took away some of the sting of Jesse's rejection.

She rapped on the door to the keeper's quarters on this bright Friday morning before Christmas. A chill was in the air, which seemed only right. There weren't any wreaths or garlands or matching bows on doors, but each front door in town displayed a drawing of the manger scene made by one of the children. Louise pressed a hand to this one, drawn by Sadie Decker, who was an exceptional artist for her tender years. Each child carried a gift of hope inside him or her, and these drawings reflected why they had this hope.

"All is calm, all is bright," she sang softly from the hymn, "Silent Night."

The door opened, and Jesse stood just inside.

"You have a lovely singing voice."

Louise felt the heat flood her cheeks. She averted her face, ashamed that an ordinary compliment from him excited such a rush of emotion in her.

She searched for something to say and settled for "Thank you."

"What brings you here so early in the day?"

You, she wanted to cry out, but that was selfish. "I— I'm collecting the toys for the children. Your whistles."

"Of course. Come in. I'll be right back with them."

She stepped inside as he headed deeper into the house. "Jane isn't here?"

He turned. "She's up to her elbows in flour."

"Oh." She should have realized the early hour would mean Jane Blackthorn would be busy. With the next three days consumed with practicing the play, Sunday service and Christmas worship and festivities, she would want to get as much done today as possible.

Jesse had vanished, leaving Louise alone in the front

hall. A hall table and receiving plate waited on one side of the room while a chair, umbrella stand and hat rack stood on the other. All manner of family outerwear was at the ready. Louise brushed a hand over a knit cap. That's what a home was like. Instead of seeking a place to hang her coat amongst those of strangers or storing it in her bedroom, parents' scarves mingled with those of their children. Each one was treasured.

Eyes filling with tears, she pulled her hand back.

"Here we are," Jesse said, coming into the room with a cloth bag the size of a pillowcase. Judging from the way it bulged, he'd been very busy.

"Is that all whistles?"

"Whistles and birds and fish."

"Fish?"

He shrugged. "It seemed appropriate at the time. Maybe some of the smaller children would like them."

"Did...did Miss Pickett paint them?" She prayed he would answer in the negative.

"Some but not all. Take a look." He set the bag on the foyer table and spread open the mouth of the bag.

A riot of color greeted her. She could not resist one of the birds, so beautiful that she had to pick it up.

"A hummingbird!"

He smiled. "That's right."

Oh, how his smile sent her emotions soaring! She turned over the bird. "So pretty, with the ruby-red throat."

"Keep it."

"Oh, no." She hastily put it back in the bag. "These are for the children. I certainly don't need something so frivolous."

She quickly closed the bag, lest she be tempted again.

Jesse placed his large hand over hers, stilling them. "I'm sorry."

"You did what you felt you must do." Though Amanda's words about adoption replayed in her mind, she could not bring herself to reveal her heart, not now, not while Ruth was still in town.

"I was a fool."

Each word hit with the impact of one of Warren's fists. She staggered slightly, off-kilter after such a declaration. "Me too. Ruth is a good woman." She couldn't quite bring herself to say that she was sorry the engagement didn't work out.

"She will leave on tomorrow morning's ship for Chicago. It should get her home in plenty of time for Christmas."

"I will wish her a safe voyage."

He nodded. "I should never have let it go on as long as it did."

Louise didn't know what to say.

"I wasn't honest with Miss Pickett," he continued, "and I certainly wasn't honest with you."

Louise trembled.

"Don't be afraid," he said. "It's no place to live. I know that now, after a lot of talking to God and reading His Word."

Jesse was afraid? "Fire?"

He took in a deep breath, and his gaze slipped far away. "I worked under the quartermaster in Vicksburg after the war ended. The soldiers were going home. They came from everywhere, from the prisoner of war camps, from every Union encampment in Confederate lands."

Louise thought of Warren, who had died before the war ended. If he'd lived, he might have gotten the political position he craved. At this moment she might be living in the New York capital of Albany or even Washington rather than in a boardinghouse in Singapore, Michigan, but she wouldn't trade places for anything. "They must have been eager to get home."

"Too eager. Couple that with greedy shippers as well as captains and army officers who were supposed to look out for the men, and disaster was inevitable."

Louise shivered. She remembered it now. The terrible explosion and sinking of the paddlewheel steamboat. She had read of it with horror and had even wondered if Warren had been onboard, since word of his death had not yet arrived. "The *Sultana*. You were there?"

"I was on it."

"Oh, my." A hand went to her mouth, as if it could stop the horror. "You were not…"

"Injured? Yes, but not in the way you think. My injury couldn't be covered by a bandage or cured by a doctor." He gripped her shoulders, his expression so earnest that it frightened her.

"You don't need to talk about this."

"I do. Don't you see? The guilt has followed me ever since that night."

"Guilt? Why would you feel guilt? You suffered through the disaster and survived."

"I shouldn't have." His expression had grown grim. "You see, I should have stopped the steamboat."

"You had that power?"

"I could have. I could have notified my commander's superior. I could have told the soldiers to leave the ship when I saw how overloaded it was. I didn't. No, I stood by, loyal to my commander even though I suspected he was taking a percentage of the bounty paid by the government for each man loaded on the ship."

His grip had grown so strong that she cried out.

He pulled back his hands like he'd grabbed hold of a

log in the fire. "Forgive me. It wasn't fair to burden you with this."

"No. I want to hear. I want to know."

But he didn't look like he believed her.

So she pleaded in a different way. "I too carry a hidden pain."

His anguish eased. "Your inability to have children?"

That wasn't it. Not really.

She shook her head. How difficult it was to speak this aloud, as if saying it betrayed Warren's memory. His parents would deny it, just as they had denied any of his shortcomings over the years.

"My late husband," she whispered, barely getting it past her throat.

He waited, holding her shoulders gently now, as if to support her.

She had to close her eyes. She could not say this while looking at anyone. "He drank spirits often. It made him mad. H-he would attack me." She touched her jaw, which had begun to ache.

"A man should never strike a woman, especially his wife."

"He did not love me. He never loved me. He married me to make his parents furious. They hated me," she said softly. It seemed excessively cruel, but it was the truth. "Each day he was home I lived in fear."

He gathered her in his arms and held her close. Her defenses broke then, washing away with the finality of a broken dam. The tears came, and she held on to Jesse like a buoy in a raging sea.

"I won't let that ever happen to you again." His voice was ragged.

She looked up into his eyes. They were stormy, filled with anger and intensity. Not the love she had hoped to see.

"You cannot stop pain." It was something she'd come to accept. So too must she accept that their relationship could never go any further. Then she noticed a sprig of something green pinned to the lintel above Jesse's head. Mistletoe? Was it a sign that he had changed his mind? There was only one way to find out. "Life has its burdens. I cannot give you or any man an heir."

Instead of holding her close, he stepped back to arm's length. "Did he do that to you?"

The separation knifed through her. She fought disappointment. "Does it matter? The past is over. The future is in God's hands. Each of us has only this day."

His jaw worked, as if he was trying to come to terms with something unpalatable.

She had one last shot, the one Amanda had suggested.

"There is adoption," she said softly. "Many orphans long for a home."

He stiffened as if ice had fallen down his neck. Then he dropped his hands. Though he said nothing, his expression gave her his answer.

She gathered the bag of toys. "Thank you for helping the children."

Then she left.

Adopt? Jesse had seen the street urchins in every city he'd entered. He'd endured enough panhandling and pickpocket attempts to last a lifetime. As a boy, his father had threatened to send him to the orphanage if he didn't behave. Pa's words still rang in his head. *Only the worst children went to orphanages. Only children that no one else will take.* Adopt?

Jesse shuddered.

What was Louise thinking? It must be desperation. No, the choice was clear. Marriage to Louise meant a lifetime without holding an infant son in his arms, without searching the boy's face for any resemblance to himself. A man needed a son.

Yet he could not forget the disappointment in Louise's eyes and the quick averting of her face. It had torn through him like a bullet and still stuck in his mind that night when he lay down to sleep.

The next day, he saw Miss Pickett off and then checked with Roland to see if any mail had arrived.

Roland looked up from his ledger. "Not this time."

Jesse felt a flood of relief. "I hope there won't be any more."

Roland set down his pen. "Have you made a decision then?"

Jesse blew out his breath. "Not yet." The desire for children warred with his love for Louise. He couldn't imagine never holding his own child. Neither could he imagine a life without Louise. It was a hopeless dilemma.

Roland shook his head before tackling the ledger again. "Is there anyone you can imagine seeing every day?"

Louise. But Jesse couldn't say that, or Roland would ask why he didn't just propose to her. That was something he couldn't answer without betraying her privacy, which he would never do. He'd already hurt her enough.

"Let's just say I'm undecided," he finally answered.

"Mmm." Roland shook his head again.

"What does that mean?"

"All I can tell you is that once you've found the woman who captures your heart, you'd better do everything you can to hold on to her."

Jesse couldn't very well say that he would. "I'll keep that in mind, but so far no one's perfect."

Roland burst out laughing. "If you're looking for perfection, you'll never find it. We're all imperfect. That's what makes life interesting. It's not about meeting a set of criteria, it's about finding someone who makes you laugh, who brings joy and excitement to every day. It's about a woman so dear that the thought of never seeing her again is intolerable. Once you've found that, you'll know she's the one."

His advice rolled around in Jesse's mind all weekend. Louise was all that and more. The thought of leaving her behind was the worst part about taking the South Manitou lighthouse keeper position, but he'd assumed that feeling would wane in time. What if he was wrong?

He watched her during Christmas service. She sang with all her heart and gave extra attention to the Evanses' niece. Seeing her with the little girl pierced his heart. She would make such a good mother. She was patient and gentle and kind. Love flowed out of her, and she didn't even realize it. How bitter it must be to know she couldn't have children.

As Mr. Calloway read the Scripture that told the story of Elizabeth, who had been considered barren but conceived late in life, he wished such things could happen these days.

Oh ye of little faith.

The words resounded in his head. But he did have faith. That story was from long ago. The impossible had happened in order to fulfill God's plan. It didn't happen today.

"...behold, the angel of the Lord appeared unto him in a dream," Mr. Calloway was reading from the gospel of Matthew.

Jesse started. He'd been lost in his thoughts instead of paying attention.

"Saying, Joseph, thou son of David, fear not to take unto thee Mary thy wife…"

Jesse did not hear the rest of the reading, for in that moment, he understood exactly what Joseph had been thinking. His wife would give birth, but not to Joseph's son. In the dream, God told him to accept the child as his own. To adopt.

Joseph had "adopted" Jesus. That was God's plan.

Jesse sat stunned. Joseph had obeyed God. Would he?

Louise got up and walked to the back of the church with the Evans girl. That's when Jesse realized that all the children had moved there, but he had no idea why. The nativity play had taken place yesterday. Were they planning to sing?

"Now we'll sing 'Joy to the World,'" Mr. Calloway announced.

The hymn began, and something lifted from Jesse's heart. The agonies of the past didn't disappear, but they were somehow overshadowed by a peace and, yes, joy.

When the song ended, a riotous sound drew every head to the children, who were blowing their whistles with all their might. Laughter bubbled to many lips, including Jesse's. Then he saw Louise, hands clasped at her throat, beaming at the children.

In that moment he knew. As Roland had said he would, Jesse knew.

The whistles were ear-piercing, but Louise couldn't help herself. She laughed and then clapped. So did many others, for these children who had lost so much were grinning and poking each other with their elbows and standing so tall and proud.

Louise brushed away a tear. Surely this was the best Christmas ever. Not for lavish feasts or special gifts or family reunions. No, this year she felt in her heart the babe in a stable, God come to earth not with great splendor and riches but in the humblest way. A tiny baby. A dirty stable. No relatives gazing on. Yet the skies were filled with great joy, just as this small church was filled with joy. The Christ had come!

For a moment, the displaced forgot their loss. Parents hugged children, tears in their eyes.

The poor forgot their empty larder. A feast pulled together from everyone's stores awaited in the hotel dining room. Sawyer hugged Fiona and Mary Clare, doubtless eager to begin.

The orphans forgot their lack of family. Dinah and Linore. Pearl and Amanda. Some had made new families. Others found a family in this tiny community.

So had Louise. God might not grant her a family of her own, but the entire town had embraced her. She could love the young ladies she taught and the children of dear friends. It was enough.

That lightened her heart. So much so that she didn't notice Jesse approach until he spoke.

"I've never seen anyone more lovely."

The words startled her. Surely he could not mean her. But he did. He looked only at her. No other woman stood near except the mothers of the children who had blown their whistles.

She swallowed and averted her gaze. "Thank you for the whistles."

His gaze never wavered.

"I've made a terrible mistake," he said, "and hurt you in the process."

She held her breath and just as quickly let it out. He was simply apologizing.

"I accept your apology." She started to move away before he raised the old obstacle between them again.

He stopped her with a light touch on her arm. "Please hear me out. I don't deserve your forgiveness, but I accept it. You have been kind and considerate and patient from the start. I have, well, I've been stuck in foolish thought and behavior. You were right, you see."

"I was?" She hazarded a glance and saw open honesty in his expression.

He nodded. "We can only do our best and leave the rest to God."

Her heart skipped a beat, but she tried to calm herself. "I learned that from a dear, old friend, now deceased."

"She—or he—was wise."

"Yes, she was, and one of my few friends in New York."

Many of the families had already left the church. Only a few people remained: the Calloways, Pearl and Roland, Amanda Decker and Fiona, who looked like she wanted to ask her something.

"I'm sorry for your loss," he said.

"Thank you." She nodded toward the group waiting near the door. "Perhaps we should leave." To push home the point, she began to walk in that direction.

Again he stopped her. "Please give me a moment."

Louise glanced at her friends, who all nodded their approval. Though they stood across the room, Louise felt as if she was a specimen beneath a looking glass.

Jesse took a deep breath, his expression solemn. "I botched this the last time. This time I want you to know there are no restrictions and no criteria to be met. Louise Smythe, I can't imagine living one day without you. I love everything about you. Would you do me the great honor of—"

This time she stopped him with a single raised finger.

Though her heart thumped wildly, Louise could not let him say what she expected he was trying to say without telling him everything. There would be no secrets and nothing withheld this time. "You need to know that I do not want to leave Singapore."

He started. "You don't?"

"It has become my home. These families are my family. The children are my children. I can't go to a barren island."

He nodded solemnly, and she steeled herself for his departure. Instead, he took her small hands in his large ones. "Neither can I."

She stared. "You can't?"

"No. I didn't know it until now, but ambition isn't everything in life. I will stay as long as the Lighthouse Service lets me."

Now her pulse was really accelerating.

"And the reason why," he continued, "is because of you. I could live anywhere if you were there. Without you, it's just another place. This is home. I love you, Louise Smythe." He dropped to one knee. "I love you and would be the happiest man on earth if you would consent to become my wife."

"But the children you wanted?"

"We can adopt."

Had she just heard correctly? He hadn't said it with absolute certainty, but he had said it. Tears filled her eyes.

"When I think of how much Dinah and Linore wanted a real family, I desperately want to take a child into my heart."

"Linore and Dinah are orphans?"

"And Pearl and Amanda."

He looked stunned. "But they're nothing like…" He

shook his head. "Apparently my father wasn't quite accurate."

Louise had no idea what he meant, but she did see the tension slip from him.

"Yes, we can adopt," he said with a great deal more joy. "I love you, Louise, and can't think of anything I'd rather do than spend the rest of my life with you and the children God brings into our lives. We can adopt. In fact, let's do it right away."

"Aren't you forgetting something, Mr. Hammond?"

He sobered. "You don't accept?"

How could she refuse that boyish disappointment. "I do. Yes, I do."

Then he broke into a genuine smile, one broader than she'd ever seen. It changed his appearance from pensive and weighty to one of pure joy, and her heart surged toward him. This was indeed the man she loved.

He stood, swept her into his arms and looked deep into her eyes. "There's something else I've forgotten." Then he kissed her, pure and yet filled with the promise of what was to come.

When the kiss ended, she gazed at her fiancé as if seeing him anew. She had no idea what had changed his mind, but she had no doubt of the change. Jesse Hammond was a new man, one looking into the future not back at the past. Freed of burden and filled with joy.

"Look who found the mistletoe," cried Pearl.

Louise looked up and laughed. No doubt her friends had placed it there, and somehow she and Jesse had managed to stand directly beneath it. Her three friends all clapped. Then they surrounded her with embraces and congratulations.

"Just think," Pearl said, "you will almost be a Christmas bride like us."

A bride. Louise let that sink in. She looked to Jesse, and their gazes locked. This time she had made the right choice.

Epilogue

June 1873

Louise looked into her husband's deep blue eyes. "Are you certain? There's still time to change your mind."

The spring breeze was gentle and the sun already high. Jesse glanced wistfully at the lighthouse. "I am."

She threaded her fingers through his, bolstered by the strength of his large fingers between her much smaller ones. "You will miss it."

He shook his head. "I will miss Lake Michigan but not the job. Almost two years is long enough to be an assistant. I'm looking forward to being in charge." His lips curved into a smile. Combined with the sandy blond curls framing his face, it transformed him into a boy.

His son would look just like him.

Lyle—such a grown-up name for a wee baby—fussed in her lap, shaking his tiny fists at her. She held him close and drank in the smell that she'd thought she'd never experience.

"Does he need changing?" asked the small voice of Grace Ellen, the eight-year-old girl from Chicago that they'd adopted at the end of their wedding trip a year ago last January.

Wonder of wonders, little Lyle was born ten months later.

"No," Louise told her daughter, "I'm just drinking him in. Babies have a wonderful smell."

Grace Ellen wrinkled her nose. "Not so wonderful to me."

Louise chuckled. In time Grace Ellen would understand. For now it was enough to play at house and get her long brown hair plaited into braids each day with a bright red ribbon on each one.

"Ready to go?" Jesse asked. "It looks like the wagon train is set."

They did look a lot like a westward-bound wagon train, but in their case, they were headed east to a location that Roland Decker had scouted eight months ago, as soon as it had become apparent to all that Singapore was dying. Upon his report of good, affordable land, each of the other families had purchased a plot. According to Roland's description, a lake stood nearby and a river ran past the land, which had been cleared but not plowed. They would have a lot of work ahead, but the six families were eager to begin anew.

Grace Ellen squeezed between her and Jesse on the wagon seat. Though Louise would have loved the comfort of her husband's strength for the journey, little Grace needed it more. She had barely become adjusted to Singapore before being uprooted again. The little girl squirmed on the seat.

"I never been on a wagon," little Grace Ellen said.

It had been a long time since Louise had ridden in one. She recalled the journey being rough and very uncomfortable, but a wagon was the only way to get their belongings from Singapore to their new land.

Roland walked toward them. When he reached their wagon, he stopped, repeating the process he'd followed for the wagons in front of them.

"One final check to make sure everyone is ready," Roland said.

Jesse nodded. "The sooner we begin, the sooner we'll get there."

Roland laughed. "You sound like my wife. Once I check with the VanderLeuvens and Sawyer, we'll get going."

The wagons were aligned in front of the boarding-house and curved past the quiet sawmill. Roland and Pearl with their year-old boy took the lead, followed by Garrett and Amanda Decker with their four children. Then came Jesse and Louise, followed by the elder VanderLeuvens with their son and his family from Holland. Sawyer and Fiona and Mary Clare brought up the rear. Though heavy with her first child, Fiona insisted they take the all-important rear position. In fact, she had directed much of the packing—for everyone, not just her own family.

After Roland returned to his wagon, they began to roll forward ever so slowly. Mrs. Calloway joined her husband on the porch of the boardinghouse, though she had stated many a time that she couldn't bear to watch them leave. Her wave triggered Louise's tears.

Singapore had given so much to her and the other three ladies who had come here nearly three years ago in answer to a mail-order bride advertisement. Things hadn't worked out the way they'd planned before their arrival, but each would leave with the family she had desired and a friendship that could not be broken. Louise would miss

Singapore, but, as Roland had predicted, when the timber ran out, the town began to die. Already two buildings had been taken apart and relocated upstream in Saugatuck.

It was time to move on.

Jesse wiped a tear from her cheek with his finger. She leaned into his touch.

"Sad?" he asked.

"In a way, but excited also. Who knows what the future will bring?"

"Only God."

She leaned close, encompassing Grace Ellen and Jesse in her embrace. "I do know that together we are strong, and we have the dearest friends imaginable joining us on this adventure."

"That we do." He kissed her ever so briefly as the wagon gathered momentum, and he had to keep his attention on the team of horses.

"Pearlman." She tried out the name the group had decided upon for their new town, a name formed by combining Pearl and Amanda's names. Though the two had objected, the rest of the group thought it perfect to honor two orphans by giving them a place where their names would reside permanently.

"It should have been Louise," Jesse teased.

She laughed. "Thank goodness it wasn't. I have all the honor I need right here with my husband and children."

As the wagons rolled up the river road and Singapore disappeared from sight, she could only look forward, confident that together they would make a wonderful new beginning.

* * * * *

Dear Reader,

Lighthouses have always fascinated me. When I was growing up, I would watch the light from the offshore lighthouse come on at dusk. Later, in travels, I've been able to tour many a lighthouse. Researching how they operated in the 1870s was a joy. The Great Lakes have many remote and island lighthouses. I always wondered how a keeper and his family endured the isolation. Perhaps that will be another story.

The real-life story of Singapore, Michigan, fascinated me for many years. Sadly, it's a familiar tale for lumber boom towns. Many disappeared, though not as literally as Singapore, which ended up buried beneath the sand dunes. I've loved setting a series there, and hope you have enjoyed the stories of Louise, Pearl, Amanda and Fiona.

That's why from the start I envisioned these characters moving on together to begin anew. You will see familiar names in my early 20th-century books set in Pearlman, Michigan. The first of those books is *Soaring Home*, set in 1919. See my website at christineelizabethjohnson.com for a full list of the "Pearlman" books and more about how the characters in this series became the founders of Pearlman. You can also contact me through the Connect page on my website. I do love hearing from you!

I wish you a joyous Christmas.

Blessings,
Christine Johnson

COMING NEXT MONTH FROM
Love Inspired® Historical

Available January 2, 2018

MONTANA GROOM OF CONVENIENCE
Big Sky Country • by Linda Ford

If Carly Morrison doesn't find a husband, her father threatens to sell the ranch she loves. So when Sawyer Gallagher arrives in town hoping to give his orphaned little half sister a home and family, a marriage of convenience is the answer to both their problems.

ACCIDENTAL COURTSHIP
The Bachelors of Aspen Valley • by Lisa Bingham

Women are forbidden at the secluded Utah mining camp where Jonah Ramsey works. When an avalanche strands a train full of mail-order brides nearby, can he avoid clashing with the newly hired—and female—doctor, Sumner Havisham?

HIS FORGOTTEN FIANCÉE
by Evelyn M. Hill

When Matthew Dean arrives in Oregon Territory with amnesia, Liza Fitzpatrick—the fiancée he doesn't remember—needs his help to keep the claim a local lumber baron covets. But will he regain his memory in time to save the land and give their love a second chance?

A MOTHER FOR HIS FAMILY
by Susanne Dietze

Faced with a potential scandal, Lady Helena Stanhope must marry, and with John Gordon in need of a mother for his children—and not looking for love—he's the perfect match. But their marriage in name only just might force them to risk their hearts.

———————

Get 2 Free Books,
Plus 2 Free Gifts—
just for trying the *Reader Service!*

Love Inspired HISTORICAL

YES! Please send me 2 FREE Love Inspired® Historical novels and my 2 FREE mystery gifts (gifts are worth about $10 retail). After receiving them, if I don't wish to receive any more books, I can return the shipping statement marked "cancel." If I don't cancel, I will receive 4 brand-new novels every month and be billed just $5.24 per book in the U.S. or $5.74 per book in Canada. That's a savings of at least 13% off the cover price. It's quite a bargain! Shipping and handling is just 50¢ per book in the U.S. and 75¢ per book in Canada.* I understand that accepting the 2 free books and gifts places me under no obligation to buy anything. I can always return a shipment and cancel at any time. The free books and gifts are mine to keep no matter what I decide.

102/302 IDN GLWZ

Name	(PLEASE PRINT)
Address	Apt. #
City	State/Prov.	Zip/Postal Code

Signature (if under 18, a parent or guardian must sign)

Mail to the **Reader Service:**
IN U.S.A.: P.O. Box 1341, Buffalo, NY 14240-8531
IN CANADA: P.O. Box 603, Fort Erie, Ontario L2A 5X3

Want to try two free books from another series?
Call 1-800-873-8635 or visit www.ReaderService.com.

* Terms and prices subject to change without notice. Prices do not include applicable taxes. Sales tax applicable in N.Y. Canadian residents will be charged applicable taxes. Offer not valid in Quebec. This offer is limited to one order per household. Books received may not be as shown. Not valid for current subscribers to Love Inspired Historical books. All orders subject to approval. Credit or debit balances in a customer's account(s) may be offset by any other outstanding balance owed by or to the customer. Please allow 4 to 6 weeks for delivery. Offer available while quantities last.

Your Privacy—The Reader Service is committed to protecting your privacy. Our Privacy Policy is available online at www.ReaderService.com or upon request from the Reader Service.

We make a portion of our mailing list available to reputable third parties that offer products we believe may interest you. If you prefer that we not exchange your name with third parties, or if you wish to clarify or modify your communication preferences, please visit us at www.ReaderService.com/consumerchoice or write to us at Reader Service Preference Service, P.O. Box 9062, Buffalo, NY 14240-9062. Include your complete name and address.

LIH17R2

SPECIAL EXCERPT FROM

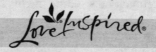

*Hoping to make his dream of owning a farm come true,
Jeremiah Stoltzfus clashes with single mother
Mercy Bamberger, who believes the land belongs to her.
Mercy yearns to make the farm a haven for unwanted
children. Can she and Jeremiah possibly find a future
together?*

Read on for a sneak preview of
AN AMISH ARRANGEMENT
by **Jo Ann Brown**,
available January 2018 from Love Inspired!

Jeremiah looked up to see a ladder wobbling. A dark-haired woman stood at the very top, her arms windmilling.

He leaped into the small room as she fell. After years of being tossed shocks of corn and hay bales, he caught her easily. He jumped out of the way, holding her to him as the ladder crashed to the linoleum floor.

"Are you okay?" he asked. His heart had slammed against his chest when he saw her teetering.

"I'm fine."

"Who are you?" he asked at the same time she did.

"I'm Jeremiah Stoltzfus," he answered. "You are…?"

"Mercy Bamberger."

"Bamberger? Like Rudy Bamberger?"

"Yes. Do you know my grandfather?"

Well, that explained who she was and why she was in the house.

"He invited me to come and look around."

She shook her head. "I don't understand why."

"Didn't he tell you he's selling me his farm?"

"No!"

"I'm sorry to take you by surprise," he said gently, "but I'll be closing the day after tomorrow."

"Impossible! The farm's not for sale."

"Why don't you get your *grossdawdi*, and we'll settle this?"

"I can't."

"Why not?"

She blinked back sudden tears. "Because he's dead."

"Rudy is dead?"

"Yes. It was a massive heart attack. He was buried the day before yesterday."

"I'm sorry," Jeremiah said with sincerity.

"Grandpa Rudy told me the farm would be mine after he passed away."

"Then why would he sign a purchase agreement with me?"

"But my grandfather died," she whispered. "Doesn't that change things?"

"I don't know. I'm not sure what we should do," he said.

"Me, either. However, you need to know I'm not going to relinquish my family's farm to you or anyone else."

"But—"

"We moved in a couple of days ago. We're not giving it up." She crossed her arms over her chest. "It's our home."

Don't miss
AN AMISH ARRANGEMENT
by Jo Ann Brown, available January 2018 wherever
Love Inspired® books and ebooks are sold.

www.LoveInspired.com

LIEXP1217

SPECIAL EXCERPT FROM

Special Agent Tanner Wilson has only one clue to figure out who left a baby at the Houston FBI office—his ex-girlfriend's name written on a scrap of paper. But Macy Mills doesn't recognize the little girl that someone's determined to abduct at any cost.

Read on for a sneak preview of
THE BABY ASSIGNMENT by Christy Barritt,
available January 2018 from Love Inspired Suspense!

Suddenly, Macy stood. "Do you smell that, Tanner?"

Smoke. There was a fire somewhere. Close.

"Go get Addie," he barked. "Now!"

Macy flew up the steps, urgency nipping at her heels.

Where there was smoke, there was fire. Wasn't that the saying?

Somehow, she instinctively knew that those words were the truth. Whoever had set this fire had done it on purpose. They wanted to push Tanner, Macy and Addie outside. Into harm. Into a trap.

As she climbed higher, she spotted the flames. They licked the edges of the house, already beginning to consume it.

Despite the heat around her, ice formed in her gut.

She scooped up Addie, hating to wake the infant when she was sleeping so peacefully.

Macy had to move fast.

She rushed downstairs, where Tanner waited for her. He grabbed her arm and ushered her toward the door.

Flames licked the walls now, slowly devouring the house. Tanner pulled out his gun and turned toward Macy.

She could hardly breathe. Just then, Addie awoke with a cry.

The poor baby. She had no idea what was going on. She didn't deserve this.

Tanner kept his arm around her and Addie.

"Let's do this," he said. His voice held no room for argument.

He opened the door. Flames licked their way inside.

Macy gasped as the edges of the fire felt dangerously close. She pulled Addie tightly to her chest, determined to protect the baby at all costs.

She held her breath as they slipped outside and rushed to the car. There was no car seat. There hadn't been time.

Instead, Macy continued to hold Addie close to her chest, trying to shield her from any incoming danger or threats. She lifted a quick prayer.

Please help us.

As Tanner started the car, a bullet shattered the window.

Don't miss
THE BABY ASSIGNMENT by Christy Barritt,
available January 2018 wherever
Love Inspired® Suspense books and ebooks are sold.

www.LoveInspired.com